Totally Bound Publishing books by Angela Addams

Single Books
Forever My Cowboy
Must Love Cats
Trouble With Cats

Wicked Distractions
Wicked Disclosure
Wicked Ways
Wicked Secrets
Wicked Trouble

Collections
Naughty or Nice?: Wicked Christmas

TROUBLE WITH CATS

ANGELA ADDAMS

Trouble With Cats
ISBN # 978-1-80250-988-5
©Copyright Angela Addams 2022
Cover Art by Erin Dameron-Hill ©Copyright October 2022
Interior text design by Claire Siemaszkiewicz
Totally Bound Publishing

TROUBLE WITH CATS

Dedication

To Ghost, Salem, Pumpkin and Wilkie,
my furever felines.

Chapter One

Crimson

Crimson had picked her hiding place carefully — downwind, in the shadows and under a heaping arch of brush, deep in the forest where she knew at least one of her stalkers wouldn't find her. The advantage of being on foot was that she could slip quickly under the trees' canopy, obscuring the eagle-eyed vision of Talon, whose shrill cry overhead made her smirk. He was frustrated, to be sure. This game had gone on longer than he'd wanted.

The echoing crack of a branch underfoot had her crouching lower, her breath barely there as she reined in the urge to bolt. A predatory snort, closer than she'd like, had her heart pounding so thunderously that she was sure she'd give herself up any second.

Unlike the eagle shifter, in his wolf form, Valor would have no trouble hunting her at ground level. The only thing she had going for her was her head start and how easily she'd wedged herself under the protection of the piled branches. If she was lucky, he wouldn't be able to pick up her scent.

With the way she was sweating, though, she'd probably need to shift to plan B shortly.

Another snort, another twig creaking. Normally he wouldn't be so noisy, but she guessed he wanted her to know he was near. He wanted her to know that her little game was becoming tedious and that she would pay, one way or another. Still she hunkered down, holding her breath now that he was so close, determined to win this round, at least. Through the thicket, a flash of gray fur strode by—so leisurely, so assured. As an apex predator in Shade, he was monstrously large, as were all the familiars, but Valor also had an air of sophistication along with his brute force, as though he were a king among his kind, even when he, along with Crimson and Talon, was an outcast.

She loved that about him.

Crimson's lungs, pushed to their limit of air deprivation, wheezed out a short gasp through her clenched lips. She froze, scanning the small area in her line of sight. It was hardly a sound, and yet...

The ground beneath her shook with the thundering approach of Valor. She had an easy escape route, but she waited, pushing down the instinct to get out and run. She didn't know which direction he was coming from, but she knew it was only a matter of time before—

The stacked branches around her creaked and groaned, threatening to collapse with her underneath as Valor pounced on top of her hiding spot. She rolled to the side and briefly made eye contact with the beast. His cunning brown gaze shone with triumph.

Not yet, wolfie. Not yet.

He shoved his snout between two branches and wedged one paw, claws out, through the wood. Crimson grinned.

"Gotcha." She kicked as hard as she could, and as the entire structure began to fall, entangling the wolf in an avalanche of debris, she rolled out of the way, clearing the mess before Valor even knew what had happened. She was on her feet, bolting to the tree line, keeping her snickers contained as much as she could as she listened to Valor's grunts and huffs behind her. He was too big to get out of the disaster of branches gracefully.

The barn was a short distance from the forest — the closest point of safety — which was why she'd chosen the hiding spot she had. She paused only briefly to look up at the sky. The summer sun was at its peak, beating down relentlessly, despite the veil of fog that Crimson had built around her safe haven. She scanned the skies again but there was no sign of Talon. Almost out of breath, her chest heaving, she made a dash for it, pumping her legs as hard as she could. All she needed was two minutes. Two minutes and she'd win.

Talon's screech sounded like fury itself, and Crimson dug deep, pushing harder toward her goal.

Fifty feet.

Forty.

Thirty.

She dared not look up or behind. She didn't need to anyway, because she felt the predators closing in. They were at her heels and above her head.

Twenty feet remaining.

She would make it this time.

She would —

One foot landed wrong, and instead of touching the wood of the barn, she face-planted right into the grass.

Oof!

Dirt rammed against her face and embedded into her hair. Bits of grass flew up her nose. She coughed and sneezed, too disoriented and out of breath to do much more than accept defeat.

Valor howled seconds before skidding over her, his giant paws caging her head while the rest of him pressed into her body. She pushed herself up — or tried to, anyway — just as Talon landed, his claws digging into the ground in front of her. Valor shoved her down with his snout between her shoulder blades. Talen dropped rope with two loops for her wrists in front of her face.

"Yeah, yeah." She spat dirt then slipped her hands through the loops.

Valor prodded her roughly, giving her enough space so she could flip over. He was grinning like a crazy wolf, his fangs bared and muzzle scrunched.

"Rub it in, why don't you?"

The rope loops tightened as Talon took flight, the force of his ascent whipping her to her feet in seconds. She stumbled backward until her shoulders pressed against the wall of the barn, her toes barely touching the ground. The rope pulled taut, letting her know that Talon had secured her. She was trapped and at the mercy of her familiars…again. Talon's cry sounded like victory. She looked up to see him circle above, letting her know what she had coming.

She kept losing this game. On purpose? No, she was too competitive for that, and yet, something always seemed to cause her to trip up at the last minute.

"You're a terrible hider, Crimson." Valor's voice rumbled like thunder, forcing her attention to him.

She pulled her gaze from Talon to see that Valor was fully clothed still, which was hardly like him at a time like this. All the same, the tight breeches he liked to wear left very little to the imagination—not that she minded. She enjoyed seeing how aroused her men got, even if it was hidden behind their clothes temporarily. His loose-fitting shirt was unbuttoned enough to give her a glimpse of the dark curls of chest hair that she loved feeling pressed against her skin, roughly warming her with every thrust. He ran his fingers through his hair, then shook the curls out, a gesture that made him look like he had no cares in the world when they both knew he was dying to fuck her silly.

She knew this for certain because her men always wanted to fuck her silly, but also because his cock strained against his pants like it was ready to burst out on its own.

What she wouldn't give to swallow him whole. To taste his cum. To lick his balls.

She squirmed, lust pooling in her every erogenous zone.

"Growing impatient, darling?" Talon spoke as he shifted, a unique talent that few familiars had.

"A taste of her own medicine, I'd say," Valor added.

"You two wouldn't have caught me if I hadn't stumbled." Crimson tugged on the ropes, even though she knew it was pointless. She could use her power to get herself out of the bindings at any time but where was the fun in that?

"Stumbled?" Valor laughed. "Is that what that was?"

"Looked more like eating dirt to me." Talon swooped in to run his fingers over her cheek, his golden eyes sparkling. "In fact, you've got some grass right here."

She flicked her cheek to the side in a vain attempt to shift away from him. He gripped her chin in response and yanked her face toward him again, all playfulness gone from his eyes. "Now, now, Crimson, no need to be a sore loser."

"I'm not a sore —"

He cut off her words with a kiss — a demanding, tongue-probing, toe-curling kiss. She melted. How could she not? Talon was not only a fierce protector and loyal familiar, but he loved her and made sure she knew it in every imitate moment they shared.

He released her too soon, turning her chin to the side. Her protest was cut short by Valor and his teasing kiss — a nip on her bottom lip, a soothing lick, then a leisurely stroking that incinerated her every last urge to resist.

Why would she, anyway? This was what she wanted — to be bound and at the mercy of her men.

Talon draped a rough swath of fabric over her eyes then tied it so tightly behind her head that she gasped. Valor nipped her bottom lip one last time before pulling away. She tugged on her arms as if she could coax him back with a touch, but the binding was too strong for her to move more than an inch away from the wall, so she only managed to make herself sway. Someone tugged another piece of cloth over her mouth, slipping it between her lips so that her jaw was wedged slightly open and her lips pulled taut.

She'd put her war gear on for their game, which meant the men had to navigate a series of buttons and hooks to unravel the layers of skintight fabric that wrapped around Crimson's body. *Hardly a challenge for these two.*

They had her stripped bare in a matter of moments. The sun's heat beat down on her exposed skin so she was slick with sweat. A wisp of a breeze, full of grass and dirt and the heady scent of her familiars' arousal was like a balm, making her nipples harden to the point of aching need. She loved fucking these men in the middle of the day, outside, without a care as to who might see.

Not that anyone visited their little hideaway. They'd all been banished a year ago, forgotten by the court in place of a death sentence for a crime she hadn't committed.

It was meant to be a punishment, but really it was a blessing — peace, quiet, the never-ending roll of days with nothing to do.

At least, that's what she told herself.

Hands cupped her breasts. Fingers splayed her pussy lips. A tongue traced the side of her neck. Sensations of exquisite torture, teasing touches, barely-there kisses… Someone hauled her ass up with strong hands, cupping her cheeks. Hot breath cascaded over her clit.

Anticipation made her squirm.

Desire and need coiled deep inside her core, every muscle tight, waiting for release.

Someone covered her nipple with hot, wet heat and a flickering tongue. Someone squeezed her other breast to the point of pain. Her men both had large hands and big mouths, wide enough to envelop her tits almost completely, which made it impossible to know who was playing with what. But that didn't matter, because her body was on fire. Every nerve-ending jolted as her lust wound around the pinnacle of release.

A flick of her clit made her moan behind the gag. The hands on her ass hoisted her higher, a feast on display as thumbs yanked her pussy open wider. A strong, determined tongue roughly licked her from top to bottom so that rolling waves of nearly unbearable pleasure made her whimper and groan. Finally, lips latched onto her clit with force and huge fingers thrust inside, seeking that special rhythm so that the bud of her G-spot roared to life.

Featherlight kisses just below her earlobe made her shiver.

Relentless pounding of thick fingers in her pussy made her gasp.

The coil of her climax tightened with each nip and flick and suck of her nipples.

She writhed and swayed and desperately wanted to pull away from the intensity, but instead her body pleaded for *moremoremore*.

When her orgasm crested, it was a rising peak that seemed to stretch beyond the sky. She held back for as long as she could, reveling in the waves of power that built it higher and higher. Her breath caught. Her body froze. She was on the edge with a sheer drop seconds away.

One more flick.

One more suck.

One more kiss.

She arched into the dive, her body contorting and rolling and spasming. Her synapses fired all at once then short-circuited with the bombardment of sensations. Light exploded behind her eyes as she rode the wave through every pulse-pounding, pussy-quivering second of it.

Her men didn't let her go—not even when her legs shook, not even when she moaned from the pit of her desire. They were relentless, caressing every tiny bit of pleasure out of her until she was limp, out of breath and complete putty.

Someone untied her arms so she could collapse properly into his arms. By the way he kissed her, so sweetly, she knew it was Talon who cradled her. It was

Valor, then, who undid the gag, then the blindfold. She kept her eyes closed to protect against the blinding sun.

"Time for a bath, Crimson. You're a mess." Talon's voice was a gruff command. No debate. He loved to bathe her, and she loved the way he worshipped her body, so he'd get no resistance from her — not that she could move of her own volition right now anyway.

She blinked her eyes open to smile at Valor, who was only a step behind her.

She expected to see the cocky smirk of a job well done, so when his beautiful face twisted into a pain-filled grimace, Crimson jolted and a knot tightened in her gut.

Talon's next step landed wrong, and instead of carrying her forward, he began to fall. He curled himself around her body, clearly trying to protect her from hitting the ground, even though his arms shook and tears streamed from his eyes. He rolled so she landed on top of him, bearing the brunt of a hard landing on his shoulders and back.

"What's wrong?" Crimson split her attention between her familiars.

Valor clenched his chest, like his heart was about to burst from his flesh. She felt Talon's body vibrating beneath her fingers, his pulse probably racing at the same pace as Valor's.

Valor's eyes flashed between wolf and human, taking on a predatory gleam as he struggled to stop himself from shifting.

She moved off Talon's body just as he contorted then rolled into a ball, holding his gut, moaning in obvious agony.

"Something's wrong —" Valor sputtered. "Can't keep hold —"

"No shit!" Crimson grounded herself, connecting with the natural magic of the earth while at the same time yanking her magic from its resting place. Her familiar marks flared in hues of red, coursing power from her toes to her scalp. She put one hand on Valor, one on Talon, hoping to tap into whatever was causing them pain so she could obliterate it. As soon as she laid her hands on them, she flew back like she'd touched a lightning bolt. Searing pain roared through her body, tearing over her from sternum to groin. It felt like her head was splitting, her limbs ripping from their sockets...

Death. Death was all around them...in them, taking violently from somewhere. Echoed screams ricocheted through her conscious mind, and she knew... She just knew.

*My sister...*one of three witches in the Court of Shade—a triad that maintained balance in their world. *My sister is dead.*

"Aria—" Crimson gasped.

Talon, now in his eagle form, took flight with a screeching wail. Valor, now a wolf, limped toward her.

They'd been forced to shift, and the only thing that could do that was the death of one of their own. A Brother of Shade had died and so had her sister.

Their sanctuary. Their blessing. It all shattered.

Crimson didn't know who the enemy was, but she knew her peaceful days were over.

Chapter Two

Valor

Valor was having trouble fronting his human form. His wolf clawed and growled just beneath the surface, desperate to be out so he could protect his witch. What the beast didn't understand was that Crimson needed counsel, not fangs, right now.

"I can't pierce the veil *and* keep us undetected." Crimson sat at the small wooden kitchen table, nursing a cup of tea that smelled strongly of whiskey. Talon hovered near, his face showing that he was doing his own version of battle with his eagle. The beasts only wanted what was best for Crimson, and in their world, when facing an unknown threat, what was best was ferocity and aggression.

"If Aria has died, your remaining sisters will want you back at court." Valor leaned forward so he could take Crimson's hand. "They will demand that you take your rightful place in the triad." At least, he hoped they'd see the error of their ways in elevating a weaker witch, Aria, above Crimson a year before. Enough time had passed that surely they'd reflected on their actions and realized their grave error in banishing Crimson.

Crimson scoffed but didn't pull her hand away — a good sign that she was maybe considering the possibility that cooler heads had prevailed and her sisters had finally seen the truth of her innocence.

"Valor is right. Your sisters will require your help — especially if this new foe has enough power to not only kill a witch of the triad but also several of our brothers." Talon rubbed his chest in the same spot that Valor still felt the echoing hole of fallen brothers — familiars they were bonded with in spirit, fellow champions of all witchkind.

"And why should I go back?" Crimson glared at Talon, then Valor, but both men knew that her anger wasn't directed at them.

Her sisters had reacted harshly and ignorantly a year prior when they had cast Crimson out of the kingdom. At the moment, it was her pride that prevented her from seeing what she must now do to help the very witches who'd turned their backs on her, to prove that she wasn't the witch they'd accused her of being. Underneath it all, Valor knew she was deeply wounded by her sisters' rejection and still bled over the way they'd accused, then punished her.

"I'm not fit to lead, remember? I'm a criminal in their eyes." Her shoulders slumped slightly when she said that. "Whoever this foe is, my sisters will need to find another witch to replace me in the three in order to fight our enemy. *Their* enemy."

"You really haven't changed at all in the last year, Crimson." Disappointment dripped from those words as they forced themselves through the air seconds before a gaping maw of black void opened in the middle of the room, separating Talon and Valor from Crimson.

Talon's eagle burst forth, but somehow, Valor was able to keep his wolf at bay—not because he wasn't just as startled by the intrusion as the eagle but because he knew that voice very well.

"Jaggar," Valor growled, "you're not welcome here."

Jaggar, one of the triad familiars, stepped through the portal, which stretched up and out to accommodate his huge stature. *And his huge ego.* Behind him came Zephyr, equally as huge, arguably not *quite* as arrogant. Both were Fortis, familiars whose exceptional powers made them suitable mates for the strongest of the witches. It was only the Fortis who were allowed to be closest to the witches of the triad, protecting them, supplying them added power, bolstering their rule.

"You're needed at court, Crimson." Jaggar spoke as if Valor hadn't. "Your sister is dead."

"Yes, I know." Crimson didn't bother rising from her seat, despite court protocol to bow to the henchmen of the triad. She glared up at Jaggar with clear disdain. "You pierced my veil with your portal. That's against our agreement. We're banished, remember? *'Forgotten by the court. Erased from the minds of all of Shade.'*"

Words spoken by Crimson's eldest sister, Tabitha, at the time of her banishment. Her crime? Being more powerful than her three sisters combined, in Valor's opinion. The reason given by the new queens? Treason.

Crimson had been accused of having had something to do with the formerly reigning queens' disappearance—as if she would ever harm her grandmother, mother and aunt. Their mysterious disappearance had created chaos and rattled the peace in Shade. Even without ample proof, Crimson's sisters had banished her and threatened to strip her of her power if she caused any further problems.

They all knew that had been an empty threat because Tabitha, Wyvern and Aria were no match for Crimson, but all the same, it had been a blow that Crimson hadn't been prepared for, a betrayal that had shattered her soul—and her confidence had suffered greatly for it.

"Things have changed." Zephyr muttered his words like he wore a muzzle. "Your magic is needed."

"No—"

"You stubborn witch—" Jaggar roared as he closed the gap to Crimson, yanking her up by the collar of her war suit so that the chair she'd been on tumbled backward.

Talon dove at the same moment, using his claws and beak to batter at Jaggar's head and shoulders.

Valor stepped in the way of Zephyr, knocking him back as best he could without shifting. Not that it really made a huge difference since both Jaggar and Zephyr completely outmatched Valor and Talon in both human and familiar forms. They both bore the markings of magic, which made them the powerhouses that they were. Fortis were the only type of familiars who could wield spells. Similar to how familiars marked their witches to bolster her power, magic itself had marked the Fortis, singling them out of the Brotherhood to gift them magical enhancements. It had forever been a mystery why some familiars were given those marks, but both Zephyr and Jaggar had swirling tendrils of magic markings all over their arms and chests, making them both terrifying forces of power.

All the same, Valor wouldn't let the two bully their way to their goal.

"Get this bird off of me!" Jaggar waved his hand over his head like he was shooing a nuisance from his space, but in the process, he also let Crimson go.

She stumbled back a few steps but otherwise seemed unaffected. "That's enough testosterone posturing here." She flicked her hand and sent a shockwave of magic with enough force to freeze everyone in place. "Can we behave like civilized people, or do I need to keep you boys grounded for a while?"

And no matter how powerful the Fortis were, Crimson outmatched them all.

She waited for each of them to grumble or squawk agreement before releasing her hold. She righted her chair then took her seat again. Talon shifted back to human form and took his place behind Crimson, leaning against the wall like he was totally relaxed, when everyone could see the vein on his forehead pulsing. Valor positioned himself close enough to intervene but not so close that Crimson rolled her eyes over his protectiveness.

Jaggar ran his fingers through his long hair as if it were causing his frustration rather than the witch who was sipping her tea, seated so casually in front of him. "You must come with us, Crimson."

Zephyr stepped forward. "The Court of Shade is falling. You're needed back home."

Jaggar growled at his partner, clearly unhappy with that revelation.

"What do you mean, the court is falling? Are Tabitha and Wyvern not in command of the situation? I know a triad is preferred, but they're strong enough to do without, not to mention the cousins who can help."

"Your cousins are in hiding. Your sisters are on their own. This foe, a witch named Angelica, has the crystal, Crimson."

Crimson clamped her hand over her mouth but not before a gasp escaped. "The Crystal of Shade?"

The crystal was a powerful gem that had been missing for over three centuries. It was rumored to have been stolen by a handmaiden, Isabel of Clover, so long ago. It was believed that Isabel had slipped between realms to hide, but no trace of her whereabouts had ever been detected. Crimson, for all her treasure-hunting skills, hadn't been able to find her, anyway.

"How did this Angelica get possession of the crystal?" Talon managed to rein in his anger enough to speak without spitting.

"We only know that she has it, not how she came by it. She's not the talking sort. She's out for power and, so far, she's managed to acquire quite a lot of it."

"Acquire it *how*?" Valor asked as he shared a concerned look with Crimson. This was bad news. The Crystal of Shade had enough power to level their world to rubble if used in the wrong way.

"From what we can gather, she's using the crystal to capture then transform some of our brethren from their natural shifter state to monstrous wild cats. Those who successfully transform serve her without question, and those who don't, she murders then consumes their heart for her power stores."

Crimson gasped again, but this time it was echoed by both Valor and Talon respectively. "That's grotesque, a violation of —"

"Crimson, she isn't the kind of witch who cares about violating anything," Jaggar said.

"A violation of witching," Crimson continued, cutting a glare Jaggar's way. "But yes, I know, villains don't seem to care about the moral codes."

"So, you'll come." Jaggar moved toward the black void of the portal.

"I didn't say that." Crimson stood, teacup in hand, then walked to the sink. "Why would I sacrifice my familiars, put them at risk, for a kingdom that rejected me? I was unfairly judged, without evidence, and convicted for something I didn't do." She dumped what was left of her tea then put the cup gently into the sink before turning to face Jaggar. "The way I see it, we're safe here. The veil protects us from unwanted attention, and it hides us from the kingdom so that no witch citizen can find us—which, as you know, was the demand of my sisters."

Crimson folded her arms as she leaned against the counter. She was going for indifference, her face a shield, but her eyes gave her away. The pain of her sisters' accusations and actions still sat heavy on her heart and mind for all to see. "I don't think it's the right time for us to break the decree of the triad, do you? I mean, they were the ones to sentence me."

Jaggar's mouth gaped like a fish hunting for air. Zephyr stepped forward, his hand up, as if he could actually get to Crimson in time to touch her. Crimson just smiled, baiting the Fortis to react, to give her a reason to put them in their places, again.

"I was right," Jaggar finally managed to bark out. "You are too caught up in feeling sorry for yourself to do the right thing. You don't understand what it means to put the good of the whole above your own needs, in this case your desire for vindication. You aren't seeing the forest for the trees, as usual. There's more going on here than your need to prove your sisters wrong."

"Vindication? I'm surprised you even know that word, Jaggar." Crimson smirked to cover up the look of hurt that flashed over her face. "Only those who have been wronged would seek vindication. Are you saying you think I'm innocent?" She covered her mouth in mock surprise. "What would my sisters say about that?"

It did sound like Jaggar was suggesting something...something borderline treasonous, maybe. Valor met Zephyr's eyes and the Fortis shifted them away quickly. *What is going on here?*

He opened his mouth to ask but was cut off when the ground rumbled a warning a half second before the explosion, so neither Valor nor Talon had time to throw themselves in front of Crimson to protect her. The air shimmered, then detonated as magic burst from the black maw of the portal.

The side of the house exploded, and everyone inside was blown out.

Valor tumbled over the debris, instinct flaring as his wolf pounded forward to take control. He skidded to a halt with his claws in the dirt. His ears were ringing and his thoughts spinning, and even though he stood on all fours, he felt pain in every part of his body.

There was no time to take stock of his injuries, because out of the rubble of what was left of the front of the house came four ferocious and grotesque-looking cats.

They were bare of fur and marked with black barbs of magic like Fortis but radiating evil with every step. Their fangs dripped with blood and their eyes were black, void of conscience.

Talon screeched overhead, a battle cry that Valor answered with a growl.

Jaggar's panther and Zephyr's tiger matched the size of the wild cats, but Valor wasn't intimidated by the enemy before him. What he lacked in bulk, he made up for in devotion. No beast would get between him and his mate, and right now, those wild cats were blocking him from Crimson. He'd go through them to get to her and obliterate any beast that stood in his way.

Chapter Three

Crimson

Crimson shook the shock off along with the debris and quickly checked herself for catastrophic injury. Apart from a few deep cuts and a rattled brain, she wasn't going to die anytime soon. The explosion had wedged her between the fridge and the island, but she wasn't stuck. She just didn't want to move — not with the gigantic, ugly hairless beasts that were stalking out of the portal and through the remnants of her home. *Fucking Jaggar!* He'd opened her protective veil with his blasted portal and had led the murderous wild cats straight to her and her familiars.

She didn't need to see the magical markings on the beasts' flesh to know that they held a lot of power. It radiated off them like black smog, tainted with evil. Whoever this witch Angelica was, she was a force to be heeded, with or without the Crystal of Shade.

Although, her having that crystal was definitely a very bad thing.

Crimson held steady, barely breathing as the wild cats zeroed in on her familiars. Even though Talon and Valor were big men and even bigger animals, they looked puny next to the Fortis—Jaggar and Zephyr— and these mysterious wild cats of the witch Angelica's making.

One of the cats crouched, ready to attack, but Valor's wolf didn't give it time to twitch. He dove into the crowd of them, growling, clawing and tearing apart everything in his path. Crimson knew Valor was trying to get to her. She knew that being separated by the wild cats would have her familiars in a tizzy. She rose cautiously from her hiding space, careful not to make noise, even though the beasts were fully engaged with both her familiars and the court Fortis. She didn't know if these wild cats were here for her specifically or just on a killing rampage, but she had no doubt that they'd take her down if given the chance.

No way she would let that happen.

Pulling her own magic from idle to active required nothing more than a thought. Her markings flared— golds, reds, purples and blues all swirling together to bolster her innate power.

One of the wild cats must have sensed her magic awakening, because it tore itself out of the melee and dove straight for her, its fangs gleaming, black eyes hyper-focused and brimming with hunger.

Ready to kill her without hesitation.

She pooled coils of power in her palms and waited for the thing to get too close, its fangs and claws inches away from her throat. She ducked and wove at the same time as she lobbed one handful of magic high enough for a distraction and the other low enough to get the beast right in its exposed gut. The wild cat swerved away from one blast but took the second one dead center. It screamed its fury but hit the ground, all the same. Her spell tore its flesh faster than its healing power could mend, but that didn't stop the thing from rallying.

Crimson had no compassion for abominations, even if they used to be familiars of Shade. In their transformed state, they were tainted beyond repair and better put out of their misery. She gathered two more handfuls of magic, rolled over the ground to a crouching position, then struck again. The beast was just pushing itself up when two more of her strikes hit home — one to the head, one to the shoulder. The wild cat screeched again, shaking its head like her power had scattered its brain.

It charged for her but only made it two feet when Jaggar slammed it from the side, taking the wild cat by surprise and forcing it to roll with him away from Crimson. The angry yowls the cat made gave Crimson goosebumps, and the sudden silence as Jaggar ripped its throat out was a blessing. She wasn't going to complain, even if it was *her* kill that Jaggar had stolen, not when both of her familiars were battling the same wild cat while Zephyr handled the last two.

She called her magic again, pulling it taut and amping it up so that her body vibrated with its power. The markings on her arms threw heat that made sweat drip from her forehead. She coiled it tighter and tighter, building up her spell to such intensity that it felt like her hands were about to burst into flame. When she unleashed the torrent of magic, it came out as a blue fire and shot directly into the core of the wild cat who was battering her men.

She blew a hole straight through its middle, shattering bone and shredding its guts to come out the other side. The thing dropped right then and there, dead before it hit the ground.

That left two more, and with the four familiars as well as Crimson's power, they didn't stand a chance.

Zephyr swiped his claws through one wild cat's throat, and Crimson shot magic into its belly. Valor and Talon severed muscle, tendons and arteries, before Jaggar took the final swipe and tore the beast's head from its neck.

With blood, gore and guts all around them, Crimson and her familiars assessed one another for damage while Jaggar and Zephyr surveyed the corpses, looking, no doubt, for some way to trace their magical signatures back to Angelica.

"Are you hurt, Crimson?" Talon was still panting as he checked over her arms for injury.

"I don't think any of this is my blood." Crimson couldn't blame Talon for the concern, since she was doing the same thing to him—reaching out with her power to do a body scan and make sure there wasn't anything serious to worry about. She could heal most things, from infection to gaping wounds and broken bones. It was the nasty black magic that the wild cats carried that had her worried. Too much of that would test Crimson's healing abilities. Both Valor and Talon seemed to be relatively unscathed, and none of their flesh wounds held any lingering sludge of black magic.

"What the hell are those things?" Valor wiped blood from his face then stepped over a piece of wall to get closer to one of the dispatched wild cats. "Like Fortis but worse."

"These things are not Fortis—or at least, they're not like any I've ever seen." Jaggar reached down and yanked open the chest of one of the cats. "Look at its heart."

Crimson was trying to keep herself from puking after hearing Jaggar pull bones apart that shouldn't be pulled apart outside of the heat of battle. She'd never had a strong stomach for autopsy. Jaggar was right, though. The beast's heart was deformed, half the size it should be and resembling a shriveled, petrified piece of meat.

Crimson bypassed the dissected wild cat and examined the decapitated one instead. Its magic markings were static now that the beast was dead. The magic had writhed while the wild cat was alive, but now it looked more like ink etched on skin, benign and useless. Crimson traced one line of the now-dead marking with her fingers, and it disintegrated with her touch, cracking apart and floating into the air. "It's not bound to them. If it was, it wouldn't be coming off like this."

"Probably because it's a blasphemous kind of marking this Angelica is doing. She's not infusing these beasts with power. She's layering it onto them—an exploitable weakness, to be sure." Jaggar nodded. "But no matter, they are still a foe to be wary of, and she has numbers in the hundreds now."

Crimson shook her head. Hundreds of familiars were lost to this evil witch. With the death of a familiar, a bonded witch became weaker, so for every familiar Angelica killed or turned, one of Crimson's fellow witches, courtiers and demi-courtiers of Shade would suffer and become less of a threat to their collective enemy.

With the death of a witch... Crimson snapped her eyes up to Jaggar.

"How are you even alive right now?" Crimson stood slowly, her eyes on Jaggar's, even though he refused to look at her. "Seriously, Jaggar, if my sister is dead, you should be as well."

Because her sister had bonded with Jaggar, despite the fact that he and Crimson had been born for each other, despite the fact that Jaggar had vowed devotion to Crimson when they were too young to know what that meant. Aria had not only banished Crimson from court for a crime she hadn't committed, but she'd taken Jaggar away from her as well.

"Jaggar!"

But his silence was as powerful an answer as his words could ever be.

How is this possible?

Aria and Jaggar hadn't bonded? Aria had died without his mark on her flesh, and the proof was standing right in front of her. *This makes no sense.* Jaggar was devoted to the Triad of Shade. He'd chosen the court over Crimson a year ago.

Or had he?

"Will you come now, Crimson?" Zephyr had softened his tone, somehow registering in his big dumb head that Crimson needed tender handling. "Will you help us save the court?"

Crimson tore her eyes away from Jaggar and stared at Zephyr like he was speaking a foreign language. "How?" Her mouth was dry, and her throat felt thick with lumps. "You're both unbonded? Neither one of you marked Aria?" That would have put her sister at a great disadvantage against the wild cats. A weaker witch to begin with, without the marks of these two Fortis, Aria wouldn't have stood a chance.

"She didn't want us," Zephyr said with a croak in his voice, his eyes skittering away from hers.

Crimson shook her head. "You're lying."

Aria had wanted both Jaggar and Zephyr, and even though both had been courting Crimson and been ready to commit to her, Aria had yanked them away at the same time that she had torn Crimson's freedom away.

What does this mean?

"This is not the place." Jaggar's voice snapped Crimson out of her head. "We're wasting time here when your sisters need us at court. Stop focusing on the past."

Crimson stared at him and was startled to find him staring back. Hurt pulsed out of her, and she knew Jaggar could see it. He narrowed his eyes, cutting himself off from her completely. He'd always been closed to her, reserved in his emotional sharing, but she used to be able to see through his shield. Now he was as opaque as Angelica's black magic.

The truth smothered Crimson like a weighted blanket. Jaggar had made a choice. He'd stayed away from her, even though he could have left court at any time. Sure, it would have been a great sacrifice, but he would have shown everyone that he thought Crimson was innocent. Instead, he'd chosen to uphold the punishment, and he'd convinced Zephyr to do the same. Even if they'd never bonded to Aria because she didn't want them, they'd still chosen the triad over Crimson, because they'd stayed away. They'd let Crimson believe —

"You're needed at court," Jaggar said again. "Time to step up. Do what needs to be done."

Talon and Valor shifted to her sides, bolstering her just with their proximity. Jaggar's eyes flickered to the men standing with her, and she could swear she saw a flash of jealousy, there and gone in seconds. But that was likely wishful thinking on her part.

Do what needs to be done? What the fuck does that even mean?

Her familiars' proximity told her they'd stand by whatever decision she made. She swallowed the pain of Jaggar's betrayal and Zephyr's compliance. She steadied her heart and erected her own shield so Jaggar couldn't read her confusion and disappointment.

If her sisters wanted her at court, then she'd go back and finally, maybe, get the vindication she deserved. She'd somehow prove to them that she wasn't the villain they'd made her out to be and that she had nothing to do with the disappearance of her grandmother, mother and aunt. A small part of her hoped that they'd already come to that conclusion on their own and were finally ready to give her the birthright she'd been denied.

Her seat on the throne of three.

Chapter Four

Talon

Despite being banished from court, Crimson's suite of rooms had not been dismantled in the year she'd been gone. It had, strangely, been cleaned and smelled as fresh as the day they'd left. Talon suspected that was due to a castle spell at work and not the actions of one of the staff coming in to care for the place.

He would have thought that all remnants of Crimson's existence would have been wiped clean, but her bedroom was just as they'd left it. Her huge round bed, with its plush mattress and dozens of pillows, reminded him of the first time they'd all made love when Crimson had accepted their marks, a full year before she'd been banished from the kingdom. At the time, she'd accepted Talon and Valor with the understanding that Jaggar and Zephyr would be joining their ranks. The Fortis had been courting Crimson for more than a decade but were waiting for permission from Crimson's mother, Merianna, one of the original triad, before making the commitment. It was the understanding of everyone that Crimson would join Wyvern and Tabitha in the triad when the three crones, Crimson's mother, her aunt Telli and Shade's matriarch—Crimson's grandmother, Elvira—decided to step down and retire.

What no one had expected was the mysterious disappearance of the reigning queens. They'd simply vanished without a trace. Wyvern and Tabitha had stepped up immediately, demanding an investigation, then, shortly after, insisted that the old crones had met foul play at the magic of Crimson. There'd been no concrete proof, which was why Crimson's punishment had only been banishment rather than death.

Part of the problem was that no one really knew exactly when the queens had gone missing. The window of their disappearance was over the span of three days while they were supposed to be performing maintenance on the protection spells that cloaked Shade. They'd retreated to one of the ceremonial chambers designated solely for the queens and were expected to stay inside the entire time it took to bolster the spells. It was a routine duty that the queens performed every year, and it involved such deep meditation and spell casting that they didn't eat or sleep during that time. They were completely isolated in the chamber with only one way in or out. It wasn't until late at night on the third day that their Fortis guards had suspected trouble. When the queens hadn't emerged from the chamber at the time that they should have, the Fortis had broken the door down, only to find them gone.

"Will my mistress be needing anything else from me?" Shea, Crimson's old handmaiden, proved to be just as devoted now as she always had been.

"This is fine, Shea." Talon touched the older woman's shoulder in thanks.

"My mistress's formal wear has been aired and set out so she may be presented at court properly." Shea always handled Crimson's grooming when it came to court. "Will my mistress need me to tend to her hair?" Shea grimaced as she darted a quick look toward Crimson, who was moving around her old room, tenderly touching item after item, seemingly oblivious to the world around her. "Even with it so short, I could do something nice with flowers, maybe."

As part of her punishment, Crimson's dark hair had been cut to her scalp. Once long enough to touch her knees, it had been the envy of everyone and had marked her as not only a powerful witch but also a member of the royal family. In her year of banishment, it had grown enough that it was now to her chin, cut in an angled style that covered part of her face. The style suited Crimson better than the court fashion and acceptable long styles worn by all of the witches in Shade, but it was also a reminder that she had been stripped of status and humiliated for all to see.

"I think she'll be doing her own hair." Valor stepped in to guide Shea to the door. "We appreciate your help, Shea, but this is all overwhelming for Crimson, being home after so long away."

Shea's eyes brimmed with tears, and she nodded agreement. "I wish I could have gone with her," she whispered then covered her mouth with a small gasp. "I shouldn't have said that. Of course, I'm happy here."

Talon opened his mouth to reassure Shea when Crimson cut him off.

"I would have taken you with me if I could have, Shea." Crimson turned to face the woman, and it was clear in her eyes that she meant every word. "I wouldn't make you victim to my sisters' wrath, and I won't start now. Better to leave me to my men. They know what I need right now."

Shea and Crimson shared a meaningful look, and it was clear that, like many, Shea didn't believe Crimson was guilty of treason. With a quick swipe of her cheeks, Shea finally nodded then left the room.

Crimson had been sentenced to banishment based on three flimsy pieces of evidence. One was that, according to her sisters with the help of the Fortis, they were able to detect powerful magic in the chamber that matched the scope of only one witch in Shade... *Crimson*. Jaggar and Zephyr, her closest Fortis allies, had not been permitted to inspect the chamber to determine if Crimson's magic signature was actually there. But, Crimson often reminded them, they didn't push the matter either, and everyone just accepted that evidence as truth.

And two, according to her sisters, Crimson had no alibi. Even though Talon and Valor could vouch for her because they were with her during that time, it didn't matter. As far as her sisters were concerned, Crimson's familiars were incapable of telling the truth. They were too biased in favor of Crimson.

Then three, Crimson had said some...things — hot and angry, incriminating things — to her mother, grandmother and aunt just before she'd left court on the day they were to go into the sacred chamber. They

37

were words that painted Crimson as guilty to all who had witnessed them.

It didn't matter to anyone that for the three days that the queens had been in the chamber, Crimson, Talon and Valor had been between worlds, collecting gems and power stones as a gift to the queens. It was something she always did for her mother, aunt and grandmother, even from the time that she had been little, something she *could* do because she was so blessed with magic. Powerful in a way her sisters weren't, Crimson was able to easily travel through the veils that separated worlds to hunt for the precious talismans. The gems and stones were filled with magic, so when the queens emerged from the ceremonial chamber, drained and exhausted, they could rejuvenate quickly in a hot bath drawn by Crimson, the bottom lined with the precious magical items. She might have said things she later regretted, but her actions should have spoken louder as evidence. She had returned to Shade laden with gifts for her queens, only to discover that they were missing and she was being held accountable.

"It's possible that the only thing I missed about this place was the shower." Crimson beelined past Talon and Valor with only a quirked eyebrow to indicate that she was through with reminiscing. Talon had been worried that her daydreaming would derail her focus and that the memories of what once was would crush her completely. She was there to reclaim her rightful place on the throne, to clear her name somehow. Wallowing in the past would do no good to Crimson, and Talon was happy to see that she'd returned to the present.

"It'll be faster if we join you." Talon shared a grin with Valor.

"Faster?" Crimson poked her head around the corner, her bare shoulder letting Talon know that she was back to her feisty self. "I think not." She turned, showing her splendid ass before disappearing once again. "What are you two waiting for?"

Crimson's shower was indeed one of the best ones in the castle. Because her suite of rooms was nestled into the Mountain of Shade, the stonemason who had designed her restroom had carved her shower into the actual rock. There was no roof, so the runoff cascading down the mountain funneled straight into Crimson's shower like a waterfall. With the use of elemental magic, it was always the right temperature — somewhere between scalding and inferno, just the way Crimson liked it.

It was also big enough for ten shifters and almost like a cavern, with ledges and steps that gave wonderful opportunities for experimenting with leverage. Like right now, with Crimson arched over a slab of rock, her legs spread wide, her feet hooked into small holds and her tits on display... Talon had been sucking on her clit for the last ten minutes while he stroked himself to the point of dizziness. Crimson was busy deep-throating Valor's cock while he cupped one of her tits. She was a goddess – *their* goddess — and she was ripe for a fucking.

Talon teased Crimson as he slipped his fingers inside her hole, massaging her G-spot until her legs began to quake. He gave her one last suck on her plump little nub before he tore himself away. Crimson needed to feel the hard steel of his cock. She needed him to fuck her to oblivion. He spread her pussy lips wide and licked her again from asshole to clit, not able to get enough of her delicious taste.

He stood and stared. Crimson was all curves and cushion. Her skin was marked with swirls of color, and Talon felt the usual rush of pride. She wore his colors on her thighs — swirling reds and oranges, purples and blues that undulated across her hips and down over her legs. Valor's marks were silver and gray, with white wisps fading in and out, and they spread like spider webs over her shoulders and down each arm. Both familiars bolstered her innate skill just fine, but she had been meant to wear two others' marks as well. The Fortis would have covered the rest of her skin, giving her far more power than Talon or Valor could ever give her. But that wasn't meant to be, and Talon needed to focus on keeping his witch satisfied so that she could walk into the throne room brimming with confidence and love.

Talon flicked Crimson's nipple, loving the way it bloomed red, like a cherry. He wanted to devour her. She tilted her head down, pulling away from Valor's cock, her eyes hooded, her lips glistening and parted. Talon grinned as he leaned over her, pressing his cock to her pussy while he paused to nibble on her hard nub. She moaned, moving her hands up to grip Valor's dick as she arched into Talon, urging him to pump her full of his cock. He gripped the underside of her breast and squeezed as he tried to shove the entire thing into his mouth, denying her demands for an excruciating moment longer. He sucked her nipple back in, then rolled his tongue along the top of her tit. Crimson moaned then curled her legs around Talon's waist, using her strong thighs to move him close and applying enough force that his cock slipped along her pussy lips, dipping teasingly into her hole.

Who was he to deny this sinfully sexy witch? He released her tit then, gripping her hips, and with a deep thrust, he pinioned her slick pussy, slapping his balls against her ass.

Valor met his eyes, a flash of hunger, a groan of need. He tilted her head back again then drilled into her mouth, his cock disappearing down her throat. She cupped his balls as she groaned around his shaft, her eyes closed and chest heaving with the push and pull of her familiars.

Talon slid his dick out to the tip, rolled his hips, then pumped Crimson's pussy again and again until her tits rocked from the thrusts, nearly slapping her in the face with the force.

Chapter Five

Crimson

Her worries, doubts and insecurities were wisps of smoke that she couldn't hold on to, not with her familiars paying such attention to her needs. Talon pounded her pussy like he was in a race, his sleek body pistoning so fast that her pussy clenched to hold on, only to have him slip away just as quickly.

Valor did the same to her mouth, thrusting down her throat so that her tongue pressed tightly to his shaft. Without warning, they both withdrew and, before she could blink away the hazy fog of sex, they had her flipped around on the rock, her ass in the air, tits dangling over the edge. Talon nudged her mouth with his dick, the scent of her own arousal fresh on his tip. She greedily took him in, sucking back the spurts of cum that escaped, a precursor to how close his climax was to the surface.

Valor slid his cock into her pussy with one long stroke before reaching around to stroke her clit with his fingers. When he pumped her, it was slow and steady, deep and hard. Talon had gotten her primed, and Valor would take her over the edge.

Talon teased her nipples, pinching and flicking as they hung, swaying with her movements, super sensitive to his firm fingers. He could never seem to get enough of her tits, and if he wasn't staring at her cleavage, making her hot and squirmy in the most serious of situations, he was sucking them to the point of exquisite pain. He'd even, on a few occasions, fucked her there, his hard, thick cock sliding between her breasts to nudge her chin as he rubbed her aching nipples vigorously.

She loved when her men came on her body, in her mouth, deep in her pussy, coating her with their ecstasy.

Today was a day for marking territory, revisiting old memories and writing new ones. Today was a day for beginnings, and Crimson wanted it to start with a proper fucking.

Her orgasm ratcheted like a coil tightening, winding itself up, filling her with anticipation as she reveled in pussy-pounding, throat-drilling, nipple-tweaking bliss.

Valor grunted, his dick hardened like steel, a sure sign that he was close...*so close* to spilling his load. Talon spanned his fingers across her tits, somehow managing to flick both nipples at the same time. She bucked. She moaned. She rolled her hips to meet Valor's eager thrusts. Her orgasm unfurled with a burst of pleasure. Like a spark to accelerant, her body went up in flames, and her men only added to the flare by pumping her full of cum, bellowing together as they all came at the same time.

* * * *

It wasn't until she was weighted down by the uncomfortable formal attire of her court dress that Crimson truly registered what was about to happen.

She was about to take her place on the dais. At least, she hoped that was what was about to happen. Jaggar hadn't said it outright, but if her sisters needed her help, maybe, *maybe* they'd come to see that they'd judged her unfairly. Maybe this was their way of setting things right.

Once she was elevated in rank, she would have a voice and could order a proper investigation. She'd finally learn the truth of what had happened to her grandmother, mother and aunt. They weren't dead — that was a fact, because their Fortis were still alive — but somehow they'd been cut off from their familiars, so not even their bonded shifters could detect where they were. Crimson was determined to find out what had happened, and now that she was back at court, she would make it her priority to revive the search.

The fact that her sisters had so easily believed that Crimson had had something to do with their disappearance was a testament to their deep mistrust of her. She'd always been the more powerful sister, gifted with innate abilities that Tabitha, Wyvern and Aria had always envied.

It hadn't helped, of course, that at the time of their disappearance, Crimson had been in a bitter argument with the queens over her familiars, more specifically with her grandmother, who didn't want Crimson to bond with Jaggar and Zephyr until she was formally seated on the throne — which could have taken decades to happen. But Crimson had been impatient, wanting so desperately to have Jaggar's and Zephyr's marks on her body to go with Talon's and Valor's. Her grandmother had told her she was being rash and selfish. Her mother and aunt had agreed. When Crimson had stormed off, slipping between the veil, she'd made a spectacle of it, and her sisters had seen it all go down. Of course, Crimson had calmed herself while she'd been between worlds and had fallen to her usual practice of collecting stones and gems for the queens, partly as an apology and partly as tradition. But it hadn't mattered, as far as her sisters had been concerned. She'd had motive to remove the reigning queens in hopes of taking over so she could do as she pleased.

It wasn't true. She might have been angry at the queens' decision, but she wouldn't have betrayed them to get her way. Yes, she'd declared that she wasn't going to give up fighting for her right to bond with the Fortis familiars to join with Talon and Valor as her mates, but she hadn't meant no matter the cost, even though that's what she'd shouted for all the court to hear. It had been the very thing to convict her. Her own words had led to her banishment.

The dress Shea had laid out for her was blue to match her eyes — sapphire, to be exact. It had tightly fitted layers that not only kept her spine straight and shoulders back, but also came with a train of satin fabric that collected all manner of dirt on their way down to the throne room. It was completely impractical, and Crimson was sure she'd be doing a faceplant at some point on her way to the dais.

But she was prepared to endure all manner of pomp and circumstance if it meant righting the wrong that had been done to her so she could finally learn the truth.

Talon and Valor helped her down the stairs so she didn't trip, then stood on either side of her as she waited in front of the grand double doors to the throne room. The doors were made of obsidian, shiny and smooth. Crimson's reflection was warped in the swirls of the dark glass, but the stunning blue of her dress danced along its surface.

"You're beautiful, Crimson." Talon caressed her hand briefly.

"A true high witch," Valor said as he reached forward to open the door, the ornate lion's head knob dwarfing his hand. Before he could make contact, both doors were flung open to reveal a court empty of any spectators, with only her sisters and their Fortis present.

There should have been witches in the hundreds standing along the walls of the sacred circle, but the grand room was eerily empty.

Not even Jaggar or Zephyr were in attendance, and Crimson felt the brunt of that rejection all over again. *Why aren't they here?*

Fortis guards rushed in behind Crimson then looped iron tethers around Valor's and Talon's throats, immediately incapacitating them. It was so swift that Crimson didn't register what was going on until she heard her familiars grunt like they'd both taken blows to the head. She felt more than saw them slide to their knees and knew that she'd been betrayed all over again.

I'm a fool!

Crimson barely got a wisp of magic into her palms before she was forced to kneel then to bow with her arms outstretched in front of her, held tight to the stone floor with her sisters' combined magic. The shock of so much power weighing her down kept her from fighting it at first.

What is going on?

There was no way the two of them should have been able to do that to her, not even taking her by surprise. They simply had never been that powerful.

She pushed against the pulsing magic, but it was like steel—firm, impenetrable, heavy—and there were no edges for Crimson to hook onto, no way for her to snake her own power inside to weaken theirs.

Even with Fortis bonds, neither of her remaining sisters should have the strength to keep Crimson down—not like this, not with such unrelenting power flow.

What have they done?

This reeked of something dirty, even though Crimson could detect nothing foul in the flow of their spell.

It was awkward, but if she craned her neck, she could still keep her sisters in sight. Not that she could currently do anything about being spelled to the floor, but at least she could see them coming.

"Crimson, how lovely of you to dress up for once." Wyvern stood from her throne then brushed her fingers down the front of her dress to smooth invisible wrinkles. She always wore white, *presenting herself as a saint or virgin, perhaps?* Crimson had never understood Wyvern's need to display purity when she was as mean as a whip and capable of words just as biting.

"That dress is out of fashion, I'm afraid." Tabitha didn't bother to get up and instead leaned forward, her long auburn hair cascading over her lap like a wave. "But at least she put in the effort. It almost makes me think she's ready to beg for forgiveness."

Wyvern lifted her delicate fingers to her lips. "Or maybe she thought this would be her coronation."

Both sisters laughed. The cruel ring of it echoed all around Crimson. They'd always been awful to Crimson, mocking and teasing her constantly, playing pranks and setting Crimson up for failure at every opportunity. It wasn't just that Crimson had been born with more power, but it was that their mother had so clearly favored her. She'd always made it known that Crimson would lead the triad when the time came and that her remaining sisters would have to battle it out for the two seats at her side.

Her sisters were clearly reveling in taking her down and keeping her there. There was triumph in their eyes, and their evil smiles taunted her more than their words ever would.

Crimson could have crumpled into a pitiful mess. She could have accepted defeat. She could have bent to her sisters in submission, bowed her head and apologized for something she hadn't done. Crimson had had enough humiliation at the hands of these two, however, and she would never admit to a crime she hadn't committed. They may have capitalized on her naivety as she entered the room, and they may have somehow evolved in their magic skill, but she wasn't going to let them get away with it, not after a year of punishment she didn't deserve. Enough was enough.

Valor's and Talon's grunting let her know that they were gagged by whatever magic was infused in the iron nooses, but, like her, were trying to break free. She continued to probe along the dual spells which were woven like a braid, looking for that one mistake — the one tangle that would give her a way out.

"Enough!" Jaggar's booming voice echoed throughout the room. "Is this how you welcome your sister home?"

"Oh dear, we've offended the ever-sensitive Jaggar." Wyvern frowned in a mocking way, and Tabitha laughed harder. "We're only reminding our dear sister about the way of our world."

Crimson felt the snag of misaligned power and used her sisters' distraction to burrow into their magical restraints, drilling threads of her own magic deep into the base of their spell. It took more effort than she was expecting, and she had to push everything she had into breaking through. Concerning, yes, but she took some comfort in the fact that she still knew how to find their flaws. Her sisters might be suddenly and surprisingly powerful, but they lacked discipline and had never been very good at splitting their attention. She flexed her power, found the weakest point of her sisters' spell, then forced it to crack. She flexed again and made it shatter.

She was on her feet before Jaggar could reach her. She had Talon and Valor released from the iron leashes a few seconds after that. She was feet away from the dais and moving fast, her sisters' eyes wide with fear or shock before anyone understood what was happening.

A line of Fortis loyal to her sisters closed ranks around the dais, blocking Crimson from getting to her siblings. The fury in their eyes told her that they were a hairsbreadth away from going feral, turning to the monstrous half-man, half-beast form that only Fortis could achieve. She stopped short. Crimson might be angry, but she wasn't stupid. A Fortis in that beastly form could shred her with one swipe.

"Look at you two, hiding behind your wall of mindless familiars." Crimson sneered in the faces of these blind and stupid men. "Are you so scared of me that you can't even step off your dais?" She lifted a hand and took satisfaction in the flinch that rattled her sisters' attempt at command. "Why did you demand my return if you were going to hide away?"

"Well, it certainly wasn't to elevate you to the throne," Wyvern snorted.

"I said, that's enough!" Jaggar boomed.

"Watch yourself, shifter. You may have been Aria's pet, but you've never been ours." Tabitha flicked her hand and dismissed the Fortis who were guarding them. The familiars shuffled off to the circular sides of the room and stood sentry once again. "We're not hiding." She stood to join Wyvern at the edge of the dais. "After everything that's happened, you can't blame our loyal guards for wanting to protect us from a threat."

A threat? I'll give them a threat.

Jaggar lifted a hand, motioning for Crimson to cool it—as if he could read her mind, as if he knew she was seconds away from teaching her sisters a long-overdue lesson.

It will only give them proof that you are what they think you are, his eyes seemed to say. "You called Crimson here. Tell her what you want."

"You did a fine job fetching Crimson, Jaggar." Wyvern motioned to the door. "Why don't you take our sister's familiars to the Brotherhood so they can reunite with their people?"

"We aren't going anywhere," Valor growled, the sharp edge of his wolf coming through loud and clear.

"How dare you!" Wyvern's eyes widened and her nostrils flared. "You'll go where I tell you to go."

"Stop playing your games and tell me why I'm here." If it wasn't to tell her that they'd been wrong, that her banishment was over, that she could take her place on the throne, then what was it they wanted from her?

Wyvern shifted her cold eyes to Crimson, a tight smile now on her lips. "Very well, sister. Never one to beat around the bush. I'd forgotten. Silly me." She moved backward until she reached her throne then took a seat, making sure to sweep her hand under the back of her dress to prevent it from catching on the throne's arms. "We have a mission for you."

"A mission?"

"Yes, to find the witch who trapped Angelica here." Wyvern glanced at Tabitha who nodded. "She is the only one who can retrieve the Crystal of Shade."

"You want me to find a witch—?"

"Yes, sister, we want you to find her in her realm and bring her to Shade. Then we want you to go with her to claim the crystal." Tabitha tapped her fingers against the arm of the throne. "She is tethered to it somehow, and we can't find this Angelica without her." She paused with a little snort. "Well, we could find her, but we'd much rather you be the one to do it…since you're so good at hunting treasures."

The dig was a nasty reminder of what had landed her in trouble, her quest to find precious treasures for her queens, something her sisters had always said was Crimson's way of sucking up.

"Crimson might—"

Tabitha raised her hand to cut Talon off. "Once the witch has the crystal in her possession, we'll invite her to take her rightful seat on the dais."

"Her rightful seat?" Crimson's breath caught and her world tilted.

Again... They'd do this to me again? Ofcourseofcourseofcourse.

"Who is this witch?" Valor bellowed, speaking when Crimson couldn't.

Tabitha cut him a scathing glare as Wyvern answered. "Lucki Collins of the human realm. She's powerful enough to have shifted Angelica into this world and trapped her here. The crystal — which, as you know, was stolen from us centuries ago by a deceitful handmaiden named Isabel of Clover — is still tied to this Lucki witch. She's the only one who can steal it back from Angelica. Not even you, sister, are powerful enough to do that."

"What makes you think she'll accept the role in the triad?" Crimson could barely get the words out for the lump clogging her throat, but there was no way she'd let anyone speak for her again. Not that she didn't appreciate Valor's voice, but right now she needed to show strength no matter how gutted she felt.

"Because, as you know, sister, we can be very convincing."

Crimson narrowed her eyes at Tabitha. Her tone held an undercurrent of deceit, like this was a game and Crimson was losing somehow. What was she saying? What was the underlying meaning to her words? That she had convinced everyone that Crimson had been guilty when really they knew she wasn't?

Or was she reading too much into her sister's tone? Had a year away rattled her ability to know when her sisters were lying?

No, something was off and it was more than just her sisters' usual bullying ways.

Crimson had always suspected that the evidence her sisters had gathered had been misread, misinterpreted, but what if the evidence—the power the Fortis detected in the chamber—what if it had been manipulated by them? Would they be that conniving?

Oh gods, yes. Yes, they would. Crimson's world tilted. She staggered back a step. Could it be? Had her sisters set her up?

"Oh, and one other thing." Wyvern lifted a finger as if she was just thinking of something she'd forgotten. "We'll be keeping your familiars here, to protect the court, while you're on your trip."

Crimson lunged for the dais. Jaggar captured her over his forearm. "It's not worth their wrath," he growled.

"*Tsk, tsk,* little sister." Tabitha wagged her finger. "That temper hasn't improved in your solitude? I would think you would have had much time to meditate on that."

She struggled until Jaggar set her on her feet again. "You're holding my familiars hostage?"

"Now, now, Crimson...so dramatic." Wyvern rolled her eyes. "Consider it collateral—or better, a promise that you'll behave while you're away."

"You want me to face off with an unknown witch in another realm without shifters? That could be a death sentence." Not really for Crimson, but still, she had no idea what she'd face in the human realm or how many familiars Lucki the witch would have at her side.

"I highly doubt that. For all your esteem issues, Crimson, we do know how powerful you are. It's why we've had to clip your wings." Tabitha pouted as if Crimson's banishment was her own fault. "And we're not sending you without protection."

Crimson glared. Tabitha smirked.

Wyvern spoke. "We're sending you with your old friends, Jaggar and Zephyr. They'll be able to keep you on track and focused and, most *importantly*, out of trouble."

"You know what we're capable of when you cause trouble, Crimson," Tabitha added.

Wyvern flicked her hand in dismissal, but Tabitha kept a steady stare as she curled her lips into a vicious smile.

Chapter Six

Jaggar

"Let me through!" Jaggar could easily push his way past Talon and Valor, but out of respect for the familiars, he towered over them instead, chuffing his frustration like a civilized brute, his panther so close to the surface that claws poked through the tips of his fingers.

"You misled her, practically conned her to get her here. You should be ashamed of yourself, brother." Talon didn't have to be the same size as Jaggar to gut him with a single blow. His words were as much an attack as claws or fangs could be. "You implied —"

"I did not." Jaggar had been hopeful that the queens would see the error of their ways and, at the very least, give Crimson the opportunity to prove her loyalty so that she might become a member of the triad. It was a hope he knew Crimson had shared and why she'd so passively accepted her punishment. She had always been the one to give those callous witches the benefit of the doubt.

While the high witches hadn't explicitly said they wanted Crimson home to seat her on the throne, they had made it seem like they desperately needed her and that they regretted sending her away.

He'd realized, as they pulled their nonsense in the throne room, that what they'd meant was they needed to use Crimson to accomplish a quest that they couldn't do themselves. Retrieval work of this kind was not in their skillset, and pushing it off on Crimson as if it was a continuation of her punishment was just like them to do. They played on Crimson's low self-esteem and the mistaken belief that those on the throne deserved deference. They had always loved kicking their sister while she was down.

For all her power, Crimson never gave herself the credit that she deserved. She never thought, not once, that she might have enough power to usurp her sisters and claim what she was owed. She didn't want to believe that they were the ones who deserved to be punished.

"Let me in to see her now." He let the rumble of his panther edge his words. "We have things to discuss."

"I think she's heard enough," Valor growled back. "Unless you're here to tell her that you've used your influence to allow us to accompany *our* mate into the other realm."

Their mate. Not his. Something that he planned to rectify as soon as he could. He'd chosen a year ago to put Crimson's life ahead of his need to bond to her, knowing if he insisted on leaving court with Crimson, Talon and Valor that it would be a death sentence for all of them. At least with him and Zephyr staying behind, they could monitor what diabolical plans the high witches were hatching. The things he'd seen in the last year would send a lesser familiar running. It wasn't just their warped sense of reason. It was the underlying snicker that made all their decisions seem petty and vindictive, or worse, entertainment for their pleasure only.

He'd avoided bonding with Aria, much to the deceased witch's displeasure. She'd tortured him. Humiliated him. Threatened to kill Zephyr, to exile them both. But it didn't matter, because if he bonded with Aria, he knew he'd never be able to bond with Crimson, and she was his true soulmate.

Even if she was infuriatingly stubborn.

"You will stay here as the high witches decreed," Jaggar roared and regretted his words immediately. His panther was pushing so hard to break through that it was the cat's fury the familiars were seeing.

Talon snorted, baring his teeth as if his eagle had fangs to show.

Jaggar shook his head then lunged forward so he was all up in Talon's face, while at the same time battling his panther back. "You think this is the high witches benching you when you really should be thinking of this as an opportunity to listen, watch, study who they are and how they control the Fortis. Think strategy."

Valor pushed him back but without the force Jaggar would have expected. It seemed as if the familiar was finally hearing what he was saying.

"Zephyr and I have had a year to study our foes. Now it's your turn. We're all on the same side here. We've just been playing different angles."

Talon grunted. Valor stepped back. Dawning understanding shone in both of their eyes, and they nodded. It was confirmation enough that they were on board.

This was the way it should have been from the start. This was the way it had been before they'd been separated by the high witches. A year apart had splintered them, especially since there was no opportunity to talk to them at all without drawing unwanted attention. From the moment of Wyvern, Tabitha and Aria's ascension, something rotten had infiltrated the court, and Jaggar knew that while he and Zephyr had gotten close to finding out the truth, they weren't quite there yet. Maybe Talon and Valor would have more luck.

"Let me pass so I can explain myself to Crimson." Jaggar softened his tone and released the tension in his upper body. It was as close to submissive that he was willing to give.

Talon nodded.

Valor shifted so Jaggar could pass.

"Zephyr is in the stairwell. He can show you the things we've learned about court that will aid your search for truth—weaknesses and lapses in watch, important detours you can use if necessary. Truth is being hidden here, and we need to uncover it so that Crimson may rise to her full potential."

Valor and Talon shared a look, clearly unsure about leaving Crimson alone with Jaggar. How times had changed. Before the banishment, they would never have suspected him of treachery. He bristled, but instead of lashing out again, he opted for a calm approach.

"I will protect her with my life, brothers." It nearly choked him to have to say those words out loud, but Jaggar forced them out. "You can trust me, at least, to do that. I vow it to the Brotherhood."

Talon sucked in a deep breath then nodded before letting it explode out. "Let's go, Valor."

Jaggar paused for the familiars to turn the corner. He waited to hear the backslapping and joking as they reunited with Zephyr on more friendly terms, then stood with a touch of cowardly hesitation, for another full minute before pulling the door to Crimson's suite open.

The whining noise of a blast of power gave him seconds of warning. He ducked as a magic strike ricocheted off the door and exploded next to his ear. The near miss rattled his brain and made his ears ring painfully, but he rolled across the floor before Crimson could correct her aim.

She struck again, not bothering to hide her position, still wearing her formal court attire and looking as pissed off as her attack spells suggested. A divot opened next to him in the stone wall, and he had to believe she was missing him on purpose, because there was no way her accuracy would lapse that much, even if she'd been slacking off all year.

"Crimson, enough!" Jaggar slid beside the bed just in time to avoid another blast that took out the pillows in a plume of feathers.

"Enough of *what*, Jaggar? Enough of your lies? Enough of your betrayal?"

"I've *never* betrayed you!" Jaggar took a chance, sprang up, then dove across the bed in one leap. He wrapped his arms around Crimson's waist and tackled her to the ground. Her magic markings swirled, flashing pulses of angry color as she revved up for another hit. He pinned her hands above her head and pressed his weight into her body.

Despite his bulk and strength, that didn't stop her from bucking and cursing, trying to force her way out from under him.

"Give me a chance to explain," he huffed. They'd used to do this—to wrestle and fool around so the feel of her underneath him made him very aware of every curve, every hill, every valley that he'd been denied this past year. *Gods, it feels so good.*

Her eyes told him that those days were long over, and instead of lust, all he saw was loathing. "Get off me!"

Defeat was a hard pill to swallow, but Jaggar knew when to retreat. *If only to regroup.*

Much to Crimson's obvious surprise, he complied— not because he didn't think Crimson craved dominance, she did—just not from him, and definitely not right now.

He'd thought he could repair the damage the last year had caused by reminding Crimson of their chemistry. He'd thought wrong. The fissure between them ran much deeper than he'd anticipated, and regret over so many things swirled in his gut.

He leaned against the bed and ran his fingers through his hair, swiping it from his face as he did.

Crimson was already on her feet, already bouncing, nostrils flaring, fists up, fingers ripe with magic. "Get up! We're not done. I want to knock you on your ass."

"I'm already on my ass."

Crimson rolled her eyes then took a swipe at his head, slapping him so that his hair flipped back over his face. "Get up, you coward!"

His panther clawed to be let out. Instead, he ran his fingers through his hair again and looked up at her with no ferocity. "I am a coward." His panther chuffed at that. Crimson's fists wobbled and her smirk died. "I thought what I was doing was for the best. I was attempting to keep you safe."

She tried to hold on to her rage. The struggle was clear in how deeply furrowed her brow was while her eyes softened and her lips twitched. Jaggar blew out another long breath. There was a chance, with time, that she'd forgive him, but maybe they'd never be what they once were, and that was entirely his fault. *I did what I thought best.*

"You have a shitty way of protecting me if you think ripping my heart out is the best way to go about it." While her voice held hostility, her body didn't. She slumped onto the bed then flopped backward so her arms were spread wide and her hair splayed around her head like a dark halo.

While he liked the look of her short cut, he missed her long hair. So dark, it was like an endless night sky, so shiny that he could always see the iridescent glow of her innate power. He'd loved running his fingers through it, wrapping it around his fists as he envisioned pounding her sweet pussy and plump ass until she screamed with release. But that had never happened—and maybe never would, thanks to the high witches and their ruthless rule.

"You aren't letting it grow out." It had only been a year, but the cut suggested she was keeping it short rather than letting it come back to its old glory.

Crimson shrugged. "I needed a change."

"I like it. It suits you."

"Ha! You hate short hair." She crossed her arms and glared at him over the comforter, daring him to lie.

"I like it on you. It's sophisticated. It makes you look like a warrior."

She scoffed again, but it sounded forced, and along with the slight pink on her cheeks, she seemed flustered. "Why don't we skip the chitchat and get to the shit you should be telling me?" She pushed herself up so she braced her weight on her elbows. It showcased her ample breasts, another thing Jaggar had always wanted to stroke with purpose rather than with stolen, clumsy nudges and accidental brushes. She noted his gaze and pushed herself up all the way, curling into herself. "Oh no, you don't get to look at me like that, all hungry. Nope. Not going to happen."

"Sorry. Old habit." He pushed himself off the floor then paced to the wall. "You're right. I have things to tell you, and we don't have time to fuck around."

He turned in time to see a glimpse of a grin on her lips—there and gone in an instant.

She waved at him to carry on, all nonchalant and unaffected, or so he realized she'd like to appear.

"When your sisters banished you, Aria made it clear that if we were to follow you, she'd have you killed." He raised his hand when Crimson opened her mouth. "She'd already bonded to three Fortis before her coronation even happened."

Crimson gasped, and her eyes flashed hot.

It was against the laws of Shade for any witch to mate a Fortis without the express permission of the high witches. Since they both knew that there was no way Crimson's mother or her aunt or her grandmother would have allowed that—because it would have given Wyvern, Tabitha and Aria more power than the crones on the throne — it had to have happened before the queens had disappeared. It was also forbidden to mate with more than two Fortis, because the power they offered a witch was as intense as ten suns and could be just as dangerous. That much power could scorch a witch from the inside out, overwhelming her innate powers and turning her essence upside-down. The question Jaggar always had on his mind was how Aria had done it. How had she convinced the three Fortis to break covenant and bond with her, even when the reigning queens hadn't given express permission?

It wasn't like Aria would have ever told him how, nor Wyvern or Tabitha, for that matter. There would have to have been heavy coercion to entice the Fortis to go along with the sisters' plans to build their individual power, but the Fortis weren't talking to Jaggar, either. The sisters' bonded mates had removed themselves completely from interaction with the Brotherhood and kept their own counsel.

"So that's how they did it." Crimson slipped off the bed to pace on the other side of the room. "They somehow convinced Fortis to break the rules and mark them so that they had the balance of power. That's how they made the queens disappear." She darted wild eyes to Jaggar as if she'd let secret thoughts slip, and he realized in that moment that he didn't hold her confidence any longer. She hadn't meant to say that out loud. "Go ahead, run and tell them I've committed treason again. I'd much rather be at home than running an errand for those witches." Her voice contained the disgust that Jaggar himself felt.

"Crimson, I'm not the man you think I am." And he so painfully wished she'd truly see that everything he'd done, he'd done for her. When she didn't respond beyond a slight eyebrow lift, he continued. "The high witches have abused their power and are out of control. Both of them have taken on more Fortis marks."

"How many more?" Crimson stopped pacing. She covered her mouth, unable to hide her shock.

"I don't know." Jaggar shrugged. "But I think it's obvious that it's too much for their own good." All three had pushed the boundaries of bonding and were brimming with power that was likely nearly impossible for them to truly control. It was only a matter of time before one of them pushed things too far. Aria's death might have been a result of her overconfidence when the wild cats came for her and she made a fatal mistake, or it might have been simply because her power surged when she tried to use it and obliterated her before the wild cats even took a swipe.

"So not only do I have to contend with my sisters being unlawfully super powerful, but I also have to deal with the fact that they're both likely insane?"

"I mean, they were both probably leaning that way anyway." He grinned and was relieved when Crimson quirked a smile in response. It was small but he'd take it. "But yes, they are terrifyingly powerful. Still not as powerful as you, or at least, as powerful as you are destined to be." *With Fortis marks and more training.*

She scoffed but didn't argue. They both knew that it wasn't so much the wealth of magic a witch had but the way she used it. Yes, her sisters had might, but they didn't have strategy, not the way Crimson did.

"You're cunning, and you think on your feet. The high witches aren't capable of that."

"Isn't it treasonous for you to say such things?" She raised an eyebrow. "For you to even entertain the idea that our queens are unfit to rule? That they might have had something to do with Mother, Grandmother and Aunt Telli's disappearance?"

Classic Crimson, deflecting so she wouldn't have to admit that Jaggar was right. She was a gifted witch and had never truly accepted the power she held because of that. Her sisters had made sure to knock Crimson down, to make her believe she had nothing on them. For her whole life she had wanted to be accepted by those witches, only to be rejected over and over until her self-esteem was in the gutter. It hadn't mattered that she was favored by the ruling queens, that her mother doted on her, gave her freedoms her sisters never had. It didn't matter that she had two Fortis and two familiars vying for her bond. None of that compared to the way her sisters had rejected her, taunted her, tormented her.

"You and I know that what you say is the truth." Jaggar reveled in Crimson's flinch. His words clearly had impact. She was so determined to paint him as a villain and a co-conspirator with her sisters that she was unprepared for his support in her theory. "The investigation was a farce, but by that time, your sisters already had too much power and too much influence."

Crimson crossed her arms and narrowed her eyes, daring him to say more. The time would come for that later.

"Your sisters may have brute strength with their Fortis marks, but they haven't figured out the intricacies of their magic. It's clumsy and unreliable."

"I noticed." She waved a hand. "Took me a minute to find the weak point in their 'hold and secure' spell, but eventually I got out of it—in case you didn't notice since you were so focused on trying to rescue me."

It was this kind of thing that drove Jaggar insane. Crimson was never the damsel in distress, even when it was clear that she needed help.

"I take it you didn't keep up your training?" he shot back instead of saying what he really wanted to say, that she had what it would take to rise up and claim her birthright—that he and Zephyr would help her do it.

"I trained." But the sudden blush on her cheeks told him the real story.

"You need to be in control of your power to make this trip." He switched tactics, focusing on the present problem instead. "This witch in the other realm—"

"Lucki." Crimson laughed dismissively.

"Yes, Lucki. Her power is an unknown. We have no information about how she's been marked or by whom."

"She managed to lock another powerful witch in Shade, so I'm guessing she packs a punch." Crimson flexed her fists and her markings flared. "I'm ready."

Crimson had always been *ready* to follow orders. To do her duty. To defer to those in a position of power. He just wished she'd be the one to take the lead on her own journey rather than waiting for everything to happen to her.

Jaggar walked toward her slowly, as if he was worried that she would bolt as soon as he got too near. She didn't, though. She just stopped pacing and watched him approach with narrowed eyes.

He'd always planned to be the one to help her see her potential, to boost her confidence so she would embrace what she was destined to be—a queen.

"I need you to understand that I didn't want any of this to happen."

She allowed him to get in her space, to stand so close that he could smell vanilla and citrus and see how her eyes faded from the deepest darkest blue to something closer to the sky.

"You didn't want *what* to happen?" Her voice caught but she didn't clear her throat.

He reached up to sweep a stray hair from her face, then couldn't help but cup her jaw like he always used to do. She didn't swat him away, and his heart soared with that small permission.

"I didn't want any of this to happen." His voice rumbled out like he was speaking through a mouthful of rocks.

"Yeah, well, neither did I." She took a step away, leaving his hand hovering. "But I promise you, there is nothing in this world or any other that will keep me from my mates. I may have to go with you and Zeph to the other realm, but I won't do anything to jeopardize the bond I have with the ones who stood with me. You say I'm powerful? More powerful than my sisters? Imagine what we could have done if you'd marked me when I begged you to. Imagine if you'd taken that risk for me so we wouldn't have been separated. Imagine if you'd broken covenant for me like Aria's Fortis had for her." She sucked in a deep breath. "They must have believed in her so much that they were willing to break all the rules. But you..." she spat. "You stepped down instead of up. You chose not to empower me so I could get to the truth and find my true queens, so I could clear my name. You chose that, Jaggar, and now it's too late." She turned her back and headed to the other room. "Just in case you were under the impression that everything would go back to the way it was... Nothing will ever be like it was."

Jaggar slumped, letting the weight of the guilt he carried burden him physically. She had demanded that he bond with her. Not on her knees, not as a supplicant, begging, but with her chin jutting and her shoulders back, she'd *demanded* that he help her prove her innocence, and he'd said no.

She couldn't see that at the time it wouldn't have worked. Back then, if he'd marked her, she would have failed. She had no idea what her sisters were capable of, but Jaggar had had an idea — an inkling of what was to come. He'd watched the sisters for years. He'd known the evil that lay deep inside, that rose to the surface more and more frequently as they tormented Crimson, and it had scared him enough to want to send the love of his life away, far away so they wouldn't hurt her as their insanity grew. But now, after a year of watching, of waiting, Jaggar was ready to take action.

He'd hoped for forgiveness, for enough time to have passed that the hurt of their separation would have turned itself back to longing and maybe, somehow, understanding. He wanted to right the wrongs and move past them with Crimson at his side.

That had been stupid of him.

With Crimson there was only ever frustration and stubbornness and a willful blindness to the truth, even if it was set before her on a platter — truth about herself, her ability, her destiny. He would never stop loving her, but right now he hated everything about her.

What he hated the most was that she was right.

Chapter Seven

Crimson

When they lay together like this, Valor curled behind, his cock wedged deep inside her aching pussy, Talon in front, his lips trailing heat over her skin and his fingers rubbing against her clit, she knew that nothing in this world would come between her and her familiars. Her heart was safe and needs always met by her two powerful, loyal shifters.

Valor cupped her breasts from behind, offering them up to Talon, who teased her nipples with a little pain and a little tenderness. He nipped her tender flesh, dragging his teeth to flick her sensitive nubs, one then the other, followed by a soothing suck, lick then kiss. Valor rolled his hips, pumping her full as he kissed along her shoulder then sucked on her earlobe. It was her weakest spot, an instant aphrodisiac that made her shiver and moan. This was bliss, euphoria and all she needed.

She didn't want Jaggar or Zephyr.

No matter how many times her mind twisted toward them, she didn't want to feel the longing for them that she had fought so hard to suppress over the last year.

And yet, her desire for those two Fortis maniacs was underlying her every moan, twitch and quiver.

She was selfish for wanting more than she already had, but there was no denying that she did want more... She wanted what she'd always wanted, a harem of four.

Talon circled her clit with his fingers, pressing harder then rubbing softer, alternating sensations so that she couldn't help but buck against him, one hand flung back, clasping Valor's muscled ass and encouraging him to push deeper, to thrust with unforgiving power.

She arched into Talon's touch, her nipples flushed and hot, aching for him to suck and lick and bite. They moved in unison, gasping together as Crimson pulled Talon closer, her fingers clasped to his shoulder, and he obliged, coaxing the wisp of her climax until it rolled over her in shuddering waves, obliterating any thought, any worry, any lingering anger.

Talon kissed her as she gasped the last of her climax, swallowing her pleasure and giving her more. Cupping her cheeks with his hands and deeply probing her mouth with his tongue, devouring her every moan, awareness flickered through Crimson's thoughts that he was saying goodbye.

She opened her eyes as he pulled back, and his expression said it all.

"You will do what you have to do when you cross the ether." Talon still held her face, his golden gaze both dazzling and penetrating. "If it means taking their marks, you will."

Crimson jolted back, only to be caged by Valor. He rocked her pussy gently, rolling into her as he whispered in her ear. "You may need their power to match this other witch."

"No!" Crimson fought to free herself from her familiars, but they were solid rocks of muscle, holding her in place.

"Yes." Talon kissed her again, lips pressed to lips, love in a tender touch. "We can't risk losing you."

"I won't—"

"You will if you must." Valor pulled back, his cock slipping free before he yanked her around, swapping positions so she was now facing him. He cupped her face like Talon had and drilled her with his brown soulful eyes. "You can't despise them forever."

But she could. Jaggar had betrayed her. Zephyr had gone along with it. Both had made the choice to stay away and to exile her heart, along with their betrayal.

She knew Valor saw her thoughts. She knew he understood her pain. But he also knew her soul, her desire, that under her protest lay a kernel of want. He knew Zephyr and Jaggar had always been her conquests.

When Valor kissed her, it wasn't soft and coaxing. It was brutal and hungry.

Talon hoisted her up to her knees, giving her little time to adjust her position before slamming his cock deep into her pussy hard and fast, rocking her forward so when Valor swiveled around, one hand teasing her nipple, she was ready to take his cock.

Talon squeezed her other tit while she opened her lips and sucked Valor's dick until his crown nudged the back of her throat. She unlocked her jaw and took him all the way back, cradling him in her throat while Talon pummeled her pussy in a frenzy.

She could be satisfied with her men, her devoted shifters who always put her needs first. And yet, their words, their commands swirled through her mind.

If it means taking their marks, you will.

Valor gripped her hair, pulled her head back so he could slip free of her mouth, only to drill back inside seconds later. She pressed her tongue along his shaft as he thrust deep into her throat. His dick, hot, hard and spewing pre-cum, filled her greedy mouth and snapped her brain out of its fog. *Be in the moment. Cherish your shifters.*

If this was goodbye, she needed to make sure she took everything they had to give.

Talon used his free hand to rub her clit, circling, flicking, pressing until her climax sparked all over again.

She dug her knees into the bed, attempting to anchor herself so she could cup Valor's balls with one hand, pressing firmly to his shaft with her tongue at the same time, desperate to give him as much pleasure as he gave her. His answering moan was a testament to his need.

Her nipples burned, her clit throbbed and her climax crested, fireworks ready to explode.

Valor grunted and growled, his cock like a steel rod, his balls tight, his thrusts urgent. Talon groaned, pumping until his dick pulsed and his cum spilled, coating her until it dripped from her pussy. Crimson's climax detonated, blasting waves so intense that her vision flashed rainbows and her body quaked. Valor released his load, jets of hot cum hitting the back of her throat so forcefully that she sputtered through the first few gulps, and streams ran down her chin.

They rocked together until there was nothing left — until every quivering, shuddering spasm had rolled through each of them to its end.

Satiated physically but not mentally or emotionally, they lay in a tangled mess, sweating and panting, avoiding the words that had to come at some point.

Goodbye. I love you. Be safe.

She would pay her sisters back for separating her from Talon and Valor, but she wouldn't do it with the magical marks of those who had betrayed her. She would do it with cunning strategy, organized magic and maybe, a little bit of luck.

Chapter Eight

Crimson

Crimson had known Zephyr longer than she'd known Jaggar. He'd come from the caves of the Brotherhood when she had been sixteen and had stuck close to her in his brooding, silent way. It had been clear to her almost from the start that he was attracted to her magic, but there was also a quiet intensity to his protectiveness. He'd made sure things didn't get in the way of her training and her happiness, including her sisters. He'd encouraged her to push herself past the limits she'd thought she had. While Zephyr had never been much of a conversationalist, the few words he'd said to her always had impact. Crimson had never doubted that he had her back and only wanted what was best for her, which was why it had come as such a devastating shock when he'd told her to leave Shade, to leave him behind with Jaggar and her sisters—not to fight the unfair punishment, but to go along with the staining of her name. It was as good as a punch to the face. He'd gutted her, and in the year that had followed, she'd slammed shut any possibility of their relationship ever being repaired.

"I'm not sure why you're giving me dirty looks, Zephyr." Crimson adjusted her battle suit, which twined over her body in swathes of black fabric. It moved with her like a second skin and helped channel her power where she needed it. "It's you who betrayed me."

Zephyr hadn't looked directly at her, not once since their reunion, but he had given her such a scathing side-eye when she'd entered the chamber that she'd noticed.

He snorted, one eyebrow slightly raised.

"Oh, you disagree?" She ran her fingers through her hair, a nervous tic when she was impatient. "I guess you're following Jaggar's lead now more than ever, right? His foolish ideas that are designed to get me killed."

Zephyr yanked his eyebrow higher as if to say, *oh really?* She didn't have to hear his voice to recognize his sarcasm.

Crimson wouldn't say her thoughts out loud, not in the chamber where anyone could be listening, but Jaggar's words had gotten to her. He hadn't outright said *coup*, but she knew him well enough to read between the lines. Her sisters were out of control, and he somehow expected her to fix that by overthrowing them.

And that was just...well...insane. The only way she'd have a chance to prove her innocence was if she ascended to the empty throne. Once there, she could reason with her sisters on equal footing.

Not without the marks of the Fortis.

Her inner witch was a treacherous beast. Even though Crimson knew Fortis marks would enhance her powers considerably, even though her body craved Zephyr and Jaggar to a maddening degree, even though she knew it would be foolish to face her sisters without an army of four at her back, she still refused to accept that it was the only way to beat them at their own game.

She'd have the crystal if her plan worked the way she intended and, with that, she'd be able to sway even the demented minds of Tabitha and Wyvern.

She didn't need the two shifters who'd betrayed her, and she'd prove it.

Jaggar finally entered the chamber after rushing out at the last minute to take care of something.

"About time." Crimson didn't wait for a retort, and she wasn't a fan of delays. "I'm ready."

While they could part the veil and enter the ether in any location, it was wisest to use one of the sacred chambers of Shade where the natural magic was so strong that it hummed in her ears and sent pulses colliding with her own power. She preferred this particular circle because it was the only other place in the castle that had been built into the side of the Mountain of Shade. Just like her shower, it had jutting boulders and staggered ledges. It was open to the sky so that, at the right moments, the sun's rays would hit the rocks in such a way that their embedded crystals would sparkle and shine.

Dazzling would be an understatement. It was hard to focus on anything when the light played with the crystals and their magic released — which was why Crimson had chosen to use the chamber before the sun could peak. While the magic wasn't quite as strong, it would be enough to bolster her own power. She ran her hand along one damp wall and absorbed the static shock that nipped at her fingers. The chamber was brimming with untapped power, and Crimson knew that her sisters had never fully trained to use its potential. They'd always felt it was too archaic to bother with and had found it annoying to venture deep into the castle to get to it. They preferred more modern circles that had been built in the last century, while Crimson understood the value of age.

"Crimson, you need to tone down your power signature. We don't want to signal our arrival." Jaggar ran his fingers through his long hair before quickly tying it back with a clasp. No matter how much she hated him, she couldn't deny that he was incredibly sexy with his silky waves scraped roughly away from his high cheekbones and wicked eyes. He'd always made her knees buckle with the simplest of gestures. "Bring us in soft and quiet, so we can do recon before we engage the witch. If you can manage, cloaking our arrival would be helpful, too. Battle is the last resort. Hopefully, with some luck, we'll be able to snatch her before anyone notices."

Crimson rolled her eyes. He might be hot, but he was pushy as fuck, and she didn't take orders from him. "Snatch the witch who banished Angelica here?" Crimson scoffed. "That's your plan?"

She shook her head when both he and Zephyr glared at her as if to say, *you have a better one?*

As a matter of fact, she did, but she wasn't about to tell them about it.

"All right." She cracked her knuckles then shook her fingers out.

She'd said her goodbyes to her familiars. Talon and Valor would keep an eye on her sisters while Crimson was gone, and they'd stay safe, because if anything happened to them there'd be hell to pay, and the boys didn't want her bringing the castle down in her fury.

She slid her hand along the wall one last time then centered herself in the room. There were no markings to guide her. It was more of a feeling that pressed her from all sides until she was standing in the exact spot that she needed to be in order to harness the right amount of power. It had taken her years to learn the magical rhythms of this room, and she hadn't realized how much she'd missed its hum of power in her year away.

She raised her arms, unleashing her power with barely a thought. It sparked over her skin and twirled like a tornado from her fingertips. She located the tether that her sisters said would take her to the witch known as Lucki—a velvety purple thing that pulsed with a muted but distinct otherworldly magic. *Human witch magic.* Usually clumsy and under-formed, this tether linking to the witch was residual magic that gave Crimson a pretty good idea of what she'd be facing in the human world. Lucki wasn't weak, but she could be untrained, especially considering that she'd left the tether behind to trace her whereabouts. A trained witch would know to destroy it, lest her enemies find her.

The veil parted and Jaggar then Zephyr clapped their meaty hands to her shoulders. What used to be a reassuring gesture now felt oppressive. She wanted to shrug them off but knew that would be futile. They'd cling to her like leeches until the mission was complete. She scoffed in her head. Too bad she hadn't known that loyalty was optional with these two, or she wouldn't have given her trust to them all those years ago.

Ancient history. Or at least, she was trying to keep it ancient.

She tugged on the tether. "Hang on, Fortis." Then she pushed her magic through the connection and let the magnetic pull hoist her up and suck her into the ether, the Fortis brutes coming along for the ride.

Chapter Nine

Zephyr

The plan had been to go into the other realm covertly so they could gather information first, then steal the witch and battle last, only if required.

He should have known Crimson wouldn't stick to the plan. Never one for patience, she always did like to get to the point quickly.

They landed in the human realm surrounded by familiars—a wolf, bear and lion, magic emanating felines, a few non-magical wolves and one pissed-off-looking redheaded witch.

So much for recon.

Zephyr couldn't help himself. He shifted. His tiger burst forth in a frenzy of fangs, fur and a protective rage that had him snarling viciously. Crimson wasn't his mate—not yet, anyway—but he'd always considered her his to protect.

Jaggar had done the same, his panther clawing at the dirt. So now Crimson stood, hands raised and sparking with magic, with two amped-up Fortis chuffing by her side. He had no doubt that they could put up a good fight, but he wasn't stupid enough to think that they'd win. They were outnumbered, no matter how much power Crimson could wield.

"We're not here to fight." Crimson's magic pulsed, telling a different story. "We need your help."

Huh? Zephyr cocked his head to the side, examining Crimson for a head wound. It was as good as saying that they came in peace when really, their orders, and frankly, their plan, was to drag the witch through the ether by the hair if necessary. Not that he would have followed that particular command, but he would have used force to convince her and her familiars to take care of their unfinished business in Shade. It was the witch's fault that Angelica was in Shade in the first place, causing the havoc that she was.

"We come from the Kingdom of Shade. My name is Crimson, and these are my babysitters."

Jaggar chuffed. Zephyr growled.

The redheaded witch still looked pissed, but her lips twitched as if the situation was suddenly a little amusing to her. "Why do you need babysitters, Crimson?" By the way she asked, the slight trill to her voice, it seemed that this witch knew just how protective familiars could be.

Crimson lowered her hands enough to send a message. She wouldn't strike with magic, and she wouldn't throw the first punch. "Because my sisters don't trust me to follow their orders."

She got that half right. Zephyr wasn't only there to make sure that the witch named Lucki came back with them to Shade. He was also there because his heart and soul belonged to Crimson, whether she wanted it or not. Her sisters be damned. He wasn't there to keep her on a leash, no matter what the queens had decreed.

"What orders?" Lucki lowered her hands as well but kept her magic pulsing strongly enough to let everyone know she was ready if the need arose.

"They've sent me to retrieve you so you can clean up your mess in Shade." Crimson folded her arms. "I believe a certain witch named Angelica belongs to you?"

Lucki flinched. She dropped her hands to her sides, her magic ebbing back where it came. Her beasts, clearly following the conversation, huffed and growled, a message being sent. Angelica was no friend to anyone there.

"I banished her to another realm," Lucki admitted, her eyes wide, like she truly had no idea what she'd done. "Are you saying I banished her somewhere that's inhabited and she's causing trouble?"

"Trouble is an understatement," Crimson said with a curt nod.

Lucki's face twisted up as if she were riddled with guilt. Maybe this witch was untrained. Maybe she really hadn't known what she was doing when she'd sent Angelica to Shade. It was possible that a human witch was that naïve — or maybe she was as duplicitous as the queens of Shade.

"What can I do to help?"

It was the last thing that Zephyr was expecting the witch to say, but Crimson took her words in stride. "I have a plan, if you're willing to hear me out."

* * * *

Lucki and Crimson had entered the huge yellow house after it had become clear that all the familiars weren't willing, or able, to shift out of their beasts. They'd been circling one another for the last twenty minutes at least, Lucki's three attempting to keep a wide cage around Zephyr and Jaggar the entire time, but none had made any kind of attacking move, yet. The tension wasn't as high as it had been when they'd landed in the human realm, but there was a current that vibrated the air enough for all the beasts to be on edge.

Pacing a short circuit, and pent up with frustration, Zephyr realized that somehow Crimson had gotten the better of them. She'd managed to ditch her protectors so effortlessly that he had to wonder if she'd had this planned all along. She didn't trust them, that was clear, but would she willfully put herself at risk with an unknown witch, just to spite Jaggar and Zephyr?

Yes!

Zephyr had been with Crimson long enough to know that in stressful times like these, she let her heart rule where her head should. He loved that about her. Her passion was unmatched, and he had once known what it felt like to bask in the heat of her devotion.

Crimson had made it clear that she felt they'd betrayed her by not coming with her into exile. Zephyr, not a man of many words, had yet to figure out a way to explain why they'd done what they had. Jaggar's attempt had resulted in more hostility, but he had always been the hotheaded one, blunt and to the point, just like Crimson. Zephyr needed to work out how to convince Crimson that they'd done everything to protect her—that the only way they could have been together was if *she'd* come to rescue them, not the other way around. He hadn't yet figured out how to convince a bull-headed witch that she was not the victim — not entirely the victim, anyway. He had to find a way to show her that she had the power to resist, even though she didn't see it herself. Maybe she was right... Maybe if he'd gone with her into exile, he would have been able to bolster her confidence, but that would have meant turning his back on the queens, and they were far too tricky to ever show that kind of weakness to.

Zephyr knew that Crimson wanted truth, but he also knew that for all her bluster and boom, she wouldn't make the first move to strike against her sisters. She was too entrenched in the rules, the covenants that her mother, the true queen, had instilled in her. She still, deep down, believed that her sisters were innocent — or at least, that they deserved what they hadn't given her — a fair trial. Crimson had a deep-rooted belief that loyalty was the anchor of families, despite the very obvious fact that her own sisters had betrayed her. She wouldn't strike first against them, no matter what, and that was her fatal flaw. Also, it was her most endearing quality.

Jaggar was clearly antsy. He wanted in that house, but each time he padded in that direction, Lucki's familiars would roar, laying claim to their territory. Since Crimson had called a truce, neither Zephyr nor Jaggar could assert any kind of dominance. If they made the wrong move, they'd start a battle, and that was not what Crimson wanted. They were bound to her leadership, even if they weren't technically bound to her as familiars, which was another thing Zephyr hoped to rectify as soon as possible. With, or more likely without, the blessing of the triad, Crimson needed to accept that one of the ways for her to beat her sisters at their own game was to level up and take Jaggar and Zephyr's marks.

When the game is dirty, it's necessary to play dirty as well.

At the moment, though, Zephyr needed to figure out how to get inside the house before all the testosterone-fueled magic choked him out.

Jaggar shifted from cat to Fortis, giving him a more menacing appearance caught somewhere between beast and man, but also allowing him to speak to the group.

Bold.

It wouldn't have been a strategy Zephyr would have chosen with the tension that existed in the small space, since it signaled dominance and was the way, in Shade, that familiars showcased just how powerful they were. Since Zephyr had been spending his time pacing instead of taking action, however, he really couldn't complain about Jaggar's methods.

"Brothers, we follow the lead of Crimson. She has declared peace, so I propose that we shall as well. We will shift on three and speak as men."

Leave it to Jaggar to dominate anyway.

Zephyr sighed, half expecting the other familiars to turn Fortis and wage war, but instead they grunted and grumbled, looking at each other as if they could somehow communicate telepathically.

"One...two..." Jaggar began his shift from Fortis to man, usually a painless and quick process, but it appeared that he was struggling with his beast for control.

Zephyr wasn't sure his cat would relinquish control either, but perhaps shifting first to Fortis was causing more problems for Jaggar. Zephyr focused on calling his tiger back, pulling and pushing at the same time so that he shifted from four feet to two. It was rough, a struggle he didn't relish repeating, but at least he'd managed a little more seamlessly than Jaggar had.

The bear tilted its enormous head back and roared. Its jowls shook and its fangs dripped with spit. Zephyr's hackles rose and his claws punched through his knuckles, unsure if the beast was about to attack or if the bear was doing his own internal battle for control.

Several excruciating minutes later, they were all standing as men, trying hard to not to glare but failing miserably.

"What is your witch up to in there?" The dark-haired wolf with the electrifying blue eyes was the first to lash out with his frustration. It was obvious to Zephyr that the familiar was a hairsbreadth away from losing control over his beast again. His jaw was tight, muscles popping as he clenched and unclenched his fists.

"Presumably sharing her plan with your witch." Jaggar raised his hands as if to calm the wolf down.

"And what is that plan?" the bear asked, his tone even and more diplomatic, his expression relaxed, as if this were a friendly conversation with no underlying need to protect the witches.

"We don't know. Crimson has deviated from what I *thought* we'd agreed on. She's willful, headstrong." Jaggar sighed as if he was just as frustrated with the situation as he was with Crimson's way of doing things.

"Same here, brother. Same here." The bear laughed in a hearty, deep-belly way, expelling the remaining tension. "All right, men, let's work this out so we don't all go barging inside like a bunch of Neanderthals. I'm

Reuben." He held his arm out. "And I welcome you to Weeping Falls."

Jaggar didn't hesitate. He stepped forward and clasped Rueben's forearm. "Jaggar of Shade."

Reuben nodded to his right where the golden-haired former lion stood. "Julian," he said as he took his turn grasping Jaggar's arm.

"Zephyr." Zephyr made his way through the line of familiars, clasping arms and nodding until he reached the wolf.

"Wren." The wolf's grip was strong, as was the magic that rippled along his forearms. *Unchecked magic.*

The magic marks on their flesh were an obvious sign that these familiars were Fortis, but it was clear that they had no idea what that meant. If they'd been trained, they would not be brandishing their strength as they were. A Fortis' magic should be managed so that it became part of their hidden arsenal. To display it like this was an amateur way of broadcasting to all what limitations and weaknesses could be exploited.

"When were you marked?" Jaggar, apparently thinking along the same lines, nodded toward Wren's visible magic markings.

"Three months ago," Reuben answered. "Still trying to feel our way through it."

"And how did you come to possess the magic?" Jaggar turned to face Reuben.

There were believed to be different ways for familiars to become imbued with magic markings that would elevate them to Fortis status, many still a mystery in Shade. What little they did know were mostly highly guarded secrets that only the queens possessed. There were stories, of course, a kind of mythology that had made its way through the

Brotherhood, but no one knew for certain what was truth or fiction.

"Lucki, our witch, gifted the markings to us." Reuben beamed when he said this, like his pride in his witch had no bounds.

Ah. So she is a powerful one. A witch who was endowed with surplus magic could transform a familiar to Fortis, and the fact that Lucki had done it to three was beyond impressive. In fact, if he hadn't been seeing the results for himself, Zephyr wouldn't have believed it possible, and he knew by the feel in his gut that Reuben wasn't lying. Lucki must have channeled a great deal of power at some point to mark the men. Jaggar and Zephyr had been reborn with their marks, along with no memory of their previous lives and witches that had granted them such power. All they knew, thanks to Queen Elvira's investigations many years before, was that for them both to have the markings they did, meant they'd been reborn more than once and possibly carried the magic of multiple witches.

Jaggar let his own magic markings pulse to the surface. He was endowed with layers of power that extended from his fingers up his arms to his neck then down his chest. "We can help you with that. There's some training needed to gain control, then more to wield effectively."

Zephyr crossed his arms and nodded. No Fortis should be without some basic understanding of his power. No matter where these familiars came from, they were part of the Brotherhood and therefore linked to Zephyr and Jaggar through universal oath, if not blood.

"And shifting?" Julian motioned up and down. "Are we able to shift as you do? To that in between beast?"

"You are Fortis, so yes," Jaggar said. "We can guide you through that shift as well. It takes some practice but comes in handy when communication and brute strength are equally needed."

Julian grinned. "Well then, fellas, welcome to Lady Clover's Cat House." He opened the back door and waved them in. "Let's go see what trouble our witches are stirring up without us."

Chapter Ten

Crimson

"I don't think I'd ever get used to having so many little bundles of magic walking around." Crimson stroked an orange and white cat that was sitting on her lap. It was purring so loudly that it rumbled against her thighs. "And it was Angelica who created them?"

"A by-product of the curse she'd cast on Weeping Falls. There used to be thousands, but she murdered so many in her quest to get her powers back."

Lucki had brewed them buttermint tea, a new taste for Crimson that she didn't hate, and was in the process of refilling Crimson's mug. There was a blanket of calm in this house, and Crimson had lowered her guard almost immediately. Maybe that was stupid of her, but over the last year, with the help of Talon and Valor, she'd been working on trusting her gut, and right now there wasn't a speck of unease there. Lucki was pure and open and brimming with kindness—a trait that would cause her problems in Shade but one that Crimson could relate to at a soul level, if only because she'd craved that kind of companionship her whole life from another witch.

"The wolves were orphaned and wild. They didn't start as domesticated companions, but now they act like dogs more than wolves." Lucki laughed in a soft way that only added to Crimson's belief that this woman, this witch, had no malice in her bones.

The wolves were clearly juveniles, brimming with energy but eager to stay close to Lucki. Crimson noticed that all three had taken sentry positions around Lucki's chair and had moved with her, getting underfoot at times, while she'd been making their tea and setting a plate together with desserts.

They had no magic that Crimson could detect, but that didn't always mean they weren't powerful in their own way. Loyalty was stronger than a lot of magic and bound thicker and more permanently than many spells.

"This battle that happened three months ago with Angelica... Was she injured?" Crimson sipped her scalding tea and enjoyed the burn that traveled down her throat.

"I was injured, but she was just getting started. I'd sent her into the ether as a last-ditch effort to be rid of her. I had no idea I was banishing her into another realm to cause havoc for you." Lucki shook her head, her expression contorting. "I'm sorry for that."

"Sometimes you have to do what you have to do." The back door creaked open, followed by the thud of approaching footsteps. Crimson grinned. "Seems as though the hotheaded familiars worked things out."

Lucki grinned back. "Yes, yes, it does." She turned her head slightly, a wistful expression on her face as she sought out her men.

If Talon and Valor had been there, Crimson would likely be doing the same. As it was, she set her face to show her displeasure with the circumstances. For all she knew, Jaggar and Zephyr were acting as spies for her sisters. She'd give them no glimpse of her softer side on this trip. They didn't deserve it.

Jaggar's narrow glare would have been intimidating to a lesser witch. To Crimson it was a sign of his stubborn belief that he was in control — a belief that she was determined to obliterate.

"About time," she drawled. "Tea?" She lifted her mug toward the teapot.

Jaggar growled in response.

Crimson winked at Lucki, who looked like she was trying to hold back a snort of laughter.

All the familiars crowded into the kitchen somehow. It was a large space, but with five Fortis consuming most of it, the kitchen felt suddenly cramped. They introduced themselves to Crimson with varying degrees of enthusiasm. The bear, Reuben, was by far the friendliest of the bunch, but Julian, the lion, was a close second. Although it was blasphemy in Shade, Lucki had the marks of three Fortis shifters and didn't seem to suffer from any sign of instability. That alone made her much more powerful as an ally than a foe, and Crimson hoped to tap into that by asking her for help.

"How did Angelica get the crystal?" Crimson had listened to Lucki's retelling of her experiences in Weeping Falls, from arriving with no idea that she was a witch to being marked by not only the cats but also the three familiars who stood by her now. Crimson had never heard of miniature shifters marking a witch, but the little felines didn't exist in Shade, so she tried to keep an open mind.

"It was embedded in my ceremonial mask." Lucki motioned to her head as if she still wore the mask. "The mask was ripped from my face when I got yanked back through the portal by the cats."

"And where did you get the mask?" Jaggar's voice was always a grumbly, guttural thing at the best of times, but right now he sounded like he was ready to spit rocks.

Crimson could tell by the bristling of Lucki's familiars that they didn't appreciate the tone. All the same, that crystal had belonged to the Triad of Shade and had been missing for centuries. Finding out how it came into a human witch's possession was important to Crimson, too, so, for once, she couldn't fault him for his reaction.

"It belonged to Isabel Clover and was passed to Lucki." Reuben rubbed Lucki's shoulder as he leaned over her to grab the tea pot. "I'll freshen this up."

"Isabel of Clover," Jaggar said, seconds before Crimson could. "She was a handmaiden for the Triad of Shade many centuries ago. She stole the mask."

"Isabel would never betray —"

"Yes, she would." The wolf named Wren cut Reuben off while sharing a meaningful look with Lucki.

"Wren, how could you say such a thing about your former mate?" Reuben tried again, his face masked by grief. Isabel had clearly meant something to the man.

"I say it because it's true. She could be deceitful, especially when she thought she was doing what was best." Wren huffed out a long breath, his eyes locked on Lucki's. It was clear, for all his bristle and bark, that he was deeply in love with the witch. "As misguided as that was."

Reuben grumbled something that sounded like *we'll discuss this later*. Julian nodded his agreement.

Lucki looked a shade paler than she had moments before. "Now that you know my story, what's yours — and how does Angelica come into it?"

Crimson's story was way too complicated for a tea conversation, so instead of answering that question, she decided to jump to the point.

"Angelica has been using the crystal to channel her power into creating these monstrous beasts, these grotesque —"

"Wild cats?" Lucki offered.

"Yes, I supposed that's what they are — hairless, warped-looking things." Crimson shuddered at the memory of being attacked by such abominations. "She's transforming our familiars into the wild cats and weakening our witches. We lost one of the triad as well. My sister."

"Oh no!" Tears welled in Lucki's eyes. "This is all my fault!"

Julian rested his hand on Lucki's shoulder and squeezed. "You didn't know you were sending her to Shade, beauty. Don't be so hard on yourself."

"Some might say that my sister had it coming," Crimson said with a curt nod. "Not to be flippant, but I've come to learn that Aria wasn't exactly the most honorable witch. She might have done things, bad things, that made it easier for Angelica's wild cats to bring her down." She flicked her gaze to Jaggar, daring him to say anything to stop her from sharing this information with Lucki, a virtual stranger. He pressed his lips together and folded his arms.

Lucki's unwavering stare gave Crimson the courage to continue.

"After she was killed by the wild cats, my remaining sisters sent me to retrieve you in hopes that you'd know a way to defeat Angelica and retrieve the crystal. They're offering you a seat on the triad." Saying those words out loud was a bitter poison on her tongue. To offer a seat that rightfully belonged to Crimson was painful. "If you help us, they plan to reward you in both magic and power. With power comes riches for you and your familiars, as well as respect and privilege. You'd be elevated to a very comfortable life in Shade and would want for nothing."

"I'm not following… As a sister, doesn't the throne belong to you?" Lucki frowned. "Why would you ask me to help if the reward is your birthright?"

A cascade of anger battered against Crimson so heavily that for a moment she didn't dare speak. The truth of Lucki's blunt question triggered her deepest fury. If she opened her mouth now, she'd spew a torrent of hate that Lucki didn't need to hear. She wanted Lucki to agree to help retrieve the crystal and put an end to Angelica and her wild cats, so she needed Lucki to believe she'd be rewarded. And she would be… Crimson would make sure of that, beyond her wildest dreams, but it wouldn't be with a seat on the throne. Crimson had walked away from her rightful place once because she'd been too much a coward, too much a 'yes witch' to protest, but things had changed. Crimson had changed, and she was ready to rule. With the crystal in her possession, her sisters wouldn't be able to deny her again.

"Yes, as a blood sister, Crimson should have that role," Zephyr said gruffly.

Everyone shifted their gazes his way, expressions of shock that the statue had actually spoken. Even Crimson looked at him with confusion, because he made it sound like it was hers to take, just like Jaggar had suggested. It shouldn't have surprised her that the two of them had concocted some kind of idea that she needed to usurp her sisters, since they shared one brain, but for Zephyr to say it out loud, in front of strangers, meant he really believed his own bullshit.

"I fully intend to help you—"

"Lucki, don't you think we should discuss this in private before—?"

"No, Wren. I created this problem. I'll help to fix it." Lucki speared the wolf with a firm gaze before shifting her eyes to each of her familiars in turn. All three nodded.

Such devotion.

Such loyalty.

A knot of longing curled in Crimson's gut. What she wouldn't give to have her own familiars with her now.

"But I'm not interested in being rewarded with a seat on your throne." Lucki seemed sincere as she locked eyes with Crimson. "I'll help *you* get the crystal back and put an end to Angelica, but I'm returning to Weeping Falls once it's done. I trust you can deliver the crystal to your sisters?"

"I'm afraid my sisters won't approve." Crimson tried to keep her relief from spilling over into her words. She had been planning to take the crystal from Lucki before she could return it to her sisters, but if Lucki had no interest in the power her sisters were offering and had no problem giving Crimson the crystal, then it made her plans all the simpler. She wouldn't have to betray Lucki in the process, which, if she was honest, would have been hard for Crimson to pull off. Betrayal wasn't really in her repertoire.

"They'll have to if you're in possession of the crystal," Jaggar said. "They'll have to answer for their crimes, as well."

Crimson snapped her eyes to him and couldn't help her mouth from dropping open. Now Jaggar was hinting, for all to hear, that she take the throne by force? *What has gotten into these two?*

The way he looked at her, with smug satisfaction, had her clamping her mouth shut and narrowing her eyes.

"I sense there's more to the story," Lucki said. "I understand if you don't want to share, but it would help if I had an idea what I'm walking into. It sounds like the relationship with your sisters is strained."

"Zephyr alluded, as the most powerful sister of four, that Crimson was meant to take a seat on the triad in due time, when her grandmother, mother and aunt stepped down to retire." Jaggar cleared his throat. "A year ago, there was a tragic...situation and the queens vanished under mysterious circumstances. Crimson was falsely accused and unfairly judged."

Tears burned the back of Crimson's eyes, so she dared not speak because she knew her voice would crack and show her pain. How could he share all of this so easily with Lucki? He was exposing Crimson's deepest sorrow and her hardest reality without flinching, like this had been part of his plan all along. And if it hadn't been part of his plan, then it meant he was adapting to Crimson's lead...which was more than unusual from an alpha like Jaggar. She'd never known him to be flexible.

His words rattled her, not just because of what he was saying but because they flew in the face of his normal, guarded ways. This was not the Jaggar she'd left in Shade a year ago. This was not the protocol-loving shifter who would do anything to adhere to the rules.

"They had no evidence, but they convicted Crimson anyway," Zephyr said, "to get her out of the way so the true culprits wouldn't be found and so the weaker witches would have all the power."

"You think the current queens had something to do with the former queens' disappearance?" Rueben asked, his tone suggesting he knew exactly how daring such a suggestion was, even without being a citizen of Shade.

"We think that there needs to be a proper investigation and that the rightful queens need to be found. Their Fortis live on, in forced exile in the castle, so we know the queens are still alive somewhere." Jaggar leaned forward, his eyes locked on Crimson. "Someone needs to uncover the truth and ensure that the ones who should be punished are. We think Crimson is the witch to make that happen."

The force of his words pulled a gasp out of Crimson so deep that tears slipped down her cheeks unbidden. How could she trust him now, after everything? How could he make it seem like he really believed in her when he'd left her to rot in banishment? How could he say such things?

Crimson tore her gaze away from Jaggar's, unable to accept his intensity.

"There is no need for you to be involved with the political matters of Shade," Jaggar continued. "Giving Crimson the crystal will be the start of righting some wrongs, and you have our word that we will ensure that it gets where it needs to be."

"The kingdom is unbalanced," Crimson said, finally able to use her voice again. "Tabitha and Wyvern are holding power they can't handle, and it's warping their minds, which is why Angelica has been able to unleash the havoc that she has."

"The queens grew arrogant in their hoarded power," Jaggar said, his words heavy with deeper meaning. "Crimson has the skill to unseat them, but she needs some backup. The crystal is a significant form of help and the only thing we'll need from you after we defeat Angelica. The rest will be up to us." He glanced at Zephyr, who nodded in response. "Only then will justice be achievable and balance restored."

He wouldn't look at Crimson, but she couldn't rip her eyes away from his face.

Whose help was he referring to? His and Zephyrs? Did he mean taking their marks? Did he seriously just suggest that out loud, in this room, in front of everyone?

Heat rose to Crimson's cheeks. It was an intimate detail for Jaggar to say publicly, to make it known that he desired her bond—completely uncouth in Shade society to be so blatant. Usually courting a bond happened in whispers and winks, behind closed doors, then at the right time, in audience with the queens, asking for permission. It was, again, something Jaggar would never have done a year ago, like a declaration of love shouted to the sky for all to hear. Her instinct was to cover his mouth…with her hand — or with her lips. She couldn't decide.

"Crimson would have support from the court if she rose up," Jaggar said with another glance at Zephyr. "Before Angelica attacked, there were many whispered conversations hoping for her return."

Is this a trick? Crimson shook herself out of the dizzy lustful thoughts. *Are they setting me up for another fall?*

There had to be a reason why they were pushing so hard on this plan. Was declaring it like this, so open, so sure, a way to con Crimson into trusting them again, just so they could betray her? She wanted to lash out with her questions, accusations even, but found herself too tongue-tied to do much more than listen. It didn't surprise her that there would be support if she managed to take the throne. Living in the uncertain world that her sisters had created with their unpredictable moods would have anyone craving sanity, stability. What did surprise her was that Jaggar was sharing this information with virtual strangers as if he really did want Crimson to unseat her sisters. Was betrayal in his blood now that he'd done it to her? Or was he finally seeing the error of his ways in supporting her sisters in the first place? Had he marked Crimson a year ago, they likely wouldn't be in the position they were in now.

Or was her gut, which was twisting awfully at the moment, trying to tell her that she'd gotten it wrong over the last year? Had Jaggar and Zephyr really stayed behind because they'd been trying to keep Crimson safe while also keeping tabs on the new queens?

Had they mistakenly thought they were doing what was best for her this whole time? That, she had to admit, would be so like them.

"It's my understanding that Crimson has a plan that would put her in a position of power with minimal bloodshed and more diplomacy than I'd be willing to use." Jaggar shrugged a shoulder and smiled indulgently at Crimson as if they were all on the same page, but the glint in his eyes was full of arrogance. Somehow, he'd figured out her strategy. She'd never been interested in bloodshed, but she'd intended to invoke the crystal to *coerce* her sisters to agree to her ascension to the throne. "As I said, giving her the crystal is the only request we'll make of you." He knew her well enough to know that taking the crystal from Lucki by force was not something she'd relish doing. "Any help beyond that is entirely up to you."

Crimson gulped back the boulder in her throat and returned his smarmy smile with a grin full of teeth and a glare full of toxin. *Never lower your guard.* These two shifters had betrayed her once before.

"Jaggar's right." She shifted her eyes to Lucki, softening her expression on the way. "You have no reason to help me," Crimson started. "I do have a plan that would put an end to Angelica and give me what I'm owed at the same time, without any need for dramatics." She'd use the crystal to convince her sisters of the right decision and help them see reality for the first time in a year. Then, and only then, would Crimson be in a position to find the truth. If she took the throne by force, she'd never know what happened to her mother, grandmother and aunt. Of that, she was certain.

"You can count us in for the first part." Lucki leaned forward. "I plan to finish what I started and put an end to Angelica for good."

Chapter Eleven

Talon

The Court of Shade had never been one of Talon's favorite places to be, not when the old crones had been in power – too formal – and definitely not now that Crimson's sisters were in power – too treacherous.

While he and Valor weren't technically being treated as prisoners – they did have free run of the castle, with very few places that were off limits – it was obvious that they were being watched. The eyes of the guards seemed to follow their every movement, and the handmaidens always seemed to pop up out of nowhere, asking if they needed anything, which was why Valor and Talon had been spending more time apart than together. Valor had been working recon with the other familiars and with the Fortis, using their Brotherhood bond to attempt to get some insider information.

Talon had been exploring the tunnels, networks of hidden passageways that Zephyr had shown them before he'd left with Crimson. As much as Talon didn't like traveling in the confined spaces, it was much easier to navigate the tunnels as a hawk. His vision, being far sharper when he shifted, gave him a better sense of what he was seeing — which, so far, had been a big pile of nothing.

But Zephyr had insisted that Talon explore the tunnels since both he and Jaggar were too big to do so. Zephyr, for all his grunts and limited words, had conveyed that both he and Jaggar knew there was something being hidden that needed to be found, and had left it up to Talon to figure out the rest. Since Talon wasn't a Fortis, he had no magic spells to help conceal his actions, so slipping away from the ever-watchful familiar sentries had been tough until he'd figured out the routines and guard changes — and the lapses that happened naturally at those times.

The tunnels themselves were dank and damp, with pungent moss growing in crevices along the ground and jutting rocks in odd and unexpected places. To navigate these tunnels on two feet would be highly dangerous, never mind four. Even though he had no magic to wield of his own, his hawk's senses picked up traces of magic that wafted in the stale air and coated the slick walls. The tunnels had been used by someone with a lot of power. It was impossible to tell how recently, but by the way the magic drifted, Talon would guess that someone had been through this narrow space many times, risking their very neck traveling along the darkened pathways.

It could be the handmaidens whose magic Talon was detecting, lesser witches with limited magic and no familiar marks, who worked throughout the kingdom and catered to the needs of the more powerful. He knew, from his time living with Crimson in the castle, that the handmaidens used these tunnels to get from point A to point B quickly, but he had a hard time imagining anyone choosing to come through there on a daily basis, especially anyone with errands to run and chores to do. Even with magic, these tunnels would be hard to navigate. Besides, the magic he detected, even faded as it was, was too strong for a hobbled witch such as a handmaiden, so he doubted that any of the servants had come this way.

He swooped around another tight corner then followed the tunnel down a flight of crudely carved stairs — another neck-breaker as far as he was concerned — then continued on, scanning the floor, the ceiling and the walls for anything that might hint at a secret.

Again, there was nothing but moss and more moss.

By his account, he'd covered nearly half the perimeter of the castle by now, which left only the section closest to the mountain to investigate. He angled in flight, hugging his wings tight to his body, and slipped through a low gap that would have forced any man or woman to get on hands and knees to pass through. Once on the other side, the darkness faded somewhat and natural light seeped in from above.

The castle had been carved into the mountain with magic and manual labor many centuries ago. There were parts of the castle, like Crimson's bathroom as well as a sacred chamber, that had openings to the sky. They were unique spaces, often shunned by court witches as being too raw, too untamed for their preferences. Crimson adored them for that very reason.

She'd always taken to the unvarnished above a polished veneer, and those mountain spaces called to her power in a natural, effortless way. Even the shower offered Crimson a power boost that left her more than refreshed after a good soaking. Talon didn't know the castle intimately, as it was huge and had many areas that were off limits to anyone but royal family members, but those open sky spaces, he felt, were rare.

Except suddenly Talon, quite unexpectedly, found himself soaring into another.

The stone ground fell away abruptly, and a gust of air pushed Talon up as he glided through an arched opening to find the walls gone and an open, cavernous space ahead. The natural light only penetrated so far, but the waft of magic he'd detected earlier became a battering-ram of power. He dove down, deep into the darkness, following the strong pulse of magic that seemed to beckon him. Zephyr and Jaggar had been right. There was something hidden in the depths of the mountain.

Talon swooped low, skirting the perimeter of the cave, cautious and on alert. He followed the trail of power, which grew stronger as he flew toward it, then zigzagged around two large boulders before nearly crashing into an iridescent wall of magic. He managed to pull himself up, barely skimming past the defensive spell that emanated danger with every pulse. He perched himself high enough that he wouldn't be detected or troubled by the spell that had clearly been cast to keep snoopers out. It was near opaque and streaked with black threads, but through its shimmer of pulsating magic, Talon was able to see the shadowy forms of three people.

He scanned the surrounding boulders, looking for a place to get a closer look without touching the spell that, if Talon had to guess, was likely designed to kill on contact. Nothing good ever came from a spell like this, not when it was buried deep in a cave, underground and embedded into a mountain, as if to shield its existence from any witch or familiar who might stumble upon it.

He spotted a jutting ledge that rested inches away from the spell's wall. It'd be risky, but Talon felt the absolute gut need to investigate more. He assessed one last time, taking in the sounds — echoing drips of water, skittering bugs and small animals, the scents of moss and minerals, tangy and pungent, and the magic — dangerous, powerful and meant to harm as much as conceal.

He flew swiftly and silently, landing on the small ledge without much room for error, his beak almost grazing the edge of the spell and his feathers ruffling with the pulse of its power.

The shadows inside the spell sharpened as the walls of magic shimmered. Three figures stood back-to-back, their heads bent so that long gray hair covered their faces and reached nearly to the floor. They were bound by iron manacles, linked together at the elbows and ankles, each wearing a collar that attached them to a pillar of stone that hung from above. The pedestal that they were on was magicked and rotated slowly, so each of the figures moved into his line of vision one after another.

He narrowed his hawk eyes as the third figure circled toward him. Dark magic wafted around him, stinking up the air and coating him so he shuddered. His gut churned and he stomped his feet to keep himself grounded, because his hawk wanted to take flight and get the hell out of there. The figure, somehow sensing his presence, looked up through straggly hair and locked eyes with him.

He jolted, forcing himself not to look away from the uncanny blue eyes that he'd only been brave enough to gaze into once before.

Eyes that belonged to Crimson's mother, Queen Merianna.

Not disappeared by Crimson, as all of court and Shade had been led to believe but here, held captive and being used to...

Her eyes never left his the entire time she rotated around, and the foreboding chill made his feathers ruffle in warning. As the cycle continued and the old crone's stare finally broke, Talon became attuned to another spell in play. Power wafted upward as if being siphoned from the three crones and channeled somewhere. Talon took off, soaring straight up, avoiding the wall of the spell until he found where the stolen magic was going. There was a small opening in the roof of the cavern — smaller than any of the tunnels he'd explored so far. His hawk wasn't happy as he ascended toward it, but the only way for him to really see what was going on was to follow the tunnel. With a split-second decision, he gave one more powerful push, then closed his wings around himself and soared into the tight space. He shot up, carried on the crosswind of magic, until the tunnel opened into another cavernous room. This one was a crudely carved circular space that had crystals inlaid into the bedrock, shaped into the symbol of the triad — three interconnecting curves that were a pinnacle of power.

Talon landed and surveyed with every sense on high alert. There was one door made from wood and iron, and Talon would bet his life that on the other side of the door was the high witches' private wing. The room reeked of their tainted magic, and his gut screamed at him to leave. He pushed that impulse down and observed the way the crones' power wafted from the small tunnel he'd traveled through. It billowed into the room then suctioned to the floor, slithering and hugging the rocks as it moved toward the crystals. The triad mark pinged a low vibration, almost like it was calling the magic to it, then greedily soaking it in as soon as the magic got close enough.

This was what had been hidden. This was how the triad had maintained their rule.

Fury, which had already been simmering just beneath the surface of Talon's control, burst out of him and he attacked the stone at his feet, pecking and scratching at the gems that were inlaid into the floor. How dare Tabitha and Wyvern accuse Crimson of this crime! How dare they punish her for their own treachery! He attacked the gems like he was gouging the eyes of those who'd wronged Crimson, not satisfied until he dislodged the largest of the crystals from its casing.

He fluttered his wings to calm himself down, then kicked the crystal away so that it pinged against the farthest wall.

Somehow, Wyvern and Tabitha were stealing magic to bolster their own—despicable and vile witches that they were. Not only was this kind of spell work forbidden but it was also dangerous—dangerous for the victims and for the thieves as well. Stolen magic would leave a taint when cast, a taint that could lead to insanity, violence and soul destruction. Add that to the fact that Wyvern and Tabitha had bonded with multiple Fortis, and it was a one-way ticket to crazy town.

How had the triad gotten the crones into the cavern? It wasn't as if the crones were powerless. They'd been engorged with magic themselves, their age and experience having only enhanced their abilities. And where were the crones' Fortis familiars when they'd been taken? Each had been mated to two Fortis, who would have died before they'd let anything happen to their witches. Crimson had been told that they'd been questioned thoroughly at the time of the queens' disappearance and that it had been the queens' Fortis who had pointed fingers at Crimson, saying it was her magic that they'd detected in the chamber. Crimson had never been given the opportunity to question them herself or to hear those accusations firsthand, because her punishment had been handed down quickly, mercilessly, then followed swiftly by her banishment from court.

That meant that no one had seen or heard from the queens' Fortis, other than Tabitha, Wyvern and Aria. So, where were they, and what did they actually know? It was obvious to Talon now that Crimson's sisters had been lying about detecting Crimson's magic in the chamber where the queens were last known to be. They'd somehow either coerced the queens' Fortis to lie as well or, more likely, they'd made up the whole thing.

He wondered if Zephyr and Jaggar had been able to figure out the puzzle of the Fortis guards in the time they'd been conducting their own investigations at the castle. There was no way the queens' Fortis were dead, because those deaths would have been felt by everyone in the Brotherhood. Whenever a brother-familiar died, it resonated in every familiar's bones. The depth and severity depended on their shifter strength but more significantly, how loyal they were to the Brotherhood. When a Fortis died, the entire witch population felt it like a soul stripping. Assuming the crones' Fortis were alive, there had to be a reason why they were unable to protect the queens and why no one had heard or seen them since the queens' disappearance. Talon strongly suspected, after seeing what had been done to the queens, that some kind of dark magic was keeping the Fortis gagged and hidden.

Talon and Valor would have to locate the missing Fortis and find a way to release the crones. They'd also have to warn Crimson about how deep her sisters' treachery went. Jaggar had hinted at a coup. At the time, Talon had thought the man was unhinged or maybe up to something nefarious himself. Now he knew the truth. Jaggar had somehow already guessed that the reigning queens deserved a heavy-handed approach. Crimson would have to rise up against them in order to set things right.

Talon glanced at the triad symbol, now missing one of its gems. The crones' magic swirled around the room, no longer drawn to the symbol, free to float casually now that Talon had broken the magnetic pull of the connected gems. He swooped over to the crystal that he'd kicked away then secured it in his beak, making sure it wouldn't fall. With the symbol incomplete, Wyvern and Tabitha wouldn't be able to siphon power this way. He hurried back into the tunnel. He had to get to Valor so they could figure out a way to do what needed to be done and get Crimson in position to take control.

Chapter Twelve

Crimson

"We're wasting time." Crimson was doing her best to ignore the sheen of sweat that coated Jaggar's magnificent body. She might hate his guts most of the time, but she wasn't blind to his assets. For some reason he'd been training in a pair of tight shorts— and nothing else—that he'd borrowed from one of Lucki's shifters, so it wasn't just his glistening muscles on display. The outline of his...other appealing anatomy was clearly visible. And that made Crimson hot and very bothered.

"We're making sure everyone is ready." Jaggar hoisted a tree trunk over his head as if it were a twig, then started walking toward the gathering of familiars on the other side of the forest clearing. They'd been working on some kind of Fortis obstacle course since the meeting had broken a few hours before.

"And you think fun and games is the way to go?" Crimson couldn't begin to understand how Fortis trained to be the way they were, but she had a hard time accepting that this was the best, most time-effective method of giving Lucki's men the basics before battle.

Yes, Lucki's familiars needed to learn how to wield their power and explore their range of shifting, but like this? Jumping over boulders and shimmying under logs? *Really?*

Jaggar didn't pause to answer her, so she was forced to follow him through the forest path he'd created. "We need them to be ready for whatever Angelica throws at us. This is the quickest way to train then test them."

"And exhaust yourselves at the same time."

Jaggar gave her an *oh please* look over his shoulder.

"Right, you're such a big bad tough guy that you don't get exhausted. How could I forget?" She'd grown used to Talon and Valor's limitations. While they were both strong familiars, they weren't Fortis, so they did need to rest and recharge—just as Crimson sometimes did. It had suited her fine over the last year to snuggle with her familiars on lazy days and sleep hours away together, but in the face of Jaggar's brute, unending strength, she felt like she'd been the one wasting time and, as he'd rightly guessed back in Shade, she'd been slacking on her training as well.

He heaved the trunk he was carrying over his head then hurled it at Zephyr. Even though the other familiar was standing with his back to Jaggar, he lifted his arms in time to catch the damn thing.

Fucking Fortis. So smug with their powers and uncanny senses. Why did they always have to be so perfect?

As if reading her mind, Jaggar turned toward her with a telling grin.

She wanted to slap it right off his face. "We need to talk about what you did inside."

Jaggar's grin didn't falter as he pretended he had no idea what she meant.

Playing dumb or actually dumb?

"What's your game, Jaggar? You're all of a sudden hell-bent on overthrowing our queens?" It absolutely killed her to call her sisters queens under normal circumstances, but now that Jaggar's hinted accusations swirled in her head, along with her own suspicions, it was doubly bad. Was it actually possible that they deserved a reckoning? Had she been right this whole time in thinking that her sisters had set her up to take a fall in order to protect themselves? Had they been the ones to disappear their grandmother, mother and aunt? "You clearly don't want to support my plan to claim the throne in a more civilized way."

"Civilized?" Jaggar snorted a laugh. "You mean by threatening them with the crystal? Or wait, no, not threaten them. You were probably planning to negotiate with them, right? To talk reason with them?" Jaggar crossed his arms. "Yeah, that's exactly what you were going to do."

His words dripped with sarcasm, and that made Crimson irrationally pissed. "Staging a coup isn't exactly going to encourage them to confess anything."

"It will if it's done right."

"You mean if they're tortured into a confession?" Crimson shook her head, disgust aimed at him with no buffer. "How easily you turn to your baser instincts. What would you do? Let your beast have its way with claws and fangs and brute strength until they scream what you want to hear? You think that's the way to get the truth?"

Jaggar scowled. "Don't be naïve, Crimson. There's no room for diplomacy in Shade. Not anymore. Not with what has become of your sisters."

"For all I know, you're setting me up," Crimson blurted, only half meaning to, then tore her gaze away from Jaggar when she saw a flash of naked pain cross his face.

"You would think that," he growled, but his tone held less anger and more hurt.

"You can't blame me for not trusting you." She crossed her arms to keep them from shaking. She couldn't let him know how much he still got to her. "You have a track record of betraying me."

"I don't know how many different ways I can say this, Crimson, but I did what I had to do to keep you safe." He sighed like she was exasperating him.

It was something she always found annoying about Jaggar, how condescending he could be—what an infuriating know-it-all he was. "I can handle my own safety."

"No, you can't—not when it comes to what your sisters are capable of." He lifted his hands as if to grab her arms, but she stepped back before he could. "You put too much faith in the possibility of their goodness. You give them too much trust when you should give them none. They aren't who you think they are."

"I know exactly who my sisters are." It was a kneejerk response that she'd said a million times over the years, but for the first time, her own words struck her as badly off. Did she? Did she really know who Tabitha and Wyvern truly were? She hadn't expected them to take Fortis mates without the consent of their queens. She hadn't expected them to banish her. "They're troubled...misguided. My mother always pitted us against one another, so of course they hate me. They need me now. They really do. I can fix this."

"Yes, you and I can agree about that." Jaggar's tone softened. "You can fix this, but not the way you're planning to. Your sisters are ruthless, powerful, and they don't play by the rules."

"Neither do I!" she lied. It sounded weak, even to her.

"Yes, you do. You can't even fathom what your sisters are capable of doing to you. You can't accept what they've already done."

"I...can't...*what*?" Magic sparked down her arms as his words hit home, an echo to her own thoughts from moments before. "You don't think I know what my own sisters are capable of doing? You don't think I bore the brunt of their cruelty for my whole life? Their lies? Their treachery? Their taunting and pranks? All I ever wanted was for them to see me as worthy to be a sister, to stand with them, but they only saw me as competition." She blinked away angry tears and shoved her finger toward him. "It's you who doesn't like to break the rules. You're the one who refused to bond with me. You're the one who wouldn't support me so I could find the truth a year ago, before my sisters became warped by too much magic." Crimson turned away. "I don't know why I'm so surprised that you won't support me now."

"No, Crimson, you're wrong. Your sisters are hiding something, something that is more than just a violation of witch law. They're hiding something beyond vile and treacherous. I know they are, and deep down, I think you know it, too." He stabbed his fingers through his hair, tugging it loose from its clip.

Crimson watched the hair clip hit the ground and bounce before disappearing into the brush.

"I didn't bond with you because I wouldn't let them unleash their wrath on you. I'd hoped that while you were banished, you'd take all that anger, all that hurt, and turn it into motivation to take back what they stole—to accept that your sisters did this. They orchestrated all this." He let out a deep breath. "I hoped you'd see the truth."

But you didn't. Words he didn't have to say but that hung heavy in the air between them.

She turned, latching on to the only thing she could think of, lashing out at him because his eyes said more than his words ever could. "If they're hiding something that has you so scared, what are you doing to figure it out? If I'm such a failure, so blind to the truth that you so clearly see, then what are you doing to prove it?"

His face shuttered and a chill ran down Crimson's body. "I've left orders with Talon and Valor to figure that out while we're gone."

"You did *what*?" Her gut twisted like a mini-tornado, but her words lost their venom because fear seeped into her bones and froze her soul.

"Zephyr showed them the tunnels that we've never been able to explore—tunnels that reek of magic."

"You sent Talon into the tunnels?" She knew about the secret passageways because she'd explored some of them as a child. They were dangerous, even for a hawk, full of gaping holes and bottomless caverns. Her sisters knew of the tunnels, too. They'd used to torment her in so many different ways by traveling through them and popping up in unexpected places to scare her or spy on her.

"I did."

"How could you?" Crimson lunged for him, but he caught her arms in his hands and held her up on tiptoes. It didn't stop her from spitting more anger at him. "How could you put them in danger like that?"

"We have to know what we're up against. Those tunnels hide the truth. I know it in my gut. It's worth the risk."

She let her power rise through her skin, heating until Jaggar's face showed both his discomfort and his battle to maintain his hold on her. She may have lapsed on her training, but she was still powerful. She could still have impact.

"You had no right to order my familiars to do anything without my knowledge." They needed her there to protect them. Her sisters would know immediately if someone was accessing the tunnels. They'd always seemed to know when Crimson had, anyway.

"If we were mated, I would." As Fortis, leadership would undoubtedly fall to him. He was the most powerful and the most dominant. Before everything had happened, when they'd all dreamed of a day that Crimson would bear the marks of all four familiars, it had been universally accepted that Jaggar would be alpha, second only to her.

"You made that choice a year ago, Jaggar!" Crimson couldn't keep her voice down, not after a year of brewing over that very thing—his refusal to bond with her when she'd asked him to.

He stepped away from her. "Nothing will ever be like it was. Isn't that what you said? What you keep saying?" Jaggar's face shuttered more, closing her out. "Now it's you who are making a choice, Crimson. I'm here, offering what I denied you before — denied you for very good reasons, I might add." He banged his fist to his chest. "It's you who are rejecting me. It's you who has decided that what we used to have is gone." He turned his back to her. "I'm beginning to believe that you're right. Maybe what we had has vanished, right along with the true queens."

Chapter Thirteen

Valor

Valor didn't know if his fellow familiars, non-Fortis like him, were too brainwashed or too intimidated by the reigning queens to speak up, but something was definitely keeping them from being honest. It wasn't so much in their words. They were, after all, answering his questions. It was just, well, that they wouldn't look him in the eyes, and there was no conviction in what they told him. They were leaving out important details.

When Valor had tried to get to the bottom of where the crones' Fortis guards were so he could talk to them, see if he could pry the truth out of them about Wyvern and Tabitha's investigation a year ago, the lower-ranking familiars all acted like they couldn't understand what Valor was asking. It was more than them being evasive. They stared at him with blank expressions, like his words were too hard to decipher.

It didn't help matters that he was trying to be stealthy, easing into conversations then nudging toward his goal of getting to the bottom of things without alerting anyone to his true intentions. If he could be more direct, then maybe he'd get more honesty — or maybe he'd end up in the dungeon.

Worse than the lying by omission, the familiars, all lower-ranking, tier-two shifters at court, used to be like actual brothers to Valor and Talon, and now they were virtual strangers — mistrustful strangers, who refused to even hint that something wasn't quite right in Shade.

No, that wasn't it. They were acting like if they acknowledged that something was rotten in Shade, they'd have to face it, and none of them wanted to do that.

Which made them come off as cowards, and that was as unsettling as it was seemingly impossible. Even though the familiars weren't Fortis, so they had no magic of their own, they were powerful shifters, and Valor couldn't wrap his head around how such a change in their very essence could happen in only a year.

Unless, of course, they were all under some kind of spell, but that...*that* would take a tremendous amount of power to accomplish. And if they were spelled with such powerful magic, why wasn't Valor picking up on it? He'd been close enough to all the familiars — eating with them, drinking with them, even doing some training with them — to have sensed a magic like that at play.

He needed to talk to Talon, sort out all the things that didn't make much sense.

They'd parted ways after Crimson and the others had left, dividing and conquering quietly. Talon had been investigating the tunnels Zephyr had shown them, his eagle compact enough to maneuver through the cramped space. Valor hoped that Talon had uncovered something useful that they'd be able to share with Crimson once she returned, because Valor had utterly failed in that mission.

Valor waited in a dark recessed alcove, out of the way but not suspiciously so. They had chosen the spot knowing that the queens' Fortis guards would be keeping tabs on them in one way or another, and the alcove was a junction to a lot of destinations in the castle.

But he couldn't stay there forever, and Talon was late.

His wolf was antsy, eager for a run, to stretch its legs in a burst of speed, maybe hunt down a rabbit for a midday snack. His mouth watered and his fangs punched through his gums with burning intensity, craving fresh meat. He'd gotten used to fun and games with Crimson and Talon, having ultimate freedom to spend their days doing as they pleased, as his *wolf* pleased, which mainly consisted of chasing, hunting, devouring and satiating his appetites. *All of them.*

Valor paced a short circuit, clenching and unclenching his fists, soaking in his wolf's agitation as he checked the window just down the hall to see if anything was going on outside. This part of the castle looped toward the majestic waterfalls, a natural barrier, ripe with magic, that made surprise attacks impossible. The mist from the pounding water rolled along the expansive gardens, cloaking almost everything in the same way that Crimson's manufactured protective veil had back home. A natural defense. This fog had given her the idea in the first place to use a veil as a security measure so her sisters couldn't break through without warning. Ingenious really, and only a witch as powerful as Crimson could pull it off. Wielding mist in this way wasn't easy, because it tended to have a mind of its own.

Valor frowned as he watched the magical fog snake in and around the walls of the castle. If three quarters of the castle were cloaked by the waterfall's magic, then how had Angelica gotten past it? Even with the Crystal of Shade, she wouldn't have been powerful enough to trick the fog. The fog was practically sentient. It read intentions and would only let someone pass through if there was no ill will toward the court.

So, what had Angelica done? Barged in the front gate? That was the only other way.

It was hard for Valor to accept that the many Fortis court guards would have allowed that to happen. It was unfathomable, really.

Another puzzle to work out and so many missing pieces to account for.

He pulled himself out of his head and away from the window.

Where is Talon?

His wolf urged him to keep moving, to leave the alcove behind, to find his shifter brother.

Something's not right.

The hackles on the back of his neck bristled as his ears picked up the faintest of sounds, like a roar, muffled and distant, followed by rumbling thunder. Valor checked the skies, and despite the fog that clung to the castle, the sky above was bright and clear, promising another scorcher of a day.

He swiveled toward the sound, his wolf rumbling, ready to burst free at the first provocation. The hall curved enough so that Valor couldn't see beyond the turn. He stepped back farther, because even though he couldn't see what lay ahead, vibrations rolled up his legs, the stone floor signaling that someone was coming his way. It could be Talon, but the tremors seemed too heavy for one shifter. It could be Fortis coming for him. Maybe that was why Talon was late. Maybe he'd been detained. Maybe Talon and Valor had been found out.

Valor eased back into the shadows of the alcove, biding his time, expecting a Fortis patrol to charge around the corner looking for him. He crouched low on his haunches, finding the grit on the floor with his fingers and digging in for traction. He had no magic of his own, but he knew how to blend into the darkness, and if necessary, he could shift between one breath and the next, then dive for the window. It'd be a long drop, but the guards wouldn't be expecting it, and Valor knew that there were enough jutting walls and sharp corners for his wolf to leap against. He'd done it many times before the banishment, if only to impress Crimson with his agility.

"Valor!" Talon's voice was strangled, desperate sounding. The thundering roar of pounding footsteps came into sharp focus.

Valor sprang up just in time to see Talon charge around the corner, half a dozen Fortis coming in hot behind him.

"Make sure she gets this!" He tossed something Valor's way, hardly aiming, but that didn't matter.

Valor snatched the gem out of the air then slid back into the shadows. The gem was heavy and pulsed with magic, so he knew that whatever he held was the reason for the chase.

He met Talon's wild eyes just as he passed the alcove.

"The tunnels, brother. Go!" He transformed before he'd finished speaking so his words were half human and half eagle-cry.

The Fortis shouted and magic blasted against the wall, just missing Talon's wing. He flew in a tight circle, making eye contact again, as if to say, *get going*.

Valor nodded then shifted to the side and pushed open the hidden door to the tight tunnels. He wasn't keen on going in there and neither was his wolf, but he slipped inside anyway. Just before the door slid shut behind him, he heard the window across the hall crash to pieces and Talon's victory cry as he soared away. There were very few bird of prey familiars at court, and no Fortis who could fly. Talon would be safe as long as he stayed in the air.

Valor's eyes adjusted to the darkness, his wolf vision punching through so he could take in his surroundings. The walls dripped with moisture. Being so close to the waterfall probably caused a lot of condensation in this part of the castle. It was humid, sticky, the air thick. His wolf grumbled, slinking back, withdrawing deep into Valor's consciousness so it wouldn't have to endure the discomfort of the next few hours. *Thanks, buddy.*

Valor looked at the gem in his hand, and despite the darkness, could clearly see that it was bloodstone. Normally it was a powerful stone on its own, but this one was cloudy with more than average amount of pulsating power. It was like it had been supercharged in some way, and that was wrong, all wrong. For a gem like this to have so much power was not normal and likely an aberration. Strangely, his instincts told him that it was infused with a witch's magic somehow.

How would a stone like this be able to absorb so much from a witch's magic without becoming corrupt? The source would have to be so pure that it melded with the gem's own magic.

And that was just impossible.

Talon had left him with another mystery to figure out.

Valor sighed, then shifted his shoulders to get a better sense of where he was and where he should go next.

His body was wedged between the walls in a claustrophobic way. Each direction seemed impossible to move through, but he knew Talon was buying him time, so he had to get going.

Which direction, though?

With great effort and more than the usual amount of growling, Valor coaxed his wolf to the surface once again, holding enough control to keep his wolf from slipping back into the shadows of his mind. He stretched his wolfie hearing, sniffed the stale air, even opened his mouth to let his wolf taste the dust and dirt floating around him.

His wolf wasn't impressed, but he was in tune. Talon's shifter signature, a bead of his essence, was present, however faint, and it looped like an invisible trail into the darkness.

His wolf nudged to the left.

Talon had told him to get in the tunnels because there was something there for Valor to find, and that's exactly what he was going to do.

Chapter Fourteen

Crimson

Crimson had lost track of time as she'd worked within the circle of stones that pulsed with immeasurable power. Shade had circles of magic like this — built before time meant anything, by hands that had been far more powerful than any witch who existed now. They were sacred circles that had been erected on axis points where natural magic was at its most pure and powerful. How these ancestor witches had known precisely where to build was something no one in Shade understood, and there were no historical texts detailing the mystery, either. The castle of Shade had been built in exactly the same way, and its origin story had died long before Crimson had been born. All she knew was that the castle had been built on top of at least two, but probably more, axis points. One was the sacred chamber that Crimson had used to travel between the veil, but the others were strictly for the use of the reigning queens. Crimson didn't even know where the other ones were located, but she had always suspected there was one somewhere under the castle, accessed only by the tunnels that ran throughout the inner walls.

While the sacred chamber she liked to use in Shade housed some powerful magic vibes, it had been a very long time since Crimson had felt the surge of power like she felt here in Weeping Falls. This magic circle had enough of a pulse to make her giddy.

Lucki had come to watch for a little while but had declined an offer to spar, saying she wasn't crazy or stupid. Crimson couldn't blame her, as it was the stones that were taking the brunt of Crimson's residual frustration with Jaggar. She wasn't holding back as she struck, then struck again, curling her magic around each casting she created to pack the most powerful punches. She might have slacked off for the last year, but it hadn't undone the decades of training she had under her belt.

Not even a little bit.

Of course, her thoughts circled around Jaggar's words and the suggestion that he wanted to mark her now, as if everything that had happened over the last year was nothing to worry about—like her feelings of being betrayed were foolish and unfounded. What she hated the most right now was that she actually felt as if maybe he was right. Maybe she was overreacting and holding a grudge that would only hurt her in the end.

The infuriating man was confusing her feelings, tangling them up more than ever.

She wound a ball of magic around her palm, weaving threads in and out like she was knitting an interconnected web.

That's what Jaggar does!

He always made her doubt her own feelings, her own gut instincts. She reeled back then launched the powerful blast. It tore at the ground just beyond the circle and wrenched up the roots of several trees, cracking the hard-packed earth wide open.

She wound the spell back, as she had been every time she'd cast, reversing the damage she'd done seconds before. It was all muscle memory, something Crimson did any time she trained. She reeled her magic in, the ground closed and the trees righted themselves like she'd never been there.

Her mind was on Jaggar's face as he repeated her own words to her. *It's you who are rejecting me.*

She didn't want what he was offering. Right? *Right?*

Buzzing hit her ears at the same time that she snapped back to reality and realized her power was back-building, rolling toward her like a wave of destruction. She'd never get out of the way in time.

Shit!

Strong arms closed around her then spun her so swiftly out of the sacred circle that she stumbled into a wall of muscle, dizzy and disoriented, her head coming to rest on a familiar chest. Before she could blast Zephyr with a string of curses, he hunched his back and curled himself around her body.

Then he took the brunt of her spell. She felt it like the bomb she knew it would be, and it rattled her from scalp to toes and down to her bones.

His back arched, a grimace of extreme pain flashed over his face, but he didn't let her go. Even as he crumpled to his knees, he held her tight.

"Zeph, are you okay? Oh fuck! Zephyr, talk to me." She slipped her hands around his back to assess the damage from her spell. With her body pressed so close to his, she remembered how well they fit together and how much she missed his hugs. She gulped back the growing lump in her throat then focused on making sure he was okay. She might be pissed at him and hurt by his betrayal, but she didn't want to see him in pain. The magic from her wayward spell sparked and sizzled along his skin, but his Fortis physiology was absorbing it with each second that passed. He'd be okay, but the pain she knew she'd caused made her feel like such a careless fool. Her wandering mind had no place while she was casting. She had to get her head out of the ether.

"You really need to work on that one," Zephyr grunted. "It was pretty weak."

Crimson pulled back, her mouth open and ready to snap when she saw his lips quirk. His eyes crinkled, softening the icy blue of his stare. Was he...*joking* right now?

"You're a bastard," she said, but there was no anger in her words. In fact, all she felt was a homecoming. Being in Zephyr's arms had been one of her favorite pastimes. He'd always been strong, silent and a wonderful cuddler. It should have bothered her that her body was so comfortable, but it didn't. Not at all.

"That I am." He still held her around the waist and his grin faltered a little.

"Are you hurt?" Her throat felt scratchy, and her voice creaked. Her stomach flipped upside down as Zephyr's eyes hooded and he pulled her closer, so close that there wasn't a part of their bodies that wasn't touching in some way.

He shook his head and shifted his eyes to her mouth. As if branding her with just a look, her lips grew hot, along with the rest of her body. She leaned closer. He didn't stop her.

Gods, she'd missed this. She'd missed him.

His jaw was stubbled with a touch of ginger, like his hair, which was fair and tinted with streaks of red. She remembered how his kisses had felt when his skin was bristled, rough nuzzles along her throat that had made her squirm and giggle.

He swept his hand up her back, holding her against him, forcing her to tilt her head slightly so she could see him. He leaned down, moving his lips closer.

So close.

She shuttered her eyes against the intensity of his. She just wanted one taste...just one moment of what once had been. She could have that, couldn't she? Without losing herself completely?

Yes!

She brushed her lips against his and somehow sank deeper into his body. He kept his one hand on her waist, his fingers curled along her hip, the other on her back, holding her in place. She moved her hands over his shoulders and let the smoldering burn of every inch of his muscles, every press of his firm, unyielding body, invade hers.

"Crimson," he groaned, then opened his mouth, beckoning her in.

She had to...*had* to kiss him back. He was honey, nectar, metal to her magnet. He kissed her with a ferocity that made her regret every day of their separation.

Zephyr had always managed to convey every feeling he had through his touch. For such a big shifter, he'd only ever been tender and soft toward Crimson, coaxing her flames slowly, like he had all the time in

Angela Addams

the world. That hadn't changed in their year apart. He stroked her tongue and slipped his fingers along the seams of her battle gear, tormenting her with a barely there touch that she longed to feel on her skin.

As much as she didn't want to admit it, he threatened to thaw her heart and obliterate the last of her resistance.

Crimson had never doubted that he'd cared about her—which was why it had hurt so damn much when he'd betrayed her.

Just like Jaggar, Zephyr had refused to mark her and had let her leave.

She stiffened, the memories of their parting shredding her heart all over again. He stopped kissing her and pulled back, a question in his eyes.

She put her hands on his chest. "I have to go."

"You don't." He wouldn't force her, she knew that, but his hands were still locked on her body. She'd be lying if she said it didn't feel good.

But still…

She pushed against him again, and he released his hold on her. She scrambled away from Zephyr, confused and hurt. She needed distance. She needed time to think.

The way he looked at her, still on his knees, his arms limp at his sides and his eyes full of, what? Pain? Why? Because she was rejecting him.

He had no right to look at her like that, not after what he'd done. Even if it hadn't been his idea to send her away, he'd gone along with it.

"You didn't choose me." Her voice cracked again and she wanted to tear her throat out. She sounded weak. Pathetic. Broken.

"We did choose you." His eyes were penetrating, drilling into her soul.

"To protect me? Is that how you think you chose me?" Because Jaggar had said the same thing to her. "You never came for me. You let them banish me. You let me think—" She choked on her next words because they were too raw.

Jaggar and Zephyr had let her think they'd bonded with Aria.

He lowered his head, and it was the saddest thing she'd ever seen. This big, powerful Fortis bowing, defeated. She never wanted to see him like this, but she couldn't move. Her body wouldn't betray her like her heart was right now.

"It was you who made a choice, Crimson. You chose not to come back." He lifted his head and locked his icy eyes with her, making her flinch. "You didn't fight. You accepted what was done to you and left Jag and me behind. You abandoned us." His eyes told her he believed every word he was saying—every messed-up, impossible word. "You're not the victim here, Crim—or at least, you don't have to be. Wake up, open your eyes and see what's in front of you."

Tears punched past her defenses, unbidden, unwelcome. "What's in front of me?" she whispered, scared of hearing the answer.

Zephyr stood then closed the distance between them. He didn't touch her, but his heat enveloped her, making her sway dangerously close, so close that he could have opened his arms and let her collapse against him.

But he didn't.

"*We're* in front of you, Crimson—always have been, always will be." He brushed wayward strands of hair from her face, and she wanted to nuzzle against his fingers, to let him linger, but he didn't give her a chance before he dropped his hand then took a step back. "You're going to have to make the first move, C. You're going to have to accept the truth."

"The truth?" Intoxicated from Zephyr's musky scent, Crimson was having a hard time focusing.

"That Jag and I, we're your future, and you need us to accomplish your goals."

Chapter Fifteen

Crimson

Like hell! Like hell she needed Jaggar and Zephyr to accomplish her goals. If she went with their plans, she'd be instigating a war with her sisters. A war she wasn't interested in, not when she was already facing a common foe. Angelica was the one who required Crimson's violence, not her sisters.

An hour after their encounter at the stone circle, Crimson was still pissed. More than pissed, she was hurt and confused and ready for war.

How could Zephyr use her emotions against her? How could he exploit her weakness for him like he had? He'd pulled her close, enticed her with the memory of what had once been, then he'd hit her with his lies.

"That Jag and I, we're your future and you need us to accomplish your goals."

As if! As if she needed anything from the two men who had betrayed her.

No, she was sticking to her plan, infiltrating then investigating. And yes, a part of her wanted to give her sisters the benefit of the doubt—a part of her didn't want to believe that they would do something nefarious to their own flesh and blood. Maybe she was thinking too much with her heart, but she wasn't naïve.

She knew her sisters weren't telling her the whole truth, that they probably had something to do with the queens' disappearance, but she also knew that the only way to get them to be honest was to play the game they'd started. She needed to force their hands, to make it impossible to deny her ascension. Once she was elevated to her rightful role on the triad, she'd be able to dictate what would happen next. She'd be able to prove, with evidence, that her sisters needed a reckoning. That was the only way for Crimson to gain the trust of the court, the only way for her to break the spell her sisters had woven around Shade—not a spell of magic but one of fear, coercion, force. She knew how her sisters worked and how effectively they intimidated others.

Crimson needed to do things her way so that all of Shade would see that she wasn't acting in the name of revenge or vindication, that she was acting in the name of justice and truth.

Not Jaggar's and Zephyr's version of truth, but the actual truth—unbiased, unadulterated truth.

"You sure you're okay?" Lucki wasn't calling attention to Crimson's mood. Her voice was low, her lips barely moving but all the same, she wished the other witch would mind her own business. She didn't want Jaggar or Zephyr to know they'd gotten to her.

"I'm fine," Crimson snapped, then cringed. "Sorry." She huffed out a sigh then ran her fingers through her hair. "I'm *not* fine, but you have nothing to worry about. I'll get us where we need to go."

The familiars were running through some last-minute words of advice about shifting to Fortis, but they were all predators with keen hearing.

"I'm not worried about that." Lucki tugged her aside. "Any chance we could bypass your sisters altogether?" Lucki squinted, wrinkling her nose. "I mean, with everything you've said and the fact that you're simmering, maybe we should just move ahead with our plan to go after Angelica and leave your sisters out of it for now."

"Can't," Crimson said. "My familiars are being held as incentive for me to return with you. I need them with me for our plan to work."

Lucki contemplated Crimson with a head tilt for a few seconds too long, which made Crimson want to squirm. It was probably obvious to everyone that Crimson, Jaggar and Zephyr had history. Lucki's expression hinted that she knew what kind of history that was. Maybe she was wondering why Crimson wouldn't take the mark of the Fortis shifters who were guarding her now, when it was clear they were supporting her and especially since her own familiars were being held away from her.

"It's a long story," Crimson grunted, her words hardly intelligible. "Complicated."

"It's always complicated with these men." Lucki smiled, disarming Crimson enough to quirk a smile back.

Lucki turned to look at her men, so Crimson, purely on reflex, did the same and regretted it immediately when her eyes met Zephyr's and his words came back to haunt her all over again.

"You didn't fight. You accepted what was done to you and left Jag and me behind. You abandoned us."

She had abandoned them? *Seriously?*

She'd been banished! Exiled!

And that's where her thoughts snagged, because her sisters had never locked her out of the kingdom in any physical way. Crimson had created her own veil to keep her sisters out after she'd been banished. Her actual banishment had been words only, a decree uttered with a causal wave of a hand. Deep down, Crimson knew that it had been her own doubts that had given her sisters the power to toss her away as they had. There'd been nothing else stopping her from returning—nothing but her own mistaken acceptance of a punishment she hadn't deserved.

Did that make Zephyr right? Could she have come back for them? Had she even wanted to?

Should she have fought for these men whom she'd once loved?

Her mind tripped over that thought. Her heart stuttered.

Men I once loved?

Zephyr broke their stare first, turning away so abruptly that it was like a slap. Crimson touched her lips, as if he'd branded her there, as if she could still feel his mouth pressed against hers. It shouldn't have happened—and it shouldn't have felt as good as it had.

She traced the ghost of his kiss before dropping her hand.

"We ready?" Reuben parted from the group of Fortis, rubbing his hands together like he was preparing for something exciting.

To a shifter brimming with power, the hunt for Angelica probably was exciting in a primordial way.

They were standing just outside the sacred circle, and once they were ready, Lucki would invite all the Fortis in so they could harness the natural and substantial power and lessen the drag on Crimson as she pulled everyone through.

"Remember... We need to be connected, me to Lucki, then you all to one of us. If you break the connection, you disappear into the veil, and I don't want to have to go hunting for you."

Crimson stepped over the border and was instantly enveloped by the magic. It tickled along her skin then soaked into her veins, racing to her heart then out again to ping against every nerve ending she had. If it had been electricity, it would have had her hair standing on end, and a gust of magical wind did flutter around her, rising like a tidal wave. Lucki's hair billowed like a halo of red once she stepped into the circle, as if a torrent of wind was whipping around her, embracing her, infusing her with more magic than she already had. It threatened to knock Crimson out of the circle altogether, but Lucki's power rose to counter it, pushing the wayward air back down until all was calm again.

Goosebumps rose along Crimson's skin, and a delicious shiver rushed down her spine.

"My hearts, please enter the circle." Lucki motioned to her men before turning to Jaggar and Zephyr. "My new friends, I invite you into this sacred space as well."

And with that, all five men crowded around Lucki and Crimson. It was a lot of testosterone and a lot of manly musk, enough to entice Crimson to close her eyes and soak it up. She wished Jaggar and Zephyr closer, close enough to embrace so she would be caged in muscle and sinew and feral desire.

How could she hate them so much but want them more? Was she lying to her heart? Did she still have feelings for these brutes? Or was it only carnal want?

Her body heated, magic coursing, along with lust. It radiated up her neck, across her cheeks, tingling her scalp, then raced down her body to pool deep inside where her desire was a flame, raging against her will to suppress it.

Jaggar clasped his heavy hand around the back of her neck, possession in a gesture. She knew, *knew* without a doubt, that he was zoned in on her arousal.

"Anger and lust come from the same place," he growled quietly into her ear, like he could read her mind, like he knew that she and Zephyr had already crossed that line. "And there's no denying either, once you let go."

Crimson growled back, snapping her teeth in his direction, but that only pulled a deep rumbly laugh from the shifter—a sound she both loved and hated.

Zephyr gripped her shoulder, only exerting enough pressure to ensure he wouldn't lose hold of her in the ether.

Lucki slipped her fingers between Crimson's then gave a squeeze. Even though they came from different worlds, Crimson knew that she and Lucki had an understanding, a connection rooted in witchy solidarity. Lucki knew what it was like to deal with these brutes at the heart level. She might not know the intimate details of Crimson's struggle, but all the same, her small gesture gave Crimson comfort.

Crimson squeezed back, grateful for a kindred soul to stand by her side. It might not solve her problems with Zephyr and Jaggar, but it was nice to know that someone else understood.

"Ready when you are," Lucki said with a nudge of her elbow.

Crimson checked to make sure that all Lucki's men were attached in some way to her.

"Hang tight," she said before closing her eyes, reaching into the ether for her own thread, the one she'd purposely laid on their trip to Weeping Falls. It was hidden so only she would be able to find it. She coaxed it forward so she could latch on and take them all for a ride.

Chapter Sixteen

Jaggar

"Back up if you know what's good for you, brothers," Jaggar roared as he pushed against the tight line of Fortis. They'd been crowded by the guards the moment they'd stepped through the ether into Shade. "This is no way to welcome guests."

Axle, the lead guard, gave a grunt back, his hard gaze scanning the looming figures of Lucki's Fortis familiars. He flicked his eyes to Jaggar, his threat assessment swift and complete. Jaggar lifted his chin, daring his brethren to do something stupid, to give him the excuse he needed to attack the traitors, the cowards who had allowed Tabitha and Wyvern to rule, now even without the crystal in hand.

His argument with Crimson had made him feel reckless. The scent of her arousal had nearly unhinged him completely.

Axle motioned with nothing more than a nod of his head for the other guards to stand down.

The building tension lowered a notch, decreasing the boil to a simmer.

Axel's command didn't mean the guards would let them make their way to the throne room unattended, but at least the Fortis fell behind somewhat so Jaggar could lead the group to the false queens. Crimson put distance between herself and Zephyr, which, Jaggar decided, confirmed his suspicions. The sly beast had somehow gotten to her in Weeping Falls. Jaggar didn't know if it had been something physical between them or emotional, but it was obvious that Zephyr had somehow managed to slip under her skin enough to make her squirm.

Jaggar's cat chuffed just under the surface, jealousy pricking at his skin, like the big cat was poking with its claws, needling him to do something about that. He pushed back, reminding his panther that now was not the time for possessive shit. It was bad enough he'd let the cat slip out to grasp Crimson the way he had, around the back of her neck like she was his to dominate. As good as it had felt to revisit old times, Crimson was not his, and if Zeph was able to get through to her so she took his mark, then Jaggar would accept that. Even if it meant she never took his, one Fortis bond was better than none.

Yeah, right.

Who was he trying to kid? With every fiber of his being, he wanted to be the one to give Crimson her first Fortis mark. He *had* to be the one. That was how it had always been meant to be, and his panther grumbled and growled, clawing at the wrongness of his thoughts of stepping aside for Zephyr.

Jaggar gave his head a shake, trying to dispel his cat's displeasure. Even though the rational side of Jaggar knew he couldn't be a raging Neanderthal, the primitive side of him wanted to grab Crimson right there, right now, and drag her off to her room so he could mark her properly. His cat chuffed at that thought. *Do it*, his cat was saying.

Later, panther. We'll find a way to convince her later.

He looked over his shoulder to assess the group, quickly noting that the closer they got to the throne room, the tighter the group moved, cohesive in the face of a threat.

Lucki seemed to be handling the tension as she had everything so far, with a nonchalance that was strange and slightly unnerving. The witch had power, and she was surrounded by strong familiars, but nothing rattled her, not in an expected or understandable way. The trip through the ether alone should have shaken her to some degree. It was hardly a smooth ride, but even that didn't appear to bother her. It made him curious. Was she really that confident and unshakable or was she just very good at pretending to be?

Whatever it was, Crimson needed a dose of it. Her self-doubt flickered behind her eyes so that anyone could see. It was why her sisters had always taken advantage, taunted and tormented her, because they saw her weakness plainly every day. Whatever Lucki had going on, Jaggar hoped that Crimson would absorb some of it so she would finally see what needed to be done and accept that she was the only one who could do it.

Lucki's familiars, on the other hand, were not at ease. Clearly on alert, their eyes darted to every door they passed, as if they expected an ambush.

Smart men.

They entered the throne room to find Wyvern and Tabitha in a heated argument. Their heads were pressed close together like bulls ready to ram, jabbing their fingers at one another and whispered words full of venom. Even though Jaggar couldn't hear what was being said, it was obvious that her sisters were enraged.

As if taken by surprise by the arrival of guests, Wyvern and Tabitha jolted away from one another to face the approaching crowd.

"Seize her!" Wyvern shouted, her finger pointed toward the group.

As the Fortis guards converged from behind, tension and aggression rolled off Lucki's men at the same explosive rate as it did Jaggar and Zephyr. When the guards made a move toward Lucki, it was clear all hell would break loose.

"No, not her!" Tabitha screamed. "Seize Crimson!"

In a confusing blur, the guards somehow managed to yank Crimson away before she could get a wisp of magic ready. They collared her with iron bejeweled in raven stone, which sent her to her knees with a gutted moan. It wouldn't be enough to keep Crimson down forever, but it was enough to keep her down for now.

"What is the meaning of this?" Jaggar roared. "Crimson did as you asked and completed your mission."

Tabitha and Wyvern looked disheveled and haggard. Wyvern had deep purple bags under her eyes and her hair was barely styled, with flyaway pieces making her look unkempt. Tabitha's gown wasn't clasped properly, and her skin was blotchy, like she'd been picking at herself and hadn't had the time to put herself together. Both were clearly agitated.

It was not the most royal way to greet guests...certainly not the way of the sisters. They were usually calm, collected, calculating.

"We have our reasons," Tabitha said as she attempted to run fingers through her tangled mess of hair, only to snag, growl then tug her hand free.

"This is hardly the welcome I expected." Lucki's voice rang through the cavernous room like she belonged there.

Tabitha and Wyvern took notice, both with varying degrees of offense and perhaps, Jaggar hoped, fear on their faces.

Wyvern lips twisted, something vile likely already on her tongue.

"If it pleases the Triad of Shade," Jaggar interrupted, "I would like to introduce Lucki of Weeping Falls and her Fortis guards, Wren, Julian and Reuben."

Tabitha winced like the volume of his words caused her pain. "We would welcome you to Shade if you hadn't already trespassed here twice without our invitation." Her tone was full of disapproval despite the sickly-sweet smile on her pale lips.

Lucki scrunched her pretty face. "I *have* been here without realizing that I was trespassing, and I apologize for that."

Tabitha and Wyvern shared an unreadable look before turning to face Lucki again.

"As an invited guest and, according to your sister, a triad prospect, I'd like to know why Crimson is being so forcefully detained? What has she done?"

"You're here to fix a mistake you made." Wyvern ignored Lucki's questions and seemed to be struggling to muster even a curl to her lips as she spoke, not invested enough to pretend to welcome Lucki and her men.

"I apologize for causing such trouble for you." Although her words were contrite, her body language was anything but. She stood tall, her shoulders back, eyes moving from Wyvern to Tabitha like she was ready to challenge them to a duel. "Had I known that Shade was inhabited, I would never have banished Angelica here. I'm prepared to fix my mistake."

"And return the Crystal of Shade to us?" Wyvern narrowed her eyes.

Lucki stepped forward, leaving her bristling Fortis behind. "I expect a seat on the empty throne. I expect to be part of the triad."

Jaggar frowned as he watched Lucki. This was more than backbone. This was a witch with a goal. Lucki sounded very convincing—so convincing that Jaggar had a niggling of doubt that Lucki could be trusted after all. He turned his stare to Crimson, who wasn't too caught up in her own troubles to miss Lucki's words. She, too, was watching the witch, her eyes showing surprise, hurt, doubt and worse…defeat.

Why had she trusted Lucki so much when they'd arrived at Weeping Falls? What did she actually know of this witch? She'd literally spent less than a day with her and yet she was hinging her future on trusting her? Why?

"If I'm to retrieve your precious gem, I want a share in its power," Lucki continued.

"And what's stopping you from claiming the crystal for yourself?" Wyvern sounded annoyed, but Jaggar caught the glimmer of intrigue in the queen's eyes. She was impressed by Lucki's boldness and her ambition.

"And do what with it?" Lucki scoffed. "A gem like that would cause any sole witch to deep dive into madness."

Wyvern cocked an eyebrow, no longer hiding her feelings. It was obvious that she was growing more and more fascinated by Lucki. It made Jaggar's already agitated cat claw for escape. What if Lucki had been lying about leaving Shade and lying about handing over the crystal to Crimson? What if she'd agreed so easily to Crimson's plans because she had intended to betray her all along?

"As we see with the one called Angelica," Tabitha said.

"Exactly," Lucki agreed. "I have no interest in losing my mind. I vow to hand over the crystal if you vow to honor your end of the deal and elevate me to the triad."

Wyvern and Tabitha exchanged looks before turning to face Lucki once again. "We vow it," they said in unison. Their words snapped like iron shackles locking into place. While not magically binding, spoken vows held power.

This was wrong...all wrong. Jaggar knew by Zephyr's stance that he was drawing the same conclusion. His brother cat was clenching his fists like his claws were ready to burst out of his knuckles. His jaw moved as if his fangs were punching through his gums.

Jaggar's muscles bunched under his clothes, flexing with every deep breath he took. They were going to have to fight their way out of this situation and try to take the throne now.

"We will leave to hunt down Angelica." Lucki pointed a finger at Crimson. "But not without her."

"She will not be accompanying you." Tabitha's expression soured all over again. "She must answer for some…things."

"You can't expect us to move through Shade without an escort," Lucki continued. "Release Crimson and her familiars to join us on this mission. You wouldn't want us to be at a disadvantage when facing Angelica in unknown territory, would you? You do want the crystal back, don't you?"

"You will have Jaggar and Zephyr to escort you," Tabitha said with a slight toss of her head in Jaggar's direction.

"Angelica is a powerful witch," Lucki continued. "Powerful enough to murder a queen. If you won't send me with a fellow witch, then at least tell me what Crimson's crime is. If I am to believe your vow and soon to be a queen as well, I want to know."

Wyvern sucked in her cheeks as if tasting something sour. "We suspect Crimson is behind the theft of another precious gem. Her familiars are gone, with the gem, and we know they'd do nothing without her consent."

"What do you mean they're gone?" Crimson gasped, her voice jagged. "Where are they?"

"You should know, sister." Tabitha shrugged. "This was all your plan, wasn't it? To have them snooping around while you were gone."

"You forced them to stay here! *You* were holding them here as collateral! How could I have planned anything with them?" Crimson yelled, her vibrant magic sparking along the gems of her collar, a show of power that her sisters couldn't ignore.

"Bind her!" Wyvern yelled at her Fortis. "Before she can break out of that collar!"

"That's enough of that," Lucki said, her magic marks flaring along her skin like the sun. Her power surged, washing over Jaggar, rallying him to action.

The ground shook with her familiars' roars as they shifted not to bear, wolf and lion but to Fortis beasts, towering over their witch, magic sparking like flint to stone.

Jaggar let his panther loose, holding the reins only enough to continue his shift to Fortis. Zephyr already had Crimson under his arm, nestled into his beast's side.

Lucki opened a portal all on her own, as if she always knew how, then separated the ether. She quickly looped a tether around each of them, a magical touch in place of an actual one. When she tugged them toward her, it was a force that Jaggar couldn't resist, and he realized all over again just how powerful Lucki was. Swept up in the fall, they all tumbled through the portal, escaping Wyvern's and Tabitha's frantic screams for their guards to stop them.

Chapter Seventeen

Crimson

Crimson hit the ground on all fours, her palms skidding along the dirt as she fought to hold her focus. She drilled deep into the collar's magic with her own, battering against the gems that fought back hard, attempting to contain her, to nullify her power. It might have worked on a lesser witch, but her sisters' clumsy magic was etched into the collar's manufacturing and Crimson found the exact spot where the weakest link finally broke apart. The collar shattered into pieces and fell to the ground, the gems losing all color and trace of power.

She needed to get back, to find Talon and Valor. Anxiety poked at her from all sides, prodding her to do something reckless. She fought to maintain control. She needed time to think—a moment to quiet her brain so she could come up with a plan.

"Is everyone okay?" Lucki's magic still sparked over her arms and chest and radiated a halo around her head, a dazzling kaleidoscope of color.

The familiars were slowly deescalating—huffing, puffing and chuffing to get themselves from raging Fortis beasts to something else.

"I wasn't expecting you to do that." Crimson accepted Lucki's offered hand, if only to keep the peace for now, then hauled herself to her feet.

Crimson wasn't sure if she meant she wasn't expecting Lucki to pull them all through a portal with a magical tether or if she meant she wasn't expecting Lucki to demand a seat on the throne. Both had been shocking turns from the plan she'd laid out with Lucki in Weeping Falls. Was Lucki putting on a show for Tabitha and Wyvern or was she really a duplicitous witch, laying the groundwork to turn on Crimson as soon as she got the crystal?

"I've been practicing," Lucki said, like she wasn't even thinking about what had happened back in the throne room. "I've been testing the limits of my power over the last few months and experimenting with these portal things. I figured it would make sense for us to start at the cat house where I probably sent Angelica when I dragged her through the portal with me during our battle."

Crimson scanned the area, her senses alert for any pulse of power that might indicate another witch, one who possessed the powerful Crystal of Shade. She detected nothing but a mixed-up mash of old, decaying power, likely whatever had been used to construct the building that stood before them. The house was three stories, with a turret-like circular area and a wraparound porch. It was black, made of brick and wood, and looked nothing like anything Crimson had ever seen in Shade. It did, however, resemble the house in Weeping Falls where she'd sat with Lucki and agreed on a plan...a plan that Lucki had tossed out of the window when facing Crimson's sisters.

"Isabel built this a long time ago as a kind of safe house hideaway." Lucki averted her eyes as she talked, checking to see where her familiars were, like there was more to this story than she was telling Crimson—or maybe more to the story than even her familiars knew.

The familiars had shifted to their animals and were in the process of sniffing, nudging and scouting the house, around the house and into the thick fog that surrounded it all.

Lucki's magic still pulsed brightly, which made Crimson realize that she'd probably left a blazing trail from the throne room to here.

"Hang on a minute." Crimson shifted backward, stepping into the fog as she opened a portal of her own. She was tempted to go back, to leave the others behind and land somewhere in the castle that would give her quick access to the tunnels where she could bide her time then hunt for Talon and Valor. It would be foolish to act so rashly, even if she was compelled to find her men, and her sisters would probably be expecting her to do something careless like that. So, as tempted as she was, as desperate as she felt to find her men, she reined it in and refocused on the task at hand. It took her seconds to find Lucki's signature weaving through the ether. She grasped the rope of magic then pulsed her own through the threads, eliminating any trace of their journey.

Her sisters might be clumsy, but they weren't stupid. A trail like that would have been easily found, even by some of their Fortis, and despite her desire to find Talon and Valor, Crimson knew she needed to regroup, calm down, figure things out.

"I've bought us some time," Crimson said once she stepped back into the realm that Lucki had taken them to.

"That didn't go as expected," Jaggar said as he shifted from panther to man.

His tone held an edge that Crimson knew meant he was on alert, feeling threatened. She couldn't really blame him. After what had just happened in the throne room, Crimson wasn't all together sure that Lucki could be trusted, either.

"I improvised," Lucki said, her familiars surrounding her, still in animal form, their bodies heaving with deep panting. She laid her hand lightly on the wolf's head as if to calm him, but the beast still bared his fangs in apparent warning. "Your sisters seem like the type of leaders who need to see themselves in others in order to trust them. I thought it would be a good idea to pretend to want what they had offered. That's why I decided to demand a seat on the throne."

"You were very convincing," Zephyr said as he stepped up beside Crimson, close enough that she could feel his body heat but not close enough to actually touch her. It surprised her how comforting his proximity was. She both loved and hated that.

"I can be." Lucki smiled, a gesture that should have been disarming but had Crimson on edge, wary.

Crimson narrowed her eyes at the witch, trying to see through her intentions. The bear at her side lifted its giant head and roared.

"How is binding done? What effect does it have on a witch?" Lucki's voice was calm, collected, and she kept her hand on the wolf's head, her body seemingly at ease, despite her bear's clear agitation.

Caught off guard by Lucki's question, Crimson didn't immediately reply.

"Binding neutralizes a witch's power. There are few ways for it to be done, but the most efficient, quickest and least costly to a witch is if a Fortis gives up his magic to make it happen," Jaggar said. "It's not necessarily permanent when done by a Fortis, but it has lasting impact. Either way, the Fortis will have to forfeit his life."

"So, it was a good call to pull Crimson out of there when I did?" Lucki cocked an eyebrow at Jaggar.

He hesitated, taking in her words before nodding once. Like Crimson, Jaggar seemed to have an issue with Lucki's choice in strategy. What she'd done in the throne room had damaged the trust that had been established in Weeping Falls.

"Then might I suggest we all calm down and be friends again?" Lucki looked from Jaggar to Crimson then Zephyr. "Because the tension around here is choking me."

Her words were like a slap of reality. Crimson could have laughed at Jaggar's double take.

Lucki added, "I can assure you that I have no desire to take the throne, but your sisters need to think I do. I might be new to this witch thing, but I know how to read people, and your sisters have some weaknesses that are easy to exploit. First of all, they think they're clever and diabolical, but they're just two little girls playing at being queens."

Jaggar snorted. Zephyr coughed out a laugh. Crimson's instinct was to lash out, to correct the obvious treason in Lucki's words, but she held her tongue, biting it to keep those sharp words from spilling. Lucki wasn't wrong. Tabitha and Wyvern hadn't been ready to take the throne a year ago, and it was clear that they weren't doing a good job of it now. They'd accused Crimson of betrayal twice without evidence. It was time for Crimson to accept that they weren't looking out for anyone but themselves and they *were* definitely hiding something.

"And two, they're absolutely not what they want everything to think they are — powerful, in control witches to be feared."

"They're hiding something," Jaggar growled, echoing Crimson's own thoughts.

"It's not just that," Lucki said. "They're losing control, and the cracks are showing."

Crimson immediately thought about Talon and Valor and the accusation her sisters had hurled about them stealing a powerful gem. "My familiars must have discovered something that my sisters didn't want found."

"That's what I believe, as well," Jaggar said. "We sent them on a mission to find the truth. They must have gotten close enough to scare the queens."

"They were definitely rattled," Lucki agreed.

"The gem?" What gem would be more powerful than the Crystal of Shade, though? "If Talon and Valor stole a gem, maybe it was connected to something bigger — like a sacred circle of some kind." Crimson could definitely see her sisters creating a power magnet just for themselves.

"Maybe," Jaggar said as he scratched his chin. "It feels bigger than that, though. I think your shifters may have found something that changes the game the false queens are playing."

"I need to find Talon and Valor before my sisters do." Crimson's familiars would be able to find her if she let her magic out. It would be a beacon for them, a signal to home in on. It would also alert her sisters to her whereabouts and put them all in danger the longer it took for her shifters to detect it and come to her.

"We need to get the Crystal of Shade first." Jaggar side-eyed her like he knew what she was thinking. "Your familiars can take care of themselves."

"You would propose leaving them behind. That's exactly like you, isn't it? I can't abandon Talon and Valor there. I won't." Her words were edged with fury dipped in fear. Even though she knew Jaggar was right, she couldn't bear the thought of turning her back on Talon and Valor. "My sisters will find them eventually and torture them to get to me."

"Have some faith in your men, C," Zephyr muttered nearly under his breath.

His words were an annoying smack. Before she could turn on him and spew her anger, Lucki interrupted.

"I don't know a lot about what's going on in your sisters' world, but I think it might be time for you to level up your game." Lucki shifted a quick look from Crimson to Jaggar then Zephyr before returning her gaze back to Crimson, her meaning clear.

It was time, according to Lucki, to bond with the familiars at her side.

"Your sisters are hiding something, something bad enough for them to want to bind your magic in order to keep you from discovering the truth. I'd say that it's time for a reckoning. It's time for you to become the witch everyone knows you can be." Lucki lifted her hands with a shrug. "But that's just an unsolicited opinion from a witch you barely know."

Why did it feel like she was being ganged up on at the same time that it felt like they were only speaking the truth?

"I need time to think." Crimson's mind reeled away from her, shooting out in all directions of what ifs. "I need to process…"

Process *what*? Think about whether or not she could actually take the marks of these two Fortis at her sides? The men who had betrayed her once.

But had they betrayed her? Or had she misunderstood everything that had happened since her sisters had taken the throne? Had she been seeing and judging everything and everyone with a tainted lens because she'd, all along, decided to give her sisters the benefit of the doubt, unlike what they'd given to her.

"Crimson, we need to get to Angelica first, before your sisters —" Jaggar swallowed his next words when he saw the look on her face. She wondered if maybe he was sensing that her resolve to hate him for eternity was slipping. Maybe he realized that even though they didn't have the time to spare, he needed to give her a moment to think it through, to convince herself that this was the only way, to accept that her sisters weren't what she wanted them to be. "Go. We'll find a way to track Angelica while you're figuring things out."

Gratitude buzzed against her long-held hatred of Jaggar, messing with her determination to keep him at arm's length. She wanted to hug him and hit him. She wanted to scream at him and fall at his feet to beg forgiveness, because he was right about her sisters, so maybe he'd been right about rejecting her a year ago. It hadn't been the time to show strength, but now it was the right time, and she had to reconcile that shift in thinking. She didn't want to, though. She didn't want to put her heart out there all over again for him to crush.

She was a coward that way.

What she needed, desperately, was Talon. He would be able to sort this mess out. He'd be able to untangle reason from the knots in her heart and in her head.

She wandered to the back of the strange cat house, down the tangled path of wildflowers and twisted branches. She found the stone circle that existed here, in this other world of Weeping Falls, an axis point between two worlds, cloaked in fog that enveloped her as she entered.

"Talon," she whispered into the ether, "I need you."

Chapter Eighteen

Talon

They didn't have much time, and Talon was desperate to find Crimson. He'd detected a wisp of her magic at the castle while he'd been circling the sky above. It had been a strong pulse of Crimson, there and gone before he'd been able to get to her. Then, while he'd been blindly flying through the ether, he'd felt her again, a blip of her signature, only to have that disappear as well.

He guided his eagle through the dense fog, unsure what direction he was flying but hoping that, somehow, he'd get himself closer to wherever Crimson was. He had to tell her about what her sisters had done, draining the old crones almost to the brink of death. She needed to know how Tabitha and Wyvern had become so powerful and why they were acting so out of control. He hoped that Crimson would finally see what needed to be done in order to not only prove her own innocence but also lead to the undoing of those vile witches.

First, he needed to figure out where Crimson was. Both he and Valor had the ability to detect magic signatures. It wasn't foolproof. Sometimes they'd sense echoes of centuries old magic and think it was new, and sometimes they wouldn't detect anything when magic was all around them. They were both intimately in tune with Crimson's magic, though, and if she was using even a little, he should be able to home in on it and find her.

So, he circled, and circled, swooping through the ether in search of his mate. The fog parted at times, giving him glimpses of realms that he'd never seen before. There were an infinite number of them to find, realms and sub-realms that had all splintered from Shade a millennia ago, each containing their own variation of magic.

They were all connected in one way or another to the Brotherhood caves where all familiars were born and reborn. From there, the shifters would leave in search of a witch to bond and bolster and, in the process, would stumble upon new worlds. Talon always thanked whatever gods or goddesses had engineered his destiny to land in Shade so he could meet Crimson. He couldn't imagine his world without her.

Talon spied tall mountains and lush forests, worlds brimming with untapped natural magic, enticing him to fly closer, investigate places that might be hiding his mate, giving her refuge. He flew through blue skies and skimmed turquoise water, soared over snow-capped summits and wove around magnificent buildings and roaring cities. Allowing himself a taste of the multilayered magic that lay untapped, maybe uncharted, was a glimmer of distraction from the press of anxiety that all but consumed him. He knew time was running out and he needed to find his mate.

But there was no trace of Crimson.

He flew through one dense plume of fog, moisture coating his wings, tickling his beak, cleansing him of residual magic from other realms, and when he came out on the other side, the sky was dark, black with tendrils of tainted magic. He knew in his gut that he was back in Shade and that he'd stumbled on Angelica's stronghold.

He'd felt this magic before. It had oozed from the wild cats who had attacked them at home. It reeked of sulfur and malice.

He skirted the darkness as best as he could, staying high enough that he hoped he wouldn't be seen or magically detected, definitely out of reach of Angelica's wild cats but maybe not out of reach of the witch herself.

She'd transformed a volcano into her defense, utilizing its natural activity to hide her location. It was clever, but Talon was able to see through the sputters of dirty ash that filled the sky with bad intentions. His eagle eyes zeroed in on the hundreds of wild cats that circled the base of the volcano, seemingly impervious to the hot ash that fell all around them.

Everything about this place felt wrong, rotten, evil, and he knew Angelica was at the core of it all.

Talon dared to fly lower and, as much as he didn't want to, opened his beak to take in the taste of the evil magic, to etch the signature of this foul witch into his senses so he'd be able to find her again. Her tainted power seared his throat and clogged his senses, overwhelming him with dirty magic. As he swooped low, low enough to see the hordes of demented beasts fighting and snarling at one another, oblivious to his intrusion, he knew Angelica had formed an army beyond their wildest imaginations and that time wasn't running out. It had run out.

Talon needed Crimson to rise to her full potential now or Shade as they knew it would be lost forever.

He pulled up, flapping his huge wings with everything he had, then dove back into the ether with the bitter taste of Angelica's magic in his mouth and the burning need to find his mate pulsing through him.

"Talon, I need you." Crimson's voice was a beacon in the fog, calling him with as much desperation as he felt to find her. He shifted his flight path, then soared with eyes closed and heart open, his eagle's cry loud enough to wake the gods.

* * * *

"You're here! You found me." Crimson ran to him as he shifted from eagle to man, his arms out and ready as she barreled into his chest like he was her life support. "Are you hurt?"

He wrapped his arms around her, molding her body into his so he could feel every curve pressed against him. "No, love, not hurt."

"Valor?" She nuzzled against his chest, breathing him in, her arms wrapped tightly around his waist.

"He's safe." At least, Talon hoped he was. He'd given Valor the gem that he'd plucked from Tabitha and Wyvern's siphoning chamber, hoping that his brother would find the rightful queens deep in the tunnels and know what to do with it. That gem held enough power to release the queens from their captivity — in theory anyway — if the old crones were able to utilize it. "We have to get back soon though... Your mother —"

"My sisters —" Crimson said at the same time.

He pulled back as she did the same, looking up at him while still holding his waist. "What about my mother?"

"I found her and your aunt and grandmother. They're alive." *Barely.* "We need to help Valor release them."

"You found them?" Crimson's eyes widened and swam with instant tears as his words fully sank in. "Release them from where?"

"Your sisters have been holding them captive, siphoning their power." He didn't want to tell her how terribly frail her mother had been. The siphoning had done a number on all three witches, but Crimson's mother had looked like she'd aged a century.

Crimson gasped, her hand flying to cover her mouth. "No."

"Valor is with them." He had to be by now. He would have detected Talon's signature in seconds and would have been able to follow it all the way to the cave where the queens were being held. "But we'll need to help him."

"They did this... My sisters did this? Not only stealing the queens away but stealing *from* them? It's blasphemy. A violation..." Crimson fell back, pulling completely away so she could wrap her arms around herself. "I've been such a fool."

"No, Crimson, you couldn't have known they would do something like this." Not even Talon had fathomed what Tabitha and Wyvern had been capable of. Sure, he'd believed they had been responsible for the queens' mysterious disappearance, but their level of treason was unheard of in all the history of Shade.

"No? After everything they've ever done to me?" She didn't say it, but Talon knew she was thinking about Jaggar's persistent warnings before they'd left the castle, that her sisters were not to be trusted. "I should have known." Crimson whispered hoarsely, her shoulders curling in as she hung her head and refused to look at him. "When we were younger and I was only just coming into the breadth of my power, Mother was so proud, so awestruck that I had such magic already that she told me I'd be her successor." Her body clearly held the pain of that memory—a memory that she'd never told them before. "Of course, my sisters weren't happy, even though my mother's promise that one day I'd be one of the triad was a long time away."

Crimson had often spoken of how her sisters were always jealous of her abilities. How they'd teased and tormented her. "Did they siphon from you?" Talon wanted so badly to take her into his arms and kiss her pain away. Instead, he hovered and listened, waiting for a signal that she needed his touch.

"They tried to." Crimson snorted. She uncurled herself and looked at him. "They worked together— Wyvern, Tabitha, even Aria helped. They bound me in iron shackles then chanted a spell so vile that it felt like a thousand spiders crawling on my skin—a spell that seeped into my bones and squeezed so forcefully that I thought I would snap into a million pieces. It ripped hair from my scalp and tore into my veins. It burned and froze at the same time. I was in agony and worse, my heart was breaking at the confirmation that my sisters hated me that much."

Valor wanted to rip those witches to pieces. "Crimson —"

"Even with the iron on my wrists, I was still more powerful than they were. It helped that their spell casting was clumsy and unrefined." She twisted her wrists like she was breaking free from invisible shackles. "I showed them their weakness."

"You reversed the spell?" Talon knew that Crimson's abilities far surpassed those of her sisters. Even before she'd allowed herself to be marked by both him and Valor, she'd been so damn powerful.

"I did. I siphoned their magic for seconds only, but it was enough to scare them off" — she shook her head — "for a while, anyway. It never occurred to me that they'd be bold enough to try that spell again, and on the queens... Gods, they are insane."

"They've obviously refined the siphoning spell," Talon said. "It's strong enough to contain the queens and also pull tremendous magic from them."

"That's why you stole the gem." Crimson ran her fingers through her hair. "They were furious with you about that and tried to nullify my power. They even threatened to bind me."

Talon clenched his jaw. *How dare those witches try to bind my mate!*

"Did they create a symbol? Some kind of inlay in the stonework? A circle? Triad?"

Talon nodded, not trusting himself to speak.

"Without the gem in the symbol, the siphoned magic is free floating. My sisters may still get residual effects of the stolen power, but they won't get it fully right now — which is why they were so weird today. They're going through withdrawal." Crimson closed her eyes. "I should never have given my sisters the benefit of the doubt. I should have given them what they deserved, what they gave to me a year ago...judgment without mercy. I have been so willfully blind. I knew!" She hit her thigh. "I suspected they were behind the disappearance, and yet I couldn't accept it. I've been too stubborn about this and my mother, my aunt, my grandmother have suffered for it."

"Now that you see the truth." Zephyr stepped out of the shadows. "What will you do about it, C?"

Chapter Nineteen

Crimson

She couldn't take Jaggar's mark. She just couldn't, not after a year of hating him. Her anger was too ingrained. But she had less hesitation about Zephyr, if only because they'd kissed, and it had felt like coming home. She refused to think, even for a moment, about what kissing Jaggar would feel like after so long.

Nope, not gonna go there.

Taking Zephyr's mark wouldn't seem like such a betrayal to herself. If she took Jaggar's, it would feel like salt in the deepest wound. And she only needed one Fortis to outmatch her sisters. At least, that's what she was telling herself.

"You need the mark of a Fortis," Talon said, bringing the message to crystal clarity.

"I can't..." She shook her head vehemently as she swallowed her pain. "I won't take Jaggar's mark."

"Crimson," Zephyr sighed as if his disappointment would be enough to convince her heart to change course.

Talon took her face in his hands. "You need at least one of them." He knew her hurt. He knew what this was costing her.

She gulped, closed her eyes and let her body sag. Talon wrapped his arms around her.

"Just one of them," he whispered against her ear. "It will bolster you so you can defeat Angelica, so you can use the Crystal of Shade to break the crones free, so you can put your sisters in their place, once and for all. Please, Crim, do this for your harem. Do this so we can all heal."

Minutes stretched while Crimson's mind whirred. She knew how necessary this was—not only to defeat Angelica, not only to usurp her sisters and save her queens, not only because Talon was right and they all needed to heal but also because it was what she'd wanted. *Desperately wanted.* Maybe a year away had changed her, but she couldn't deny the magnetic pull that still existed, drawing her to Zephyr. She'd loved Jaggar and Zephyr once, but it was Zephyr who offered the path of least resistance for Crimson's torn and tattered heart.

"Zephyr," she croaked as if he wasn't standing close enough to hear her.

"Zephyr," Talon agreed as he flicked his eyes over Crimson's head and nodded.

Gods help her soul.

* * * *

For once, Crimson felt as tongue-tied as Zephyr always seemed to be. He'd come to stand just feet from her, led by Talon, and now stood, his head slightly bowed, waiting for her to make the first move. Talon had left them, presumably to keep the others away — to keep Jaggar away.

The process of marking a witch need not be formal. In fact, it was better when it wasn't. Marking was a private thing as far as Crimson was concerned, not something to be showcased in ceremony like the triad had always seemed to insist on, nor to be asked permission for like her mother and grandmother had decreed was proper etiquette while they had ruled. Crimson wasn't proposing the path her sisters had taken was wise, either, to completely ignore the advice of her elders, if only to stage a coup. A witch should be able to decide who was a suitable mate and when the right time was to bond with them. The days of prearranged mate matching were long gone. The heart should be the ruling judge when it came to choosing a familiar and not the business of all the court.

When Talon and Valor had marked Crimson, they'd done so quietly, in her bedroom at the castle with no other eyes on them. It had been full of passion and deep emotional meaning, and Crimson cherished the memory of that night, not only because her two familiars had gifted her with their marks, but also because they'd proven to her that they were willing to stand up with her against her queens' ridiculous rules. It had been a short-lived act of defiance that had caused no harm and had held no nefarious intention.

At the time, she'd had no idea that her grandmother, aunt and mother would go missing. She'd had no idea that the last conversation she would have with her mother would be an argument about Crimson taking familiar mates without permission and the deep disappointment that came with her defiance of their long-established protocols. She'd had no idea that her action would be used as flimsy evidence to convince the court that she was responsible for the disappearance of the queens.

"Why did you say what you said?" Crimson sighed. "About me abandoning you." She'd pushed Zephyr's accusation away after she'd dwelled on it longer than she would have liked. It had rattled her brain because his words had made no sense at the time. How could he think she had abandoned him when she'd been the one that had been banished? But now, realizing how much power she'd given her sisters this past year by just accepting their imposed punishment...now she was starting to understand.

She'd let her sisters win. She'd let them get away with hurting the true queens. Why? Because she'd been mortally offended and her heart had been wounded so much that she'd been blind to the truth. Never in her wildest imagination would she have thought her sisters would usurp the triad and siphon their own mother and aunt and grandmother. Never would she have truly thought that they would have used Crimson as a scapegoat for their crimes.

But she should have seen it all.

Zephyr didn't answer but he did raise his head and lock his eyes with her. She saw hurt that matched her own and knew it had been there all along. She'd just been too selfish to recognize it.

She would see and hear and be aware from this moment forward. No more denying what was right in front of her.

Crimson moved to him, bold and brazen as she swayed her hips and stared him down. She wasn't sure what words to say...not yet.

Zephyr held her stare the entire way. His eyes were sparkling like diamonds, thawing the frost between them. He'd always been able to see right through her. He'd also seemed to know her better than she knew herself. She shivered as awareness dawned... He'd always known she would change her mind.

She had a moment between one step and the next where she faltered in her resolve. A year apart had done damage, but she had to believe that it wasn't irreparable. Not between her and Zephyr anyway, and right now she just wanted the last year apart to vanish and for things to go back to the way they had been between them. She wanted his silent but steady support and love. She wanted to give him her unquenchable desire to prove that he deserved her love in return.

"I was foolish to ever think you'd turn your back on me." She tried to convey everything she was thinking. Yes, he should have told her the plan. He and Jaggar should have given her the chance to understand what they were thinking. Communication hadn't been their best quality back then. She lifted his hand, holding it between her palms. His callused fingers rough against hers.

"And stubborn," he grumbled. "I'm sorry for my part in this, Crimson. I never wanted to hurt you."

Her heart flipped over on itself.

It would never have been Zephyr's choice to stay away from her. She'd forgotten that about him. She should never have doubted his loyalty to her, no matter what his actions had been.

Jaggar was more than a familiar brother to Zephyr. They'd gone through things together, things that they'd never told Crimson but that she knew were more than two Fortis should ever be made to endure. It had bonded them just as surely as marking a witch would, and that meant that if Jaggar wanted to stay at court to spy and bide his time while keeping Crimson in the dark, Zephyr would as well. Not happily, surely, but Crimson knew that he would never leave Jaggar's side.

He was very loyal.

He curled his fingers around her hand then pulled her closer — so close that she felt his exhale on her cheek. She tilted her head up, craving a kiss like the one he'd given her already.

"You want my mark?" His voice was gruff, as always, but edged with hesitation that surprised Crimson — like he wasn't sure this was really going to happen between them.

Crimson nodded. "I always have." Nervous bubbles rolled from her stomach up her throat. She wanted to giggle or puke…

Zephyr nodded too but not before she saw something cross his eyes. *Relief? Acceptance? Forgiveness?* She wasn't sure but it didn't matter, because it meant they were both setting aside what had happened and embracing what was to come.

He cupped her jaw, never once breaking eye contact. "I vow to always protect you."

"And I you." Crimson slipped her hands over his shoulders so she could hoist herself up his body.

He circled his arms around her waist. She pressed her breasts to his hard chest, a tantalizing tease for her nipples that ached for more friction. He moved his hands to her ass then heaved her higher, so she was eye to eye, seeing him in a soul-deep way. No words necessary, his love shone back at her. When he pressed his lips to hers, it was more than explosive, it was incendiary. A year of missed kisses all in one. He devoured her, stroked her, nipped at her bottom lip then started all over again.

She wrapped her legs around his waist and slipped her fingers up the base of his neck into his hair. She kissed him back just as fiercely, letting everything she'd felt over the last year cascade through her lips. She'd hated him. She'd missed him. Mostly though, she'd longed for his touch. The pain she'd felt in her heart melted away with each second that passed — lips to lips, heart to heart.

She let her guard down but called her magic, coaxing fog to roll into the sacred circle. The fog would cloak them from prying eyes, but as an extra precaution, she wove a simple spell to cocoon them in privacy and keep others out, so they could have their time together.

He moved them to the stone altar, a fitting place for a sacred rite.

He laid her down, breaking their kiss only long enough to help her out of her battle clothes, then out of his. He cupped her breast and wedged his knee between her legs so he could rub her pussy with his thigh, the friction enough to make her gasp and writhe, all the while devouring her mouth. She gripped his ass and reveled in how taut his muscles were. She'd fantasized for years about how deep his thrusts would go, how powerful his ass and muscled legs were, how well he'd use them to pump into her. This was not the first time they'd touched and teased and kissed.

It would be their first time taking one another, however, becoming one, mating in the most profound sense.

Zephyr pulled back to look down at her, his lips curled into a smug grin that said more than words ever could. She grinned back, feeling just as triumphant.

Yes, this felt right.

Yes, it had been too long.

Yes, she wanted him as much as he wanted her.

The wicked gleam in his eyes made her shiver. He moved, with slow and steady kisses, along her throat, over her collarbone, then down to one breast. He sucked her nipple hard, pulling a moan from her parted lips as he slipped his fingers to her clit. So many sensations piled on top of one another that her pussy ached and wept. She wanted his cock wedged deep inside and her body pulsed for more—more kisses, more touching, more Zephyr.

He obliged, of course, shifting focus from one tit to the other, simultaneously teasing erogenous zones with his lips and tongue, fingers and palm until she was rolling her hips to meet his fingers, moaning, her orgasm rising with each flick, rub, lick and suck.

Somehow...somehow, she pushed him away and when he began to protest, she shushed him with her hand wrapped around his shaft and a gentle squeeze of his tip. It was her turn to slip down his body, to worship the cut of his muscles, to suck and lick each nipple on her way to his magnificent cock.

She cupped his balls, caressing the delicate skin. His eyelids grew heavy with a look full of lust and need. She kept her eyes locked with his when she licked his dick from base to tip then back down again. He grunted and reached for her hair, tugging his fingers through then gripping tightly. She took him down, swirling her tongue over his crown, flicking along the sensitive ridge then sucking him back to the gate of her throat. His girth stretched her lips, but her mouth was generous enough to accommodate his size, and she eased him deeper into her throat, then purred so he'd feel the vibration along his entire length.

He groaned, bucking his hips and tugging her hair. She pulled back, letting his cock slide along her tongue as she slurped and sucked and licked her way to his tip once again. She wrapped her hand around his shaft while she cocooned his sac in the warmth of her mouth, licking until he thrust forcefully against her palm.

That was the cue, the message she'd been aiming for. She didn't give him time to fully register what she was doing until it was done. Swinging her body up and over him so she could straddle his waist then lower her pussy over his dick, she speared herself swiftly and took great pleasure in the look of surprise that resonated over his face. He arched into her, his hands on her ass as she rolled her hips and ground herself against his cock.

She teased her nipples, tweaking hard enough to make her eyes water with one hand, then with the other, rubbed her clit, pressing roughly, without mercy. With her head tilted back, she rode him hard, and their magic swirled around them so it was impossible to tell where his ended and hers began. With their bodies linked, their power fused and her climax rose with shocking urgency and unrelenting ferocity.

He bellowed his own orgasm, his cock rigid and thick, pumping her with hot jets of cum. He flipped her under him so he could pinion her, riding his climax until they were both wrung out.

As he hovered over her, braced on one arm, his cock still pulsating deep inside her pussy, he used his fingers to trace patterns into her skin.

"My magic will bolster you." He splayed his fingers under her jaw, raking gently down the tender flesh of her throat then over her collar bones. "My power will be your armor." He curled his hand over one breast, then the other. She arched into his touch as his mark infused along her flesh, burrowing deep and taking root. "My soul belongs to you." He swept his fingers like a brush over her stomach.

His magic melded into her skin, sinking deep, sparking along her nerve endings, entangling with her own power, taking root and making it shine.

She clasped his hand then brought it to her lips. "Thank you," she whispered as she tried not to think about the year she'd wasted and instead focused on the time they had ahead.

Knowing deep down that her heart would never endure this same thing from Jaggar.

Chapter Twenty

Jaggar

No. No. No!

Jaggar didn't need Fortis magic to sense what had changed in Crimson. As she walked hand in hand with Zephyr out of the fog and into the clearing where Jaggar and the others stood discussing plans, he saw her glow and knew. She'd been marked. She'd willingly, seemingly happily, accepted Zephyr as a mate, and that burned like a thousand suns, scorching his heart so it took everything in Jaggar's power not to cover his chest with his hand and show his weakness.

He turned his back on them, tried to collect himself and cursed under his breath.

"It was the only way to keep her safe," Talon said quietly as he stood next to Jaggar and over the crudely drawn map he'd made. "She'll come around and take your mark, too."

Jaggar clenched his eyes shut. "Quiet," he growled through clenched teeth. "I don't want your sympathy."

When he opened his eyes, Crimson was on the other side of the map, watching him like he was a grotesque curiosity. The sting of her stare made a lump of his dying heart rise to his mouth, cutting off any words. Her throat, her collarbones, even the part of her chest that he could see radiated new magic. He knew she couldn't stop it from ebbing out of her, since it was so fresh upon her skin, soaking into her very soul, but he wished she wouldn't stand so close — not right now, not while he could feel the intertwining of her magic with Zephyr's.

At least Zephyr had enough respect to keep his distance, not that he'd done anything wrong. Neither of them had… It was just…Jaggar's need for Crimson had never abated. Yes, he'd made hard choices to protect her. Yes, he'd foolishly thought she'd forgive and forget. He'd said to her that he was losing faith in her ability to see the truth, but he hadn't really believed that she'd shut him out. He knew that what he was feeling was the loss of possession. Possessing *her*. His panther roared from within. To be the first to claim her as a Fortis didn't make Zephyr more important to Crimson, but all the same, to Jaggar it felt like a door had closed permanently to him.

The look in her eyes told him he was right.

"Angelica's stronghold is in the mountains, where the volcano stands." Talon's attempt to draw Crimson's gaze to him, or perhaps where he tapped the map, failed.

She continued to stare brutally at Jaggar, seeing into his soul, demanding he say something.

"What?" It was all he could muster, and he knew how harsh it sounded coming out of his strangled throat, his heart still wedged in there, along with his words.

"I've done what you wanted. I've bolstered myself so the battle can be won." There was a hint of triumph in her voice, like she'd won the war before the battle had even begun.

"Is that why you did it?" His voice wobbled, cracked. Pathetic, weak, he wished he could spit out his heart and never feel the crushing agony of disappointment and loss like he was right now.

"No."

Then why? He wanted to ask. *Why take Zephyr's mark first? Why make it seem so easy to forgive one man but not the other?* But he knew why. Zephyr was the path of least resistance. He was the easier choice, so she wouldn't have to admit that Jaggar had been right, so she could go on with her stubborn refusal to accept his authority in this.

"Zephyr followed your lead," Crimson said, her words hot, brimming with adrenaline from the magic coursing through her body no doubt. "He didn't keep me at arm's length because he wanted to."

"Neither did I!" Jaggar roared, his cat punching through so claws slid from his fingertips.

Is that what Zephyr told her? Did he make me out to be the villain?

As soon as those thoughts entered his head, Jaggar knew they were wrong. Wrong because his brother would never tell such lies, not even to get Crimson to forgive him. No, this was all Crimson.

Talon and Lucki motioned for the others to step away, corralling the Fortis from the clearing until they all piled into the house. The door thunked closed with finality that made Jaggar want to storm off — to leave and never return.

But he was no coward, even in the face of Crimson's stubborn refusal to hear the truth.

"You should have given me a choice!" Crimson shouted back. "You should have told me your plan."

Her anger was justified. Deep down he knew that but couldn't say those words. He wouldn't admit she had a point.

"I couldn't. Don't you know that?" Jaggar ran his fingers through his hair, forgetting about the claws, wincing as they dug into his scalp. "If I had told you then, you wouldn't have listened. You wouldn't have believed me. You were so blind to your sisters' true nature. You were so hurt by their actions. How could I tell you then that I needed time to get to the truth? How could I do that and keep you safe?"

"I would have understood." Her eyes didn't even flicker with that lie. It was like she truly believed her own bullshit.

"No, you would have told me that your sisters had the best interest of Shade in mind. You would have told me that they were going to find out who disappeared the queens. You would have told me that they'd only made an error in judgment, but that the truth would prevail." These were the things she'd said to him when she'd asked him to mark her. She'd wanted his mark so she could elevate herself in hopes that her sisters would see her as an equal, when in reality that would only have made her more of a threat.

Crimson narrowed her eyes and studied him, her arms folded, nostrils flaring. "You decided lying to me and breaking my heart was the way to go?"

"I didn't lie!" he roared, unable to contain his rage and frustration. How he wished he could take her back to those moments when she'd been spinning out of control, confused, hurt, desperate for a solution.

"Maybe not in your black and white world, but in my world, lying by omission is still lying." Crimson dropped her arms to her sides, and the magic of Zephyr's markings flared like they were already in tune with her emotions. "You could have explained. You could have said you'd mark me later… You could have said, 'Bide your time… I'll come for you.'"

"How could I come for you when your sisters watched my every move? How could I come for you when Aria had me at her beck and call? Isn't it proof enough to you that I denied her repeatedly, even though she tortured me, spelled me, tried everything to coerce me to mark her?" He'd done everything he could to keep Crimson safe. "She even, once, threatened to go to your sanctuary and punish you more if I wouldn't bond with her." Jaggar let his panther flash fang to punctuate his next point. "That, she learned, was a mistake — one she didn't make again."

Crimson stared at him, disbelief still shining there, but he saw her shiver, like his words had hit home in some way, and damn it, he wanted to hit home again. He wanted to hurt her as much as she was hurting him.

"Ask Zephyr. Now that you're bonded, he can't keep anything from you. Ask him. You'll know how hard we fought to keep ourselves pure and available for you." Jaggar leaned forward, letting the stone table bear his weight as he speared Crimson with his most ardent stare. "We waited for you to rise up, Crimson. We prayed that the day would come when you would finally see the truth, when you'd understand your worth and why your sisters did what they did to you. We waited for you to come when the time was right." He let his next words land as heavy as they could. "But you never did."

Crimson flinched. She swallowed. For the briefest of seconds, she flicked her gaze away.

"It doesn't matter now," she whispered before turning toward him again, chin jutting, lips a thin line. "The damage is done."

Jaggar sagged, all fight seeping out of him. Why did he have to go so heavy with her? Why did things always escalate so fiercely between them? Why did they bring that out in one another?

He knew that nothing he could say would change her mind, but he tried anyway, regretting his harsh words, regretting how he'd lashed out. "Damage can be repaired, Crimson."

The look she gave was full of red hot, searing heat. "No matter what your intentions, how can I ever trust you again? When you thought so little of me that you couldn't even tell me what was going on? When you watched as my heart shredded to pieces in front of you? When you told me with sincerity in your eyes that you couldn't—no, you *wouldn't*—bond with me." She stabbed the air. "You crushed me, Jaggar. You embarrassed me, broke my heart and confused me. You said those things to me like you'd never had any intention of marking me. You were so cold, so determined. You kicked me when I was already in the dirt. *You* did, not Zephyr. You looked me in the eyes and told me lies, and I don't care what your plan was, if you loved me like you'd claimed to, you wouldn't have hurt me like that. You wouldn't have been able to bear it." She stopped to catch her breath then said, "That kind of damage can *never* be repaired."

Chapter Twenty-One

Crimson

"Ohhhhh, shit!" Crimson wasn't expecting to open a portal into chaos but that's exactly what was awaiting them as they all stepped through into Angelica's territory.

Complete insanity.

Magic ricocheted off every conductive surface, wild cat growls echoed through the fog cloaked area and her sisters' massive army, beastly in their Fortis forms, were attempting to push forward, battling against the hordes of wild cats, presumably to get to wherever Angelica was hiding.

This is not good.

Crimson, along with the others, dove behind a ledge of overhanging boulders as power bursts tore at the ground where they'd been standing seconds before.

"What the—?" Lucki radiated magic, glowing a rainbow of iridescence that pulsed rapidly, as if matching her racing heart.

"The Shade army," Talon said, his expression grim. "They're here to retrieve the crystal."

Of course, her sisters had rallied to action now that Crimson had gone rogue. They would have sent the best they had to capture the crystal before Crimson could get her hands on it.

"We need a new plan," Lucki said. "Taking Angelica by surprise isn't going to work."

"Well, maybe we still can," Crimson said, her mind leaping ahead, reworking the plan they'd started with. There was a chance that Angelica and her abominations hadn't detected their arrival in the maelstrom of the raging battle. The Fortis soldiers were countering everything Angelica shot their way, and with that amount of magic flinging around, a portal entrance might not have been a blip on anyone's radar.

"She isn't expecting us," Jaggar said, like she needed his back-up. "We can flank her wild cats, create a distraction, ferret Angelica out, then Crimson and Lucki go for the witch and the crystal."

"I can help them home in on the crystal, watch their backs," Talon offered.

"We're not leaving Lucki's side," Wren growled, with her other familiars nodding in stubborn agreement.

"We won't be separating from our familiars." Crimson hated how much it stung to have to say that out loud. Was Jaggar so thick-headed that he'd forgotten about the loyalty of bonded mates? She knew she'd been the one to draw the line in the sand and that this very oversight should confirm to her that he wasn't remotely prepared to be a partner to her rather than a dominating ass, but still, it hurt that he was so clueless after everything she'd said to him. Hadn't any common sense rattled loose during their argument?

"We move together, en masse," Reuben said, exuding as much alpha as Jaggar. "Clear the area so Lucki and Crimson have a path—"

"They'll see us coming," Jaggar growled, chest puffed. "It's more dangerous your way. We need to find a means to nullify Angelica's power, to bind—"

"Are you crazy? No one here will bind themselves to Angelica," Crimson said to each of the familiars, commanding them in her tone not to sacrifice themselves like that. "We aren't losing one of our own to get her under control. We'll find another way to take her out."

A blast rumbled a warning seconds before the top of their hiding spot blew to bits, the percussion enough to knock Crimson on her ass. Reuben shifted at the same time, using his bear to shield Lucki from the falling rocks while Zephyr and Talon used their backs to take the brunt that would have fallen on Crimson.

With the boulders blown to smithereens, they were exposed. The energy of the battle shifted immediately as the wild cats caught sight of them. One by one, they lifted their grotesquely deformed heads and howled.

Shivers prickled over Crimson's scalp as she slowly stood, pulling power up her body from the ground and the litter of natural magic that lay untapped. No one said another word. The plan would have to wait while the witches took care of things.

The air around them crackled as Lucki and Crimson revved their powers then stepped forward to face their attackers.

The wild cats let loose another eerie yowl, then charged.

The men all shifted to Fortis, except for Talon, who leaped, transforming mid jump to his eagle, then soared into the fog. Crimson knew he'd find Angelica's location, and she had to trust that he wouldn't do anything reckless. It took everything in her willpower not to encase him in a protective bubble before he disappeared into the murk. A spell like that would draw Angelica's attention, and Crimson would put Talon in more danger with her precaution, so she let him be and refocused on the imminent danger around them.

Wild cats barreled toward them with spit and snot flying from their monstrous heads and death in their eyes. Fangs the size of babies' arms gleamed with gore and their claws raked through the ground like it was made of paper. Crimson wound up the heaviest hitter she had, a swirling bomb that was hell to keep in her hands. She rotated her arms, then lobbed the magic overhead, putting everything she had into sending it toward the storming cats. It whistled as it fell, a warning too late for some of the beasts. They flew apart, some taken out by the spell, some diving out of the way just in time. The spell bounced along the ground once, twice, then picked up speed again and hit one of her sisters' Fortis soldiers, dropping him dead on the spot.

Fuck.

The soldier next to the fallen Fortis swiveled toward Crimson with fury on his raging face just as Jaggar dove, practically over her head to sideswipe two wild cats at the same time, hooking his arms around their necks and taking them down in a heap of fists, claws and teeth.

The Fortis soldiers shot rapid fire at Crimson, so relentlessly that the shield she hastily created cracked. Lucki stepped beside her and added her power to the wall, her extra layer keeping the magic bullets from penetrating. Lucki's men worked alongside Zephyr and Jaggar to battle the raging wild cats, but for each one that fell, two more took its place.

"We're definitely outnumbered," Lucki shouted, her face strained and sweat beading along her brow.

Being on the defensive wasn't a great strategy for Crimson. It was time to turn things around.

"Maybe not outpowered, though." Crimson entwined her fingers with Lucki's then pushed some of her magic along Lucki's forearm. It swirled gold into her rainbow of magic, glowing as Crimson pushed more through.

Lucki gasped, closed her eyes briefly then looked over at Crimson with sparkles literally blinging from around her eyes. "Didn't know we could do that."

"It's better with three witches, but this'll do." Crimson flared her power, watching Lucki's face for signs of discomfort. "All good?"

Lucki sucked in a deep breath, then let it out. Her eyes calmed as she adjusted to the magic infusion. "Very good."

"Follow my lead." Crimson curled their fingers together, leaving their thumbs and pointers straight. "I'll act as the conduit."

In the triad, it was always the most skilled, not necessarily the most powerful, witch who pooled and distributed the collective power. Since Lucki had very little training in magic wielding and Crimson had very little experience in combining power this way, she knew it was a fifty-fifty chance that they wouldn't blow each other off their feet.

But hey, they needed an edge, and no one was expecting perfection.

"Ready?" Crimson locked her magic in, doing everything she could to keep control of the writhing, whirling mass of power that surged through her body.

Lucki was a force, that was for sure, but so was Crimson, and she was sure she could handle this.

Mostly sure.

Lucki nodded.

Crimson linked her magical threads with Lucki's, twining them like a braid, then yanked, hard, to not only meld them seamlessly but to wield them forward. She opened her other arm wide in a sweeping arc and Lucki did the same, then the two of them brought their hands together with a thunderous crack. Magic rolled forward like a tsunami, rumbling over the ground, taking wild cats and soldiers down simultaneously, knocking their feet out from under them. She tried to spare as many of the Fortis as she could — they were, after all, only following her sisters' orders — but controlling so much power strained her most tried and tested skills. She was more concerned for her own Fortis allies and focused the bulk of her attention on sparing them.

The power surge pushed Lucki and Crimson back a step or two, but both women held fast, digging their feet into the dirt like they had claws of their own to hold them in place. Crimson drew more magic from the volcanic vents beneath her feet and the ground trembled, cracks opened, giant fissures that widened enough to take more wild cats down. She tried to control how and where the cracks spread so she didn't accidently take her own team out in the process.

Lucki caught on quickly and pulled power from the fog, something Crimson hadn't considered because it was so wispy, but somehow, intuitively, Lucki knew what to do. She swirled the mist into a densely packed ball of sparking power then funneled it through their clenched hands.

Their familiars fought hard, blood and fur flying as, inch by inch, they moved deeper into the melee, headed, hopefully in the right direction.

An eagle's cry alerted Crimson that Talon was close. She spared a second to look up but when she couldn't see him through the fog, she reached out, nudging the tether of their bond and confirmed that he was just above, circling closer.

The volcano roared, black smoke pluming from its guts and the acrid sulfur stench of evil deeds and black magic wrapped itself around the battle. Smoky tendrils snaked and slithered along the ground. The thread connecting her to Talon flared along with a panicked sounding screech, then everything froze.

The battle, mid-strike, mid-growl, mid-death, stopped. Dark magic pulsed against the power of every wild cat, every familiar, everything except for Crimson. She squeezed Lucki's hand and got an immediate squeeze back.

"This will go on forever," a sultry, thick voice echoed from the dense fog, "if we don't stop it."

"You have something that doesn't belong to you." Crimson was disoriented, seeing the world around her—Zephyr, Jaggar, the others all held in place, frozen like statues, the desperate strain to break free clear in their eyes. She kept her fingers laced with Lucki's, ready to strike when Angelica showed herself.

Mad laughter filled the air, buzzing along Crimson's skin, making goosebumps rise and her skin crawl.

"Oh, and I assume you believe it belongs to you?" Angelica still didn't appear, her disembodied voice flowing through her dark magic. "It's funny. That's the very same thing your sisters first said, right before they learned their place."

"The Crystal of Shade belongs to the queens." She had no intention of clarifying which queens she meant.

"Which *we* could be," Angelica said, her words hanging for a long pause. "Did you know that your sisters offered me a seat on the throne?"

The truth behind those words hit Crimson like a hammer to the chest. Her sisters had offered her Aria's seat after Angelica had killed her? Even a mad sorceress was more appealing than their very own sister? Crimson simmered, the rejection hurting her in an absurd way. She knew her sisters had to have lost their minds to even consider Angelica a suitable queen. Or, more likely, they were being their usual duplicitous selves and luring Angelica in for some dark purpose.

Determined to find the witch, Crimson kept her lips shut and stabbed the darkness around them for any sign of Angelica. She couldn't target what she couldn't see, and she didn't want an errant shower of spells to blow back onto her own people.

"They made a deal with me to remove the weakest link, and in return, I would take her seat."

Crimson shuddered and she stumbled back a step. They did *what?* Her heart forced itself into her throat and her stomach flipped, churning with the truth of Angelica's words. Lucki pulled her back into place, holding her firm against her side.

"So I did, and you know what those treacherous hags did?" Angelica walked out of the shadows. "They demanded I hand over the crystal as a sign of my commitment to the triad."

Crimson and Lucki staggered back at the sight of the witch. She wore head-to-toe black war garb, like she was one of the queens' battle witches, a symbol of loyalty to the crown. It was the same battle gear that Crimson wore, except Crimson's had been stripped of the magical talisman that was embroidered over the left breast, signifying the queens' embrace. Angelica bore that mark for all to see. She also had the Crystal of Shade embedded at the throat, glinting with power and radiating magic.

"Where did you get that battle garb?" Only the queens could weave such a garment. It had to be magically stitched onto the recipient's body for it to take the first time.

"I told you." Angelica speared her with a knowing look. "Your sisters and I had an alliance."

There was no other way for Angelica to get possession of the queens' mark or a battle garb, not without her sisters creating it for her.

"I did their bidding, ended the one called Aria, then stepped forward for my coronation—and those fiends betrayed me. They told me they'd only elevate me if I gave them the crystal...so cloying...so innocent sounding. *Angelica*," she said, her tone a mocking version of Tabitha's, "*hand over the Crystal of Shade, and we will give you what you're owed.*" She tilted her head. "Did your sisters really think I'd fall for that? What nonsense! I don't have to be a citizen of Shade to know that having the crystal means holding the pinnacle of the power balance in the triad."

Jaggar had been right all along. Her sisters would never have been capable of repenting their sins. They'd orchestrated the murder of Aria. They'd kidnapped their rightful queens and were siphoning their power. They deserved to be punished. No more benefit of the doubt, the evidence was right in front of Crimson. They were responsible for it all, and they'd dared to punish Crimson for their crimes.

She flicked her eyes to Jaggar to find him staring at her, like he knew. Of course, he knew! That was

Jaggar's thing. He was always thinking ten steps ahead. To Crimson it had come off as paranoid and an excuse to be controlling by being overly cautious, but his foresight had practically predicted this.

She was finally seeing the truth.

She swallowed her pride and set aside her need to be right.

I'm sorry, she mouthed, because she was. She'd been stubborn...blind. She'd allowed her self-pity to consume her and to cloud her judgment. She'd been driven by anger, frustration and the need to be right.

Something in his eyes flickered, and she glanced down his body to see his fingers twitching. He was working against Angelica's spell somehow. She'd always known that his power was immense, but she'd never considered the breadth of it until now. He was strong, maybe stronger than she'd imagined, and he would have given it all to her willingly, to bolster her. She'd turned him down again and again over these last few days. If she had taken his mark, would they be in this position right now? Guilt pummeled her thoughts.

Regret was too simple a word to describe what she felt when she met Jaggar's eyes again. What she saw there made her want to scream, to rail, to tell him 'don't you dare', because she knew...in her gut, that he was willing to sacrifice everything for her, even at the cost of himself. She saw in his eyes that he was willing to give up his life in order to bind Angelica's power.

"I let you go once!" Lucki revved up, her magic pulsing along their connection, snapping Crimson's attention back to Angelica. "I'm not going to do it again."

"Now, now, little witch, I know we have history." Angelica waved her hand and sent Lucki's familiars to their knees with powerful groans. "But you don't have the upper hand here. I've harnessed the power of this very earth. The fog and the volcano itself belong to me."

She flipped her hand again and a burning rush of pain roared through Crimson and Lucki's connection, searing heat that lit her to her core. She couldn't help it. She and Lucki both dropped to their knees.

"I indulged your mighty display of power, tapping into the elements was clever, would have probably worked on a lesser witch, but I've learned a lot while I've been here. Your sisters also shared some knowledge with me...before...well...things turned bad between us." She waved her arms around. "This territory is mine." She pulled her arm down, and with it came a deafening whistle.

Talon fell with a thunderous thud at Crimson's knees, every part of his eagle form crushing under the weight of Angelica's power.

Chapter Twenty-Two

Jaggar

Jaggar twitched his fingers, control slowly returning to his body as he flared his magic again and again. While the witch was powerful, she wasn't omnipotent, and she also wasn't paying attention to what he and Zephyr were doing. They'd experienced this spell before, when Aria had been murdered. They'd conquered it then, too.

Jaggar felt Zephyr's slow success with each pulse of his power, something Angelica couldn't detect, simply because she wasn't Fortis.

Crimson, on her knees, was back building her power, a technique Jaggar had taught her a long time ago. He knew she was skilled enough to do it without drawing attention to her actions, and right now, even while Angelica taunted her with Talon's crumpled form, Crimson was a master at disguising what she was doing. A surge of pride radiated through Jaggar's body. He wished he hadn't been so bullheaded and had given her words deeper thought. He wished he could better balance his innate need to be in control.

But wishes were for dreamers, and Jaggar couldn't spare a moment for that kind of thinking, not with so much at risk.

"I recognize the advantage of having a triad on the throne. I'm willing to admit that you two are considerably powerful and would bolster my rule threefold." Angelica lifted her chin. "I will offer you alliance in return for your vows of loyalty—unbreakable vows from you and all court familiars, of course. I won't be fooled twice."

Crimson glared daggers at her. An unbreakable vow would tie Crimson and Lucki to Angelica for all eternity. They'd be under her thumb and unable to act without explicit permission.

"Accept my generous offer or perish now."

Lucki shifted her eyes to her familiars, who were locked in place by Angelica's spell and too new as Fortis to know how to battle against it. Jaggar felt the pings of Reuben, Wren and Julian pushing against the spell, clumsy in their effort but not completely without effect. Angelica's attention was torn, her power split as she repaired the tiny cracks in her spell to keep them contained…too many cracks for her to track completely. Jaggar flexed his power, testing the limits of Angelica's awareness. She didn't flinch. She didn't even glance in his direction.

Jaggar looked at Lucki and Crimson.

It was clear that Lucki didn't know what move to make. She wasn't sure what to do, and for the first time since he'd met her, she lacked her usual confidence, her eyes flashing fear. Jaggar felt her effort to break away from Angelica's spell. She was attempting to pull magic from the ether, but it wouldn't work. Jaggar knew by the pulse of his own power that Angelica was far stronger than they'd given her credit for and that she'd cut Lucki and Crimson off from the natural magic around them. Angelica truly owned this land, and all the magic it offered was at her beck and call. She'd been playing with them earlier, leading them into a false sense of mastery.

"Release me," Crimson growled, "as a sign of good faith. I need to heal Talon before he dies."

Angelica laughed. "Is this your way of saying you agree to my proposition?" She flicked her hand and Crimson fell forward. "Just know that any attack will mean death to your Fortis."

As if to punctuate her threat, Angelica clenched one fist and sent Jaggar and the others to their knees as well, forcing painful groans and frustrated growls out of each Fortis. Even so, the cracks Jaggar had created in Angelica's holding spell remained. He had a chance. He just needed to rally his strength and push everything he had into breaking free so he could do what needed to be done.

Crimson swept her power over Talon, mending whatever was keeping him down and unconscious. She funneled some of her back-building power toward Jaggar, as if knowing intuitively that he was willing to sacrifice everything to put a permanent end to Angelica. He'd love to think they were of the same mind, for the same reason. His unyielding devotion to Crimson's well-being and her future meant he'd do anything to empower her. His dark thoughts swirled toward a more likely scenario. Maybe he and Crimson were of the same mindset because she was willing to sacrifice *him* rather than lose her mates.

It was a sobering thought, but it didn't change his resolve to end this in their favor. And there was only one way to do that.

He collected Crimson's offering, pulled her magic deep into his core, wedging it into the tiny fissures he'd already created before amping it up until it exploded. He broke himself and Zephyr free from Angelica's spells before launching himself at the witch, giving her no time to react.

"I bind you," he roared as he took Angelica by surprise, using his Fortis fangs to latch onto her exposed throat, dirty blood soaking into his mouth, as his own life force funneled into her in exchange. His panther roared as it took over tearing at the muscles and sinew of her neck, while Jaggar's clawed fingers found the Crystal of Shade and tore it free. Angelica, with a strangled scream, tried to call her magic forward, to pull it to her defense, but without the crystal, she had no ability left to harness it all, and instead the magic blew outward, taking her wild cats down like trees in a wind storm. Jaggar tossed the crystal out, aiming for Crimson, satisfied when Zephyr plucked it from the air. Then Jaggar turned inward, forcing all his magic, all his essence, to flow from his core into the binding spell that wove and tangled around Angelica, choking her black magic, threading through the tendrils of dark deeds and raveling them together like a spider cocooning its kill.

He might not have ever been a shifter meant for bonding, a partner to a powerful witch, but this he could do. He could sacrifice everything he was for Crimson.

It took seconds, Jaggar's life ebbing with the final tremors of his heart, pouring into the binding spell that would take Angelica out of the game forever.

The last thing he saw was Crimson's eyes, which shimmered with tears and shined with pride that he could only hope was for him.

Chapter Twenty-Three

Crimson

With Angelica's magic tamped down, her wild cats disintegrated into lumps of ash and bone. The evil that had soaked the fog, those dark tendrils of magic, dissipated. For a moment, one tiny blink of time, Crimson felt a collective sigh, a loosening of tension through allies and foes alike.

At the same time, Jaggar's binding spell grew more solid, sealing both him and Angelica in the incasement he'd woven with his magic. He'd cast it to look like a part of the terrain, a large bolder with no discernable features that might alert someone that a binding spell was in play. With time, he and Angelica would be forgotten—at least, their resting place would be—and no one would be able to undo what he'd done, even by accident, if only because they'd never be able to find them. That, Crimson knew, was how he'd intended to prevent Angelica from rising again, because, with the right kind of magic, a binding spell could be undone—

but only if you knew where to find it. While Jaggar had sacrifice himself to contain Angelica, the witch wasn't dead, just in a holding pattern for as long as the binding spell existed.

Tears burned the back of her eyes, but she had no time to process the loss of Jaggar, because her sisters' soldiers, now unlocked from Angelica's spell, were tuning into the change in the air. They looked to Crimson, some confused, some seemingly ready to take up the battle again stopped only by the crystal Zephyr held up for them to see. It shone like a star, pulsing its powerful magic to coat everyone who stood near enough.

"This is how it should be," Zephyr bellowed then handed the Crystal of Shade to Crimson.

The crystal infused her with its power like it belonged in her hand, twining with her magic as if made for her. Her body shimmered as the crystal's natural gifts flowed from her fingers, up her arm, across her chest, igniting her Fortis marks, until she too glowed. She sent the new magic out, letting it cascade in a wave to give the soldiers a taste of what she could do with it.

They saw the magic coming but could do nothing to stop it from pushing them back, step after step, the entire battalion forced to retreat.

"Tell your queens that we're coming for them," Zephyr said with a rumbling bark to his words. "Justice is coming for them. You, brothers, have from now until then to decide which side you'll fall on."

With spinning thoughts, Crimson barely held on to the crystal's power, her grief over what had just happened threatening to overwhelm her completely.

As if sensing her emotional turmoil, Lucki latched onto Crimson then tugged her backward as she opened a portal. "Time to go."

Zephyr had one arm around Crimson and one around Talon, and they all tumbled through the ether, the reality of what Jaggar had done sinking Crimson's heart like an anchor.

* * * *

Lucki had taken them back to Weeping Falls, to her cat house, where they debriefed then scattered — to rest, to regroup, to mourn.

"He's gone," Crimson whispered into Talon's chest. He'd coaxed her to lie down on the grand canopy bed of the guest room. Even though the crystal's magic pulsed toward her from its perch on the nightstand, coaxing her to grasp it, to take action, to bring her sisters the reckoning they deserved, she couldn't raise her hand to take it…not yet.

She couldn't deny, even with all the power flowing through her, residual magic from wielding the crystal even briefly, bolstering from Zephyr, Talon and Valor, her own power stores, she was tired. She was so tired of the sorrow, the heartbreak and disappointment that life consistently brought her.

Knowing what she needed, Talon grasped her face between his palms then kissed her, consuming her with love, his lips a balm to her soul and a reminder that for all the sorrows of her life, she had joys as well.

Zephyr climbed onto the bed, his bulk making the mattress sag as he made his way up her body, no hesitation as he curled himself behind her, then nuzzled against her throat.

Sparks flashed over her skin where Zephyr kissed her, his fingers busy working at the clasps that kept her battle garb secure. Talon continued to probe her mouth, delving so deep that he stroked her soul. For this blissful moment, with two of her familiars giving over their love and devotion, she could push her grief to the side and let the sensations they offered consume her.

Zephyr expertly removed her garments, exposing her body to his roving lips, tongue and fingers. He cupped her pussy from behind, using his thumb to spread her lips in a sweeping caress that made her shiver and moan. Talon stroked her nipples as he continued to kiss her, taking her moan into his mouth and returning one of his own.

She liked that sound. It blasted away the thoughts swirling in her brain and focused them on the men surrounding her. She wanted to bring them pleasure, too, to give them what they were giving her, to help them forget the grief for now.

Crimson took Talon's cock in hand and glided her thumb over his tip, spreading the pre-cum along the ridge of his crown so he'd moan again, this time long and low, a vibration that moved through her mouth to the pit of fire that smoldered in her belly.

Zephyr slipped his cock between her ass cheeks, guiding himself along the seam of her pussy as he curled himself tighter along her body. He moved his fingers so he could tease her clit, tapping and flicking the sensitive nub while she stroked Talon's shaft lazily, reveling in the noises he made.

She opened her legs enough to let Zephyr in then gasped at the sensation of his cock stretching her out and filling her. He pierced her deeply, forcefully, possessively, and she curled her leg so they undulated together, rolling into one another, desperate for that deep connection.

Talon slipped down her body, taking her nipples, one by one, between his lips. Sucking hard, nipping lightly, teasing furiously. Then he moved on, kissing his way down her stomach, over her one hip then flipping around so his glistening cock was at her mouth and his lips were already taking over from Zephyr's fingers, stroking her clit.

She parted her mouth wide enough to take Talon's cock down to the hilt, relaxing her jaw so she could hold him in her throat, her tongue pressed firmly along his shaft. She used her fingers to cup then gently kneaded his balls before pulling her mouth back, flicking her way along his dick until she could trace the ridge of his crown and tease the tip of his head, only to start all over again.

With her men in her, she could forget the present and get lost in the sensation. Their magic marks on her body combined, flaring in a continuous cycle that she sent out to Zephyr, back to Crimson, to Talon, then back again, sparking euphoric pulses that swept from her core to her scalp, raising goosebumps and coaxing the flame of her desire to the height of intensity, on its way to an inferno.

Zephyr cupped her breast, his lips back on her throat, kissing up to her earlobe then sucking her there. She melted into his touch, then bucked her ass against him, encouraging his thrusts to go harder, deeper, to claim her with his hot cum.

She continued to gorge on Talon's cock, and he sucked her clit relentlessly, giving her back what she was giving him, the urgency in his lips making her writhe—making her tighten her lips around his shaft, making her rub his balls with more purpose.

As Zephyr pounded her from behind and Talon licked her from the front, Crimson's orgasm spread like wildfire through her body, igniting every nerve, every synapse exploding. She groaned against Talon's shaft, vibrating her rising climax over his sensitive skin until he bucked hard against the gate of her throat. Zephyr's cock hardened like a steel rod, pummeling her G-spot so her orgasm went nuclear, exploding in a rush of heat and ecstasy that looped again and again. Talon groaned as his cum hit the back of her throat, his cock pulsing against her lips. Zephyr exploded deep into her pussy, filling her, heating her from within. They rode each other, pulling from the depths of the explosive sensations until every last shudder, moan and quake had wrecked them all.

Chapter Twenty-Four

Valor

The queens were chained midway down the gaping maw of a deep cavern, on a pedestal of stone, reeking of dirty magic and at the mercy of the dark spell Tabitha and Wyvern had cast around them. It was clear that they were suffering, not just from their disheveled look, lank, unkempt hair, the withered stoop of their bodies and sallow tone to their skin, but it was like they'd been sucked dry of their innate powers. The glow Valor had always known them to exude was long gone.

Despite his best guesses, he hadn't found a way to use the gem that Talon had given him to release them. Valor wasn't magical, not the way the Fortis were, and while he could sniff power out and trail magic signatures, he couldn't wield it and he couldn't, apparently, detect any means of harnessing the gem to set the queens free. He couldn't even breach the wall of magic that kept the crones cycling on the platform. The vibration of the spell alone made it hard for him to hold on to the boulders and keep himself from tumbling into the depths of the cavern.

"I'll bring help. I promise," Valor said, not even sure if the queens could hear him or even knew that he was there. He had no pockets to hold the gem, so he secured it in the waist of his pants then started the treacherous climb back to the tunnel.

He needed to get to Crimson. She'd be able to fix this. Of course, he had no idea where she was, but he'd figure out how to find her once he was free of the tunnels and away from the chaos of dirty magic that sucked at his very essence, making him want to peel his skin off rather than feel the creepy crawl of dark spells.

He was midway up the cavern wall, hanging by claws that his wolf had forced through his fingertips, when the crones sent him a collective message, *Bring Crimson.*

The words came as a whisper in his ear and an echo in his head, rattling his already jarring thoughts.

He scoffed. *I have to find her first*, he shot back.

Then, his wolf, somehow understanding the command in a way he hadn't, gave him a vigorous shake, dislodging the useless gem from his pants. He tried to catch it, but it hit the ledge at his feet and spun out past his reach. Instead of falling deeper into the cavern, a wisp of magic scooped it out of the air mid-bounce, then brought it to Valor's eye level. It spun like a top, blurring into flashes of power that sparked with electric pulses.

This will give you the means to find her, but only if you're willing to give a piece of yourself.

He stared at the swirling gem, and his wolf nudged him to grasp what the crones were saying.

Give a piece of myself?

Everything worth something comes with sacrifice, they said.

Then, like a switch flipping, he understood.

What he'd always thought was a myth was suddenly within his grasp. If he shifted with the crystal, if he took the magical stone into himself so it became one with him, with his wolf, it would forever alter his life. *Give a piece of yourself.* The outcome, the transformation that resulted from absorbing a gem like the one hovering in front of him, could be an absolute monstrosity. He could turn into an unhinged, deformed creature, like the wild cats that Angelica had created. Taking the gem's magic, shifting with it, could transform him into a mindless beast…or…it could make him Fortis — and as Fortis, he could find Crimson.

This move wasn't just about giving up a piece of himself. It could obliterate his conscience and his soul.

His wolf howled, demanding he take the risk, urgency clawing at him. *Find Crimson.*

There's no time to waste, the crones echoed.

The gem flashed rainbows, sparkling prettily, like it was coaxing him to grab hold.

Do it.

Take the gem.

Give yourself over to its power.

He trusted that the crones knew what they were doing. His wolf believed that they did.

With a deep breath, Valor swiped the gem from the air, sent a prayer out to whatever gods might be interested, then called his wolf forward.

* * * *

208

Valor clung to the side of the cavern wall with claws that punched through the stone as if it were paper. His body, still contorting with muscle-twitching spasms, was double the size it had always been, which was throwing him off balance and made finding a foothold a challenge. But that didn't matter as much anymore since his arms, roped with cords of sinew, bore his weight like his increased size and bulk were nothing.

Magic that he would normally only smell or taste in the air was coursing through his body, electric pulses tweaking along his nerves. He let his head fall back, opening his throat so he could howl.

Find Crimson. The triple thread of the queens' voices echoed in his mind. *Bring her to us.*

Valor's new powers as Fortis told him that the crones were being siphoned so relentlessly that they were dying. Their collective voices in his head were weak, brittle. It was going to be the end for them if he didn't act fast. They needed Crimson. She'd know how to release them, how to restore their power. She would be their hero.

With one last look over his shoulder at the witches and a silent nod to reassure them he knew what to do, he pushed off the cavern wall then climbed the boulders in two giant leaps.

There was no way he'd be able to navigate the tunnels as Fortis. He was much too hulking now, but that didn't matter because his new powers brought magical solutions to sharp focus. Calling a portal came on instinct—just a thought, a desire for escape and before he could blink, a swirling black hole opened right in front of him.

He stepped through the portal and found himself at the tunnel entrance he'd started from, in the alcove where he'd been waiting for Talon, what seemed like an eternity ago. Right across from him was the broken window, Talon's escape still evident in the shattered panes. His brother's shifter essence, like a magic signature, was a tether Valor knew only he could sense. It beckoned him to grab hold, and Valor knew it would lead him to Crimson, because there was only one destination Talon would have gone and that was straight to their mate.

With his Fortis power, he called the tether toward him, teasing it from the ether beyond the castle's walls. Fog snaked into the corridor and the ether swirled. A wisp of Crimson's magic signature played against his senses and he did what he would never have considered doing before... He ran, then dove straight out of the window, praying to the gods that he wasn't making a grave error. After all, being Fortis didn't give him wings.

Instead of taking a nosedive to the solid ground, the ether stretched itself, cocooning him so he could float through the dense fog. It was disorienting to be wrapped in so much sparking power. His head spun as he floated, suspended, it seemed, and at the mercy of the ether's currents. He panicked at first, lashing against the magic blanket that surrounded him, but his wolf grunted for him to stay calm, to trust. After the initial rush of adrenaline subsided and his heart and lungs slowed their rapid fluttering, he gave in, relaxed his tension and let his wolf take over. He shifted from Fortis to wolf, yielding conscious thought over to the beast, fading until Valor had only a whisper of awareness as his wolf took him to his mate.

When his two feet hit the ground sometime later, he was back in his human form, except now, instead of being average height and build, he knew his center of gravity had shifted and he was bigger, taller, wider, bulked up and brimming with magic. He glanced at his arms, which were now host to swirls of colorful magic, iridescent and beautiful, glowing with power.

He stood outside a giant yellow house and knew, without any doubt, that Crimson was inside. He could feel her like his own heartbeat, thundering through his body.

"Valor?" As if just thinking her into existence, Crimson opened the front door looking as stunning as ever. She wore the Crystal of Shade at her breast, embedded by her own magic into the fabric of her battle gear. She'd always been formidable, but now she was unbeatable, he was sure of it. She stepped onto the porch tentatively, like she wasn't quite sure he was actually there. "What has happened to you?"

Talon and Zephyr hovered behind her, taking up all available space in the crowded doorway. She'd changed since he'd last seen her. New markings swirled over her skin. She'd bonded with Zephyr. He could smell it on her, feel the new layer of magic she wore. She'd been infused with Fortis power, just as he had.

"The crones gifted me a blessing." Valor lifted his arms wide, inviting her to take him in. "They showed me how to turn to Fortis."

"The gem," Talon said as he stepped onto the porch.

Valor nodded, meeting his brother-familiar's eyes. What passed between them was acceptance, pride and a mutual understanding that this didn't change anything about their relationship. Valor might be more powerful than Talon, imbued with magic, but they were still on equal footing.

Crimson rushed toward him, leaping from the porch, knowing he'd be there to catch her. She threw her arms around his shoulders as he hoisted her up his body.

"I was so worried about you," she cooed into his ear.

"I'm fine. Better than fine." He kissed her face all over, just as she was kissing his, using their lips to ensure that they were whole and safe and really together again.

She pulled back enough to look at him. "My mother? The queens, they're alive? Talon disrupted their spell to stop the siphoning. Are they okay?" Crimson croaked as if her heart was burdened with sorrow.

Valor frowned, eyes flicking to his brothers. Their expressions were solemn. He noted that Jaggar wasn't among them. *Fuck.*

"Your sisters have figured out how to siphon them again, and they're taking relentlessly. The queens don't have long," Valor said, his heart heavy all over again. "We need to put an end to this before it's too late. The amount of power your sisters are taking, the way they're draining the queens, it seems likely that they're expecting an attack, building up their power to confront you in battle."

"Then it's best we don't disappoint them," Crimson said as she nudged him to let her go. "We need to go back now."

"We're coming with you," a tall redheaded woman said from the door as she stepped out to join Zephyr and Talon. Three Fortis shifters came out of the house behind her.

"Lucki, it's too dangerous." Crimson turned to face the other witch. "You've completed your mission. Angelica is gone. This isn't your battle."

"Maybe so, but the chaos Angelica created lingers like a nasty fart." Lucki grinned.

Valor snorted on a laugh as the others snickered and chuffed. The tension of the moment dissipated.

"We're coming to help you set things right," Lucki said. "Because that's what sister-witches do."

Chapter Twenty-Five

Crimson

Crimson knew the second they stepped foot anywhere in the castle, Tabitha and Wyvern would detect them. Her sisters might not be the most skilled spellcasters, but every witch, no matter how powerful, mastered the simple trespass spell by the time they were toddlers, if only to keep snooping siblings out of private spaces.

So, they had to make their return to Shade count. They had to enter with a bang.

For that they'd need to split up, and thanks to Lucki's generous offer to help, Crimson was sure they'd have the element of surprise.

Working together, Crimson and Lucki wove multiple portals, set to open at intervals in different locations around the castle. Each would create thunderous noise, meant to shake the walls and disturb the peace. Their plan was to distract Tabitha and

Wyvern, keep their Fortis soldiers busy as a cascading set of portals opened and closed all over the castle, while Crimson rescued the crones.

The spell to create the portals required a lot of precision, even though most would only be used as decoys. The intention was to create chaos, but each spell had to be layered exactly right so that the one carrying the team would work properly and not send them into the abyss of the ether or tear them apart along the way.

Crimson had guided Lucki through the complicated series of spells so that once they landed in the castle, their initial portal spell would trigger another set, like strands of the same web, spreading out into more and more branches. taking them where they needed to be, while at the same time, hopefully, confusing any kind of trespassing spells her sisters may have cast.

Crimson's plan relied on Tabitha and Wyvern's predictability, that they'd cower, staying on the dais to be protected by their Fortis guards, and let the threat come to them. As much as Crimson wanted to believe her sisters would stay true to their natures, she had a niggle of doubt that she might be wrong. While she'd been grieving the loss of Jaggar on a more personal level, it was this moment that Crimson truly mourned the absence of his counsel. He was domineering, bullheaded and unapologetically alpha, but he was also perceptive and cunning and he'd been studying her sisters for the year of Crimson's banishment. He would know for sure if her sisters would be most likely on the defensive or offensive, no second guessing. If Crimson was wrong in her plans, he would have told her flat out.

She would have argued bitterly with him, but he'd be there to correct her course if she needed it, or at least, give her something to mull over. And if she did make the wrong decision, he'd be there to back her up and help her get out of it.

Now he was gone, and while Zephyr had agreed that her plan was the best one, they all knew they were taking a huge risk without Jaggar there to lead them.

Wait, no…that was the wrong way to look at things. Crimson gave her head a shake. As much as she deeply mourned Jaggar's absence, he'd want her to stand tall and believe in herself.

She would lead them, and even if her sisters didn't react as Crimson expected, she'd be ready.

"We good?" Lucki and her men stood waiting, magic emanating in waves from the three shifters and their witch.

Crimson checked with each of her men, nodding along with them as they all agreed it was time to go.

Zephyr would lead Julian and Reuben to the secret chamber that Talon had discovered, the site of Tabitha and Wyvern's siphoning spell anchor, in hopes of disrupting it once again. They wouldn't be able to access it the same way Talon had, through the roof vents of the cavern, but based on Talon's description, Zephyr felt he had a good idea of where it was located in the castle. Lucki, Wren and Valor would distract Tabitha and Wyvern in the throne room and Crimson and Talon would rescue the crones.

Once the rightful queens were free, Crimson would ignite another spell, this one meant to pull her allies together again, joining Lucki and crew in the throne room, hopefully taking Crimson's sisters by surprise with the living evidence of their crimes.

Her sisters would have to admit their guilt when the entire court laid eyes on the true queens.

And, if need be, they'd face their punishment then, too — swiftly, permanently.

The time for benefit of the doubt was over. Her sisters were guilty of atrocious sins, and Crimson would make sure they paid in one way or another.

Jaggar would be proud — of that, she had no doubt.

Chapter Twenty-Six

Talon

He wasn't Fortis, so the only help Talon would be able to offer Crimson was as a guide. He'd protested at first, when she said he'd be the one going with her to free the crones. She needed the Fortis with her, to help her conquer the spell holding the queens. A shifter with magic would be a better partner to her right now. But Crimson had insisted that she needed *him*, because he was the only one who could lead her to the cavern through the tunnels quickly. There were too many ways for her to get lost in the maze, and time was running out. She couldn't build a portal to take them directly there without setting off all kinds of alarm bells for her sisters. It was too risky, and Talon was the only one left who could maneuver through the tunnels with her.

The others were buying them time, using the portal-created chaos as distractions and decoys, but that didn't mean they had plenty of time to spare. Talon knew that they had to be lightning fast, or they'd risk losing the element of surprise they were counting on to throw the queens off.

He flew through the tunnels just ahead of Crimson, angling his wings to avoid the jutting stalactites and warning her when it was time to duck. Despite not having an eagle's eyesight, Crimson kept up, maneuvering over and around jutting rocks and navigating steep declines. She wasn't a stranger to the tunnels. According to her, she'd used them over the years of her childhood to escape her sisters' tormenting, but like everything from childhood, memories fade, and the tunnels were confusing in the best of time.

Crimson and Lucki's decoy portals opening all over the castle made the rock walls vibrate, even as they raced farther down and away from the main parts of the court, each explosion a bomb blast meant to create terror but no destruction. He hoped it was enough to keep Tabitha and Wyvern busy so Crimson could do what she needed to do.

Even with all the rumbling from above, small rocks and stones tumbling around them, they didn't slow or stop. They continued to barrel forward, despite the darkness that choked them and the eerie web of residual magic that reeked of evil.

His eagle let out a wail that echoed back to them, a signal that they were close to the end of the tunnel where the cavern space opened. Talon swooped low, intent on diving straight down along the wall as he had the first time he'd found the queens, sticking to the sides in order to avoid the spells in play.

The darkness faded to gray shadows as the eerie light from the containment spell reflected on the walls.

"Talon, hold up!" Crimson's voice held a note of urgency that made his eagle swivel a look her way. "There's something weird happening ahead."

His eagle, now alerted to a problem, could detect something dark, like a snake slithering just at the edge of the tunnel opening. The black magic he'd been feeling along the tunnels pulsed differently here.

He perched on a jutting rock and waited for her to catch up. She was huffing, sucking in deep breaths as she leaned against the damp tunnel wall.

"The spell they're using, there's something very wrong with it." She closed her eyes for a few breaths and her magic markings flared along her arms and chest, then, as if a suction had attached itself to her skin, the markings began to pull away in wisps of color. "If we go in there, we'll be siphoned, too."

She yanked her markings back with a full body shake then waved her hand. Talon sensed a barrier snap into place, separating them from the dark spell in the cavern.

"We need a plan." Crimson ran her fingers through her hair. "We can't go in there without some way to disrupt that siphoning spell. It's much too strong."

His eagle zeroed in on the Crystal of Shade on Crimson's breast.

"Spell a talisman," Talon said as he shifted from eagle to man, crowding them both in the tight space. "I can go down there alone, breach the containment spell and place it as a conduit for you to wield from here."

"No, that's a terrible idea." Crimson shook her head vigorously. "It's too risky."

"I'm the only non-magical entity here, so I can't be siphoned." Talon tried to keep his tone firm and insistent. He was no alpha, and it wasn't his style to bully, but this needed to happen. "And I'm the only one who can fly straight down to the crones."

Crimson lifted her fingers to the crystal at her breast. Talon's gaze followed her movement.

"My eagle thinks that the Crystal of Shade is powerful enough to funnel your magic." He nodded. "It can be used as a talisman, and it'll fit in my grip without throwing me off balance. Once I break through the containment spell, you'll be able to disable the rest of the dirty spells and stop the siphoning, then we can free your mother and the others."

Crimson shook her head the entire time he spoke while also caressing the crystal, her eyes locked on his. "I can't."

"You can." Talon moved forward and laid his hand on top of hers, flattening it against the crystal and her heart.

"Talon, this may kill you." Crimson's eyes pleaded with him, even though they both knew this was the only way. "The blowback—"

"Don't worry about me, Crim. I'll get out of the way before I get caught up in the maelstrom." He squeezed her hand. "Promise."

Crimson shook her head again. "I can't lose you."

He leaned in then kissed her softly. "You won't." He pressed his forehead to hers. "I'm small and fast. I'll get out in time."

"Talon…" She let out a small sob, and he knew she was grieving more than the idea of losing him. Jaggar was gone, and even though the big cat and Crimson had a complicated history, he was in her heart as securely as the rest of her shifters, Talon included.

"I'll come back to you, Crimson. I vow it." He pressed his lips to the top of her head and held her close for as many heartbeats as he could.

She sucked in a deep breath and let it out on a sigh. "Okay."

He stepped back as she wrapped her fingers around the crystal, her eyes locked on his, then pulled it free from the fabric of her battle gear, tearing a hole as she did. It sealed seconds later while the crystal pulsed in her hand.

Talon moved as far away as he could so Crimson would have space to work her magic. Since the tunnel was so cramped, that wasn't very far at all. Her signature flared, the scent of clove and lavender took over the sulfur stench of dark spells all around them. Crimson's magic markings wove into and around the crystal, threading inside and out. It responded, blasting heat as an ember of light deep in its core flared.

"This will let you break through the containment spell." She held the crystal up. "But you have to fly fast and far once you drop it inside. Try to have it land as close to the crones as possible. There's a second protection spell that will shield them from its blast, but it won't shield you, so you'll need to fly fast to get out of the way."

Talon nodded. He'd fly the speediest he ever had, if only to spare Crimson the heartbreak of losing another person she cared about. Instead of drawing the moment out and dwelling on the fear of what might happen, he called his eagle forward. With an answering yell, his eagle swooped down then took the crystal with his claws. He circled Crimson once, crying out again as he did, before soaring into the cavern.

The spell containing the crones pulsated like a living thing. It was now a cocoon, different from what Talon had seen before. It seemed like it was made up of a gelatinous membrane and had black streaks that lined the containment spell from base to tip, putrid veins pumping dark magic to keep the membrane fresh. It had evolved and was clearly growing from the evil magic that fed it.

He circled once, twice, dreading the feel of that membrane on his feathers, then dove from the side, punching between two black magic streaks, pushing through the, thankfully, thin layer to explode out on the inside. The crones looked worse than they had when he'd last seen them. Their bodies seemed like husks, hollowed out and wrinkled beyond recognition. Crimson needed to do her thing now. There was no time to waste. He shook the clinging pieces of membrane from his wings then dove toward the base of the pedestal, letting the crystal go close enough that he was satisfied it wouldn't tumble off the base.

It fell, and he watched, wanting to make sure it hit just at the crone's feet, praying that he'd aimed correctly. It bounced once then stopped moving, the burning ember in its core flared and Talon felt a blanket of protection whoosh up to cover the crones. *Time to go!* Talon lifted his head, pumped his wings and beelined back through the hole he'd made seconds before.

A jarring bang followed by intense heat pulsed up along the walls of the cavern, scalding air billowing in a rush after him. As fast as he pumped his wings, he was sure now that he'd made a mistake. He'd waited too long inside the membrane, and he was never going to make it to safety. The fiery air was definitely going to consume him. He pushed harder. He couldn't die like this. He couldn't let Tabitha and Wyvern win this way. He wouldn't leave Crimson to mourn him, too.

Crimson stood at the edge of the tunnel where he'd left her, a tight expression on her face. He raced toward her, still hoping to make it back to the tunnel in time, but the heat wave came faster, singeing his wing tips, so his eagle cried out, then wobbled mid-air.

Crimson, her eyes wide, leaped toward him, her body alight with magic.

The last thing Talon saw was Crimson soaring past him as if she suddenly had wings of her own. She turned her body toward him to flick a spell his way, coating him in a cocoon of healing magic, a balm to his burning wings. She sent a second one quickly after the first, nudging him off in another direction while she headed straight for the crones.

Chapter Twenty-Seven

Crimson

She had to get close enough to her family to see the extent of the damage, because what she was feeling from her perch in the tunnel was devastating. Her mother, grandmother and aunt were at death's door, their power waning with each second. The pain Crimson sensed, like thousands of razor blades slashing the surface, while deeper within, at the core of the crones' very essence, daggers twisting and turning, stabbing and gutting were beyond bearable, even to her. The fact that they'd had to endure this for as long as they had was heartbreaking to her.

As the explosion racked the cavern and it was clear that Talon wouldn't make it far enough away to avoid the blast, Crimson did what she felt she must. She dove straight into the melee. As she passed Talon's eagle, she enveloped him in a healing spell and sent him off toward the tunnel so that if he lost consciousness, he wouldn't hit the cavern floor, however far down that might be. She used her power to billow air beneath her, like a cushion that carried her to the platform where her mother, grandmother and aunt were being held captive.

The spell she'd woven into the Crystal of Shade had caused the containment membrane to short circuit, unable to maintain its hold on the witches and keep Crimson out at the same time. The siphoning spell, however, was going strong — protected, it seemed, by some wicked, dirty spell that reeked of Tabitha and Wyvern. It yanked continuously at Crimson's magic markings, greedy to siphon her, too. It was so relentless that Crimson had to erect another barrier to protect herself, but even with that, the siphoning spell battled her for what it craved like it was a sentient thing, an addict to magic. She needed to get her family out of this cavern and far away from the dark magic before it consumed them all.

Crimson forced herself to look, to see what her sisters had done to the crones. Their bodies were ravaged, bloodied and bruised, so emaciated that their skin suctioned to their bones, and they were filthy with dark magic grime. Their magic markings had bleached to nothing. The only sign that they were witches at all was in the way their skin faintly glowed where their marks should have burned bright. Their siphoned magic swirled above them, streaming straight up to the ceiling and beyond. Crimson could only hope that the others had found the secret chamber that Talon had described and were right now working on a way to disrupt the magic circle that anchored her sisters' spell. If they could break the circle, then Crimson would be able to get her mother, grandmother and aunt to safety via a portal.

"Mother," Crimson croaked as the pedestal turned the witches toward her like a fucked-up carnival ride. "I'm here."

As her mother's withered form swung to face her, Crimson gasped, certain the woman was dead. Her eyes, staring blankly, seemed not to see Crimson there. "Oh, gods, what have they done to you?"

Tears trailed down Crimson's cheeks. Her fingers twitched, desperate to reach out and touch her mother's decrepit body, to bolster her with healing magic. She sucked her emotions back and rallied her resolve. This was not the time to break down, no matter how bad things looked. If she acted too soon, the siphoning spell would take her healing magic then drain her dry, too. She had to tear the siphoning spell away.

With an angry lash, Crimson severed the magical cord that turned the pedestal and halted the demented merry-go-round. She needed a closer look. Her sisters always made mistakes in their spellcasting, it was just a matter of finding the error, the weakest point, then tearing it down from there.

As Crimson scrambled to climb up so she could reach the crones, her mother's voice halted her next step. "No!"

Crimson froze, her body buzzing as she battled against the siphoning spell while trying to keep her magic focused on finding a way to release her family, urgency clawing at her to end their suffering.

"Don't." Her mother's voice was broken, jagged and raw. "Don't come close."

"I need to find a way to free you." But Crimson knew what her mother was trying to tell her. If she stepped onto that pedestal, she wouldn't be able to step off. She'd be trapped instantly. That was how powerful the siphoning spell was, even without a containment spell in place.

The siphoning spell was a constant thud against Crimson's own protection spell, battering her with more and more intensity, so Crimson had to double, then triple the power she fed into her shield. On some level, deep down, Crimson realized just how hungry her sisters were for stolen magic. They were lost to their cravings and so desperate that they were willing to kill to serve their needs. This was beyond the desire for power and control. This was a disease, and her sisters were riddled with infection.

Crimson couldn't free the crones in hopes that it would end the siphoning spell simply by breaking the connection. She realized that now. She couldn't rip the crones down and, she knew, even if the others found the sacred circle, they'd never be able to disrupt the powerful flow, not a second time. The way the siphoning spell was hammering at her, Crimson knew her sisters had learned their lesson. Talon had gotten lucky when he'd plucked the gem out of the sacred circle, and her sisters wouldn't let that happen again. They would make it impossible for another gem to go missing. Their magic addiction was that intense.

It was all on Crimson to figure it out.

She took a step back, then cautiously stretched her senses to tap into the flow of the siphoning spell, looking for faulty joints or weakened elements, looking for her sisters' usual clumsy spell work. As she explored, she found jagged edges that lay like traps, pricking at Crimson's senses like sharp needles, making her wince and draw back. This was not her sisters' usual spellcasting. They had never mastered snares like that before — especially not the kind that lay hidden as these were, so cunningly concealed that Crimson trapped herself too many times to count, then had to backtrack her way out. They'd upped their game in the year she'd been away. This kind of careful skill spoke of training and patience. For her sisters to lay the spell as they had, with traps in play? Well, it meant they were on a different level than Crimson expected them to be.

She'd be impressed if she weren't so horrified.

Crimson's heart twisted the more she explored, the more she found unending loops, layers of spell work and no weak spots at all, no shadows, no wobbling threads. Her sisters had taken their time with this. They'd enmeshed their spell into the very essence of the crones, and it was drawing from their core, sucking the life right out of them.

A spell like this wouldn't stop until there was nothing left to give. It was too entwined with the crones, too connected to their magical souls. It had been naïve of Crimson to think she could simply cut the cords then bundle the crones up and carry them off like that would solve all the problems. This situation was beyond what she had given her sisters credit for.

New plan.

She needed to figure out a way to end the siphoning *first* then get her family out of there before her sisters could stop her. There were two problems with that. One, it was clear that as soon as she attempted to sever the connections of her sisters' siphoning spell, they'd know what all the distraction explosions had been about and they'd come to stop Crimson from freeing the crones, their power source. And two, cutting the cords of this spell at this point would cause a magical bleed out and would, within minutes — maybe seconds — kill the crones.

She rubbed her hand over her face, drawing in a deep breath then regretting it instantly when the burning stench of sulfur roared up her nose and choked her.

Where did my sisters learn such evil magic? What did they do to themselves to be able to wield dark spells like this? What kind of monsters have they become?

As she swayed back, something crunched under her foot. She looked down. The Crystal of Shade was nothing more than chunks of gem scattered on the stone pedestal at her feet. She looked closer. It still pulsed faintly with magic, gleaming in the eerie light of her sisters' evil spell. The crystal wasn't completely dead yet.

Crimson swooped down and coaxed the shards into her palm, spinning them in a mini-tornado so they sparkled and flashed, igniting against one another as they rotated. She'd always been good at thinking outside of the box, of figuring out inventive ways to use her magic as a complement to the natural power around her. She'd spent many years hunting gems and crystals and had seen them in many stages of fracture, yet still vibing energy. To anyone else, the broken crystal was useless, but to Crimson, the remnants were exactly what she needed.

If she couldn't find a weak point in her sisters' spell, she'd have to make one. To break this siphoning spell, she'd need to layer multiple strands of magic and weave through her sisters' warped layers of gunk. She would need to funnel healing magic to the crones at the same time. Their weakened state wouldn't stand up against Crimson tearing apart the siphoning spells. She'd layered spells before. Not like this, but she had trained to use different spells at the same time. In this case, it was super complicated and would divide her attention so much that one slip, one mistake could sever their souls. What was required was precision, a steady hand and a solid mind. There was no room for self-doubt or for interruption, and there was no time to lose.

Be bold, her grandmother's voice echoed in her thoughts.

Be brave, her aunt whispered.

Crimson, just…be true to yourself, her mother said.

Warmth spread from Crimson's head to her heart to the place where her courage lived. She squared her shoulders, tilted her chin and brought the Crystal of Shade to eye-level.

"Let's do this."

Chapter Twenty-Eight

Zephyr

Castle soldiers to his right. Fortis guards to his left. Zephyr and the others were being corralled away from the secret chamber that they'd gotten so close to entering and toward whatever grand scheme the false queens had devised. The pulsing of the sacred circle's power taunted him, and the farther he was pushed back, the mightier his sense of loss. He wasn't helping Crimson free the crones. He was failing her.

While Reuben and Julian were doing their best to wield their newly honed magical skills, it wasn't enough. What Zephyr needed was a Fortis like Jaggar, a shifter who knew just how to manipulate his magical gifts. His heart, already heavy at the loss of his brother, sank lower in his gut with the realization that they were outmatched and going to lose this battle if he didn't do something quickly.

He knew Tabitha and Wyvern weren't holed up in the sacred chamber. No way they'd lock themselves in that room and risk being trapped, no matter how hard the Fortis guard pushed them back and away from the room. Zephyr could sense the pulsing of the queens' power emanating from all directions, stained with dark deeds and immoral acts. They'd cast widely, like sticky webs, sending out their black magic to cause havoc, to bolster their Fortis, to keep Zephyr and the others busy, but the heavy beat emanated from the throne room. They were cowering on their dais while their minions did the dirty work. He knew, just by the feel of it, that Lucki and the others weren't having much success either. The queens were winning if only because they were willing to use devilish spells to get their victory.

Who, then, was doing the distracting?

Even if their plan had been to keep the queens occupied, by now Tabitha and Wyvern had to know that Crimson wasn't present for a reason. He just hoped that they didn't realize it was because she was busy with a rescue while the rest of the team were trying to keep the queens' focus at ground level.

They had to hang on, continue the distraction and make it count so Crimson had time to do what she needed to do.

His tiger chuffed for the hundredth time deep in his core, nudging him to do more…to be more.

"I know you say this is the best way to fight," Reuben roared above the clatter and clang of magic blasts and ricochet. "But I'm done with this strategy."

Zephyr's tiger roared along with the bear as the other shifter transformed, shedding his Fortis form for fur and claws and animal rage. A heartbeat later, Julian shifted to his lion and Zephyr, finally understanding his own tiger's agitation, gave up control and let his animal take over.

The bear lifted his giant head and bellowed a war cry so loud that it echoed down the halls. Zephyr dug his claws into the stone floor and bared his fangs. The tension ratcheted up, choking the air as the baffled-looking soldiers realized what was happening.

Zephyr heard the answering call of wolves, one eerie howl followed by another, and he knew that everyone was on the same page.

The pack of mismatched shifters launched themselves into the fray.

* * * *

Valor

Even with Lucki's tremendous magic abilities, Valor knew they were going to lose the battle against Wyvern and Tabitha. The queens had surrounded themselves with more Fortis guards than seemed possible, all presumably bonded to the deranged witches who were so amped up with stolen power that they pulsated like dying stars. Sickly streaks of dark magic raked their exposed skin, and their eyes were the color of coal.

Being Fortis meant nothing without training, and despite having magic of his own, every attempt Valor made to use it resulted in spells shooting off in all directions, so dangerous and unwieldy that he was worried he might hit one of his own team.

He didn't have control, and Lucki was obviously doing everything she could to keep them all protected, her focus on preventing the queens from doing harm to them so intent that she wasn't able to cause any herself.

Wren was the only one shooting blasts toward the witches, but it was having little-to-no effect. The queens' guards had enough culminative power of their own that the queens barely had to lift a hand to send bolts of power every which way.

They were losing. They were going to die. They were going to fail Crimson if they didn't change tactics.

Retreat wasn't an option. They needed to keep the battle going long enough for Crimson to do her thing.

Tabitha let out a terrible unending screech, and Valor fought the instinct to cover his sensitive ears, his wolf howling, clawing his insides to be let out. Tabitha tore at her skin, her jerky movements echoed by Wyvern. The black streaks of their magic shot out like tendrils searching for something…someone. Lucki lashed back, forcing the dark magic to swerve away before it hit her and her men. She shot an arm out to stop another tendril from whipping across Valor's face.

Something was happening. Maybe, just maybe, Crimson was pulling the crones free from their confinement and the false queens were feeling the impact of that. Even as he watched, the demented witches' pulsating stolen magic glow faded by a fraction, confirming to Valor that their power feed was wavering, that they were losing control.

Now was the time, their only chance to keep Tabitha and Wyvern from realizing what exactly was going on. And when they did figure it out, keeping them from going after Crimson.

The rumbling roar of fury that echoed into the throne room, a bear's rage, sent a rush through Valor's body and his wolf, ten steps ahead as usual, knew immediately what to do.

He shifted from Fortis to wolf, threw his head back then howled, and was bolstered when seconds later, Wren joined him.

They met eyes for the briefest of moments before turning toward the line of Fortis guards. This was the time for beasts. If he was going to die, he'd go down with the fury of fangs and claws.

Chapter Twenty-Nine

Crimson

Crimson had been careful, so careful not to rip the last of the siphoning spell away from the fragile crones, but she was at the point where if she didn't sever the connection immediately, she'd lose them for good. She knew that up to this point, her sisters probably hadn't felt the slow separation Crimson had been working tirelessly on because the siphoning was still happening, but she was at the point where it was now or never. Crimson had to end this spell.

Crimson had used the shards of the Crystal of Shade to slowly cut away strand after minuscule strand of the dark threads binding the spell to the crones. She'd been able to work quickly up until now, knowing that her time was limited, because each shard of crystal was wicked sharp and so in tune with her will. But the crystal was spent, and all that Crimson had left were her own hands and her own raw desire to see justice done.

She knew what she needed to do—rip the last threads completely while pumping as much healing magic as she could into the crones. She knew what to do, she knew she could do it and yet she hesitated.

If she miscalculated, if she put too much of her power into tearing the rest of the spell away and not enough into healing the crones, they'd die.

If she didn't put enough power into tearing the spell away and too much into healing the crones, it would be a useless waste, because they'd die anyway. They were already at the brink of being siphoned dry.

Talon, now recovered and standing behind her on the pedestal, put his hand on her shoulder, letting her know that he believed in her. Now was not the time for her confidence to get shaky.

What she wouldn't give to have Jaggar there. He'd demand she proceed, push her with fiery words to amp her up and do what needed to be done.

Be bold.

Be brave.

Be yourself.

Words that had been whispered in her mind while the crones had been capable of projecting their thoughts. Now they were silent, leaving Crimson to coax herself into doing what she knew had to be done, even though it scared her to death. One wrong move...

Jaggar... She wanted him here with her. Not because she needed him, she knew he'd always been right that she was powerful on her own, but because she'd taken him for granted. She'd pushed him away and now she suffered for it, regretting her stubborn actions to keep him at arm's length. He'd sacrificed himself to give her this opportunity so she could be right here, right now.

"Did you feel him go?" Talon said, like he was reading her mind. "Because I didn't."

"What do you mean?" she croaked as she looked over her shoulder at him, her thoughts jumping ten steps ahead, hope flaring.

"Here, I didn't feel him go here." Talon rubbed his chest with his fist. "A spell like that could take time to fully form. It's possible he isn't gone yet."

The truth was, no one really knew how a binding spell worked. The theory was that the Fortis gave up his essence and his life to make the spell work, but that it took years, sometimes centuries, to fully bind a witch like that. What if the theory was only partly right? What if the binding spell siphoned a Fortis' magic slowly, not killing him outright but taking from him as the spell solidified? Her mind leaped to a wickedly tempting conclusion. *Jaggar isn't dead.*

"There still might be time." But only if she asserted her power now.

She lifted her chin and called her power from that tiny flame of possibility that Jaggar could be saved. Somehow…maybe…

"Let's do this." She pooled her magic, swirling pinpricks of power at her fingertips, homing in on the last threads of the siphoning spell as she also pulled healing magic into her palm.

With one swipe, she severed the connection then threw a wave of healing over the crones, rushing in just as Talon did to catch them as they fell.

* * * *

Her sisters' untethered spell was like a living thing, darkly swirling around Crimson, Talon and the crones, trying to latch on to something, someone, with magic. Crimson lashed back, forcing the spell to continue to unravel as she and Talon struggled to keep the old witches from crumpling to their knees.

"Take us to those vile creatures," her mother spat. Her trembling hands clung to Crimson, but she fought to stand on her own feet.

"I'm going to get you three to safety first, then I'll face them." Crimson wouldn't put her family at risk any more than they already were.

"No!" Her grandmother's voice was surprisingly forceful and firm. She reached up and grasped Crimson's face as she pushed herself to stand. "We will fight them." She let out a gasp. "Together."

"Grandmother—"

"We've waited too long," her aunt said. She took a step away from Talon, teetering a little on unsteady legs. "Take us to them *now*."

Crimson closed her eyes for half a heartbeat then opened them to see Talon's gaze on her. He nodded once. The queens would have their way, as they always did.

And Jaggar always said I am the stubborn one.

Better to use her own power to get the crones where they needed to go rather than letting them waste any more of their own.

"All right," Crimson sighed. "Everyone hang tight."

Her mother stood fully as she linked arms with her sister and mother, a glimpse of her old self in the way she straightened her spine. It bolstered Crimson's confidence. Tabitha and Wyvern were about it get a smackdown like they'd never experienced before, and a childish part of Crimson felt the thrill of that. Talon completed the circle, his hand on Crimson's shoulder, and with that touch, she ignited a portal, all the while pumping the queens full of healing power they'd need to stand tall against her sisters.

The spinning portal opened with a roar, chaos unfolding before their eyes.

Her sisters were shooting dirty magic in all directions, dark stains that streaked across the room, some blasts hitting their own Fortis guards and dropping them in writhing masses. Lucki was fighting back, pulses of glowing light arcing from her fingers while her shifter and Zephyr, both in beast form, launched themselves directly at the dais.

It was a suicide move, Crimson saw that right away, going for the throats of the queens, but her sisters weren't expecting it—at least, not when Zephyr sideswiped Tabitha, knocking her next shot off course so it blasted into the wall instead of into anyone living. Wren didn't have as much luck. Wyvern turned at the last second and froze him in mid-air, then with a flick, sent him slamming to the ground with a bone-shattering crunch.

"That is enough!" Crimson stepped through the portal, her hands raised and pulsating with densely packed spells.

Even though the battle raged on, deafening in its fury, Crimson's words reached her sisters. They both turned, the cocky smirks sliding from their faces as they realized who was standing behind their sister.

"Your stolen rule is over, Tabitha and Wyvern," Crimson shouted and as she did, the familiars and Fortis soldiers under their command stopped fighting.

Their arms fell limp at their sides as the long absent waft of her mother's magic soared through the space and invaded every crevice, every breath, every fiber of being.

Crimson blinked back unexpected tears. She'd forgotten how comforting her mother's signature was, how powerful, how determined.

Her sisters rallied, pulling their shoulders back and jutting their chins out, their defiant eyes glaring at the woman who now stood at Crimson's side.

"I'd love to see you try to take it back, sister." Tabitha's hair was wild, tangled and like a nest of grime on top of her head. Her skin was equally as dirty, tainted by her dark spells. Her eyes darted like her attention was being pulled in ten directions at once.

Wyvern, looking no better, stood shoulder to shoulder with her sister. "You think we weren't expecting this?" She laughed, dark and menacing, and the sound of it made Crimson shiver. "As soon as you cut our spell, we knew."

"What you don't know, dearest Crimson," Tabitha said, "is that all you've done is brought our meal to us."

Wyvern and Tabitha linked arms, then cast a swirling dark net out from their bodies, like a putrid growth sprouting right from their bellies.

It was grotesque, monstrous and it rushed at Crimson and the crones, dripping with evil, swirling like a whirlwind.

"I said," Crimson screamed as she flung her readied spells at the web, "that's *enough!*" Her layered work crashed through her sisters' dark magic, and as her spells hit their target, Crimson reversed the web's trajectory and sent it flinging back toward Tabitha and Wyvern.

She wasn't expecting the power behind her sisters' web when they fought back, stopping the web midair as they attempted to redirect it again to the real queens. Crimson had to divert her magic away from her mother, grandmother and aunt, cutting off the healing energy she was feeding them so she could push it to the web.

As her multi-layered spells wobbled unsteadily, exhaustion hit Crimson hard. Her arms shook as she strained against her sisters' combined and stolen powers, but she gritted her teeth and pulled everything she could from the ground, the air and her own familiars to bolster her.

Like a lifesaving breath and a shot of adrenaline, Crimson felt the magic unifying. Her mother, her grandmother and her aunt joined hands then linked into Crimson so that they could collectively finish what she had started.

Now her arrogant siblings didn't stand a chance.

The combined power sent the web spinning at her sisters like it was made of nothing but silk. They screeched as the magic hit them, then roared when their own spell battered them to the ground, siphoning their own magic and weakening them within seconds. They lay in a heap, powerless to even lift a hand, their magic ebbing like a dying pulse. Their Fortis lost strength as well, crumpling to the ground like toy soldiers, the link to their queens making their life essence seep into the web of the siphoning spell.

Her mother squeezed Crimson's hand before letting go and, in a swirl of casting, transformed herself and the queens into their former selves. It was a glamour, Crimson knew, making them appear healthy, whole and clean, dressed in simple shimmering gowns that denoted their rank, their hair luxurious and untattered, their skin no longer sallow, but it was enough to pull a collective gasp from courtier familiars, the guards and any soldiers not bonded to the queens finally realizing who was in the room with them.

"Your foul deeds will not go unpunished," Crimson's mother said as she walked steadily, each step seeming to empower her. She moved toward the dais, leaving Crimson behind, her arms still linked with the true queens.

"You girls have been very bad little things," Crimson's grandmother said, a gnarled finger pointed to the lump at the base of the thrones.

"Remove them to the dungeon," Aunt Tilly commanded.

Even with their appearance transformed and knowing that a rightful queen spoke, the remaining Fortis hesitated for a second too long.

"You will follow my orders or find yourself in the dungeon along with them." Aunt Tilly snapped her fingers, whipping the guards with a lash of power that got them scrambling to do her bidding.

"There will be a reckoning for all involved," her grandmother said, scanning the crowd around them. "Now leave us alone with our champions."

The rest of the guards, the Fortis and familiars, jumped into action, filing out of the throne room quickly.

Lucki raced to Wren, who still lay crumpled on the floor. "Wren, are you okay?"

Wren, still in wolf form, moaned as Lucki touched his snout.

Crimson's grandmother made her way to Lucki, her steps unsteady but determined. "He'll be fine, child.

Just banged up a bit." She waved her hand toward the fallen wolf, coaxing him to stir. "A little of your healing magic will set him right. Pulse it out, and it will find the place it needs to be."

Crimson hadn't bothered to ask if Lucki even knew how to wield healing power, but the other witch nodded like it was something she hadn't thought of before, then closed her eyes and glowed.

"She's a powerful one," Crimson's mother said with a nod toward Lucki, "if untrained." She slid down to her seat, her throne the one in the middle that Tabitha had been using in her absence. "I see there's a lot we've missed in our time away." Her voice sounded weary once again.

Crimson barely registered her mother's meaning as she checked her men, making sure they were unhurt and sending a pulse of power through the tether of their bond. They responded with a pulse back to her, letting her know that all was well, and they were unharmed.

"Mother, we must find a way to save Jaggar. He's—"

"It's Queen Merianne, Crimson. You know court protocol." She gave Crimson an assessing look. "You've bonded with a Fortis."

Crimson, caught off guard by the change in subject, winced, knowing her mother's familiar tone of disapproval like a second voice in her head.

"It was necessary to—"

"No need to explain," her mother said with a weary wave.

The other familiars filed into the room finally—Valor, Reuben, Julian, striding in as men rather than beasts. Wren groaned as Lucki helped him rise.

The queens surveyed the lot of them with assessing eyes. Crimson winced, waiting for their judgment, biting her tongue to keep from blurting out again.

"And Jaggar, where is he?" her grandmother asked, still scanning the room.

"He's trapped in a spell." Crimson rushed to the dais, no longer able to contain herself, knowing she was bucking protocol but not caring. "There's time to save him, but we have to go now."

Zephyr, now back in human form, stepped around the dais. "How?"

It was one word, but it stopped her in her tracks. "I don't know!" She scanned her family, her eyes locking on her mother's. "His heroic actions got us here. If it weren't for him —" She choked back a sob. "He's trapped in a binding spell with an evil sorceress, but he's not dead yet. I need to pull him out and find some other way to contain Angelica."

When her mother snapped a confused look her way, she rushed to fill her in. "There was an attack by a witch who had the Crystal of Shade and —"

"I sense this is a long story and better suited for another time," her mother said. "You say Jaggar is alive?"

"Yes. None of his brothers felt his death." She scanned the familiars and each one gave a variation of the same response. Jaggar wasn't dead. *Yet.* "We still have time to reverse the binding spell."

There was a drawn-out beat of silence as the queens seemed to share a moment of eye contact and subtle nods.

"You believe he deserves this, Crimson?" Aunt Tilly asked, her expression serious, eyes steady, boring into Crimson's soul.

Crimson gulped then nodded. "Yes," she croaked.

"Jaggar was always most devoted to you, Crimson," her mother said, no judgment in her voice. "I'm surprised he used himself for a spell like that. He would have known the consequences, that he'd die and be forever separated from you."

"He thought he was doing right by me." Crimson's heart twisted and tears burned the back of her eyes. "He thought there was no future for us." *I pushed him away. I told him we would never be bonded.*

Her mother held her gaze, surely reading her unspoken thoughts for a tortured minute before nodding.

"Mother, please. I know there has to be a way to set him free."

"There's only one way to do that," her grandmother said. "And it'll take a heavy sacrifice."

Chapter Thirty

Jaggar

It had been foolish of him, but Jaggar hadn't expected death to be so...annoying. Beyond annoying actually, death for him seemed to be unbearable. Perhaps it was the way he'd died, trapping himself in a binding spell with Angelica—who, for some reason, wouldn't get out of his head. All Angelica did day in and day out—or whatever it was time did in the afterlife—was whine, complain, moan, curse, sob even. It was constant, this disembodied voice drilling into his brain, coming from every direction, and it was going to drive him insane.

Where was the peace everyone said came with death? The obliteration of thought, sound, all senses? For Jaggar, this was hell, and he had to wonder if he'd made some kind of grave error in this spell casting, because this was definitely a punishment of some kind.

Free me...free me...free me...

It had been her mantra for the last eternity of hours. He wanted to punch something, to claw his way out of the spell somehow. His cat was ready to rip Angelica's head off—if there was a head to take, which there wasn't. Although Jaggar felt every muscle spasm, cramp, strain, he couldn't see anything. It was pitch black, and he was frozen in place, stuck by the sticky threads he'd created to bind Angelica, tied to her in some telepathic way.

His cat roared alongside Angelica's moaning, frantic to get away from the mess they found themselves in.

This is the sacrifice we made, Jaggar reminded himself and his cat. *We did this to save Crimson the trouble of dealing with Angelica for a second longer than she had to. We did this to give Crimson the chance she needed to save the queens.*

As determined and sure as he'd been when he'd cast the spell, the time he'd spent here, in this limbo, thinking, had made him question if he should have included Crimson in his plans. Maybe she would have been able to bind Angelica without his interference. Maybe she would have done it properly and spared him this hell.

For all his bluster about her claiming her destiny and building her confidence, in the heat of the moment, he'd gone all Neanderthal on her and had stepped in to save the day...without her input. So maybe he was being punished for that, too.

Freemefreemefreemefreeme.

Lady, if I could, I would. Trust me.

Then he'd kill her for real.

His panther roared in agreement and the rumble vibrated through Jaggar like an earthquake—or a volcano erupting, which would be just wonderful...if the volcano bowled them over with black lava and encased them with more finality.

Wait... He snagged on that last thought, backtracked. That rumble was definitely outside of wherever Jaggar currently existed—as if he was still in the moral realm somehow, as if he wasn't actually dead.

Another vibration rocked the bindings that held him tight.

His panther perked up, swiveled internal ears, listened.

A low murmur of sound echoed against his confines. It wasn't identifiable as voices, not with actual words or anything, but there was something about the cadence that hit him right in the heart.

His heart, which was still beating.

Crimson! He knew in his gut that she'd come for him. She'd figured out a way to untangle the mess he'd made and deal with Angelica.

The vibration became more intense, shaking Jaggar from the foundation of his spell all the way up to the top of his scalp. He tried to help, frantic to send his magic out, but when he attempted to ignite his power, there was nothing left to give. He'd exhausted everything he had to stop Angelica. Instead, he pushed, or at least tried to push, with his whole body, hoping to create fissures or cracks by flexing so that Crimson could seep her magic in somehow and get him out.

"Hang on, big boy," a gravelly voice, not Crimson's, laughed.

Jaggar froze for a millisecond, confused, on alert, his hackles rising, then pushed even harder against whoever was coming for him. Maybe it wasn't Crimson at all. Maybe this was another enemy.

"I said, be still, ya big, dumb cat," the voice snapped.

Jaggar lost his breath. He recognized that voice, the snap of her words. There was only person who ever spoke to him that way. *Grandmother?*

She'd always treated him like he was part of the family and had insisted, like Crimson, he call her 'Grandmother' in private rather than 'Your Majesty'.

"You've gotten yourself all tangled up in this ghastly spell you made, Jaggar." She huffed. "All tied up, indeed."

He felt her snipping, cutting away the bindings that held him tight, her magic signature a welcome balm.

Wait...no...you'll let Angelica loose if you —

"Are you telling me you know more about magic than I do, boy?" Grandmother snapped again. "Shut up and leave this to me."

Even though she sounded in control, full of power, there was a wobble to her voice that hadn't been there before, and an edge of exhaustion that sounded fatal.

She'd been depleted and, Jaggar realized, she was using the last of her strength to free him.

No, Grandmother, don't do this. Fix the spell so I can take this burden on. I'm committed to sacrificing myself.

"Oh, Jaggar." He felt her warmth as she reached him, cocooning him in her special signature as she stepped into the spell beside him.

He could finally see her tattered hair, her weathered face. She'd aged a hundred years in the time she'd been away.

"My time is done." She reached up to cup his cheek. "And she's going to need you."

She...Crimson.

"She doesn't want me." Jaggar's voice felt raw as it tumbled out of him.

"Don't be a fool," Grandmother tsked. "That lie must taste bitter on your tongue."

"She doesn't need me," he croaked.

"Maybe not in the way you've always thought she would — not as yours to dominate. Yours to guide, to bully, to lead. Maybe she needs you as a partner."

"I don't have my magic anymore."

Grandmother shook her head then reached up with both hands to take his face and guide him toward her. She locked eyes with him, and in hers swirled mysteries he'd never known, magic he'd never experienced. "You'll have what is mine, and you'll use it."

"No...I can't. That will kill you." He wanted to fight against her, to demand she stop whatever it was she was doing.

She gripped his face firmly. "Yes, it will, but my heart?" Her voice cracked. "It died when those girls betrayed us, and I'm tired, Jaggar...very tired. Your power is meant for the next witch in line...for Crimson."

This couldn't be happening. He wouldn't allow it. He wouldn't let her sacrifice —

"Of for goodness' sake, boy, have you learned nothing?" She smacked his cheek. "You're not the one calling the shots, and the sooner you accept that, the happier you'll be. She has given it to you, Jaggar."

Crimson passed Grandmother's magic to me?

She nodded. "Will you accept it?"

Jaggar sucked in a deep breath, knowing that the queen had spoken, and the choice wasn't really a choice at all... Of course he'd accept her gift.

"Yes."

"Wise man...finally." She closed her eyes then pushed up on tiptoes so that her lips were a fraction away from his. As she blew her breath out, her magic went with it, entering Jaggar, refilling his magic coffers, infusing him with more power than he'd ever known. A new binding spell pinged against his senses, one woven by Grandmother as she gave away her gift to Jaggar. The new binding spell unraveled what was left of his, pushing him out with a sudden tear.

He found himself standing next to a statue that was slowly taking form and solidifying.

"Welcome back," Crimson said, her voice full of warmth, brimming with something else.

He turned toward her, the sudden sunlight blinding him. "Thank you," he said to the silhouette in front of him. "I hope you can forgive me."

"There's nothing to forgive. You were just being you." She took steps toward him, hesitant, slow. "And that's the you that I've always loved."

His heart melted, his vision cleared and there she was, glowing with confidence and power. Not needing him, but wanting him, and he finally understood the significance of that.

"With my heart in my mouth, I would ask you again if you'd allow me to be your mate." He quirked a smile. "I vow to stand by your side from this day forward and promise that I'll continue being me...with a few adjustments."

"I'm glad you finally came to your senses." Crimson beamed as she leapt to his arms. "I accept."

She kissed him, full of passion, possession and desire, and he, in turn, kissed her back, knowing that they were claiming one another as they were always meant to.

Chapter Thirty-One

Crimson

Where there had once been three queens now stood two. The rightful queens. Crimson's mother and aunt.

Her grandmother had made the ultimate sacrifice. She'd used her dying powers to rescue Jaggar and bind not only Angelica, but also Tabitha and Wyvern. Together they would slowly petrify until they were nothing more than a giant fearsome statue, reminding anyone who stumbled upon them what the consequences were for betrayal. The spell, done properly, had put a final end to the witches, and the last of Crimson's grandmother's energy had been used to restore Jaggar's power...and then some. Now her grandmother rested in peace, and Shade was in the hands of benevolent leaders once again.

"Today we are gathered to crown the next generation to the throne," Crimson's mother said, her voice strong, firm, daring anyone to contradict her.

"This will be a proper ascension, one that was always meant to be." She scanned the gathered crowd, making eye contact with those she suspected were complicit in their yearlong captivity.

The court members knew it, too. Crimson could tell by the way their eyes shifted and how they cowered under her mother's openly disapproving stare. A few had come groveling already, bending knee to the queens, humbling themselves in a desperate plea for mercy on their lapse in judgment. They were eagerly providing information about other betrayers, and Crimson had been making notes, following leads, tracking down a few who had hidden themselves away after Tabitha and Wyvern had been dethroned. There were courtiers in attendance who Crimson wanted to speak to soon, but they would have to wait until the day's official business had been concluded. She wasn't worried about losing them, even if they attempted to run, Crimson would find them, and they'd be brought to justice.

Even before her coronation, Crimson had been appointed the official investigator, so she had ultimate power when it came to ferreting out those witches and familiars who may have had knowledge of what Tabitha, Wyvern and Aria had done. She'd already uncovered the location of the queens' familiars, who had been held captive while the queens suffered. Crimson's sisters had put the poor men in the walls of their sacred chamber, using the Fortis' power to help contain the siphoned magic so that no one was the wiser. Once they were found and freed, the Fortis who still lived—her grandmother's familiars had died when she had—told of Tabitha, Wyvern and Aria's evil ruse, using deceptive magic to con the men into the sacred chamber they'd newly constructed, only to be snared in a spell so dark that they couldn't find their way out of it. Just as Crimson suspected, the queens' Fortis had never accused Crimson of being responsible for the queens' disappearance. They'd been trapped before they could alert anyone of the truth. The only signatures they'd found in the sacred chamber after the queens had disappeared belonged to Wyvern, Tabitha and Aria.

"Crimson of Shade," Aunt Tilly said as she turned toward Crimson, a crown in one hand and a battle mask in the other. Both glowed with power that radiated toward Crimson like the sun. Decorated with gems and crystals, they sparkled and flashed reds, blues and purples, a representation of Crimson's own magic. "Rise and be made queen."

Jaggar's hand was on the back of her neck as she stood slightly in front of him. He squeezed gently, letting her know that he was with her every step of the way, then nudged her forward.

She swept her gaze to Talon and Valor, Zephyr, then over her shoulder at Jaggar. They were dressed in formal court regalia – black tailored coats, embroidered with magic threads fitting for their rank. Their billowing cream shirts had ruffles down the front and sleeves that poked out to partially cover their hands. Crimson thought they looked handsome and regal, mates suited for a young queen, but she knew the men longed for simpler clothing, something they weren't afraid to get dirty in.

All the same, she was proud of her men, no matter what they wore, and was eager to have them officially made queens' Fortis.

She and Jaggar hadn't yet bonded, but that was a foregone conclusion. These were her men, and a heated rush of possession and love made her glow brighter, if only in her heart and soul.

She grinned at the thought of stripping each of them out of the pomp and circumstance later, but for now, she had a crown to claim.

Crimson stepped up, moving carefully so her long black gown didn't snag on anything as she made her way up the dais stairs toward her aunt and mother. They both looked at her with piercing eyes, only a quirk of a smile on her mother's lips, letting her know that this formality was for the benefit of the crowd. In her mother's mind, Crimson was already a queen.

"Crimson of Shade, with this crown, we anoint you as Queen of Shade, one of three, in unity, in loyalty, in sisterhood." Her aunt placed the crown on Crimson's head.

It weighed heavier than she'd imagined it would, probably because it came with so much expectation and responsibility.

"Crimson of Shade, my dearest daughter, I am so proud of you." Her mother's soft voice was only meant for her ears, and they smiled at each other, sharing this moment as only a mother and daughter could.

Her mother's eyes flickered, a cold veneer shuttering the warmth. She hardened her tone and projected her next words to the crowd, the smile gone from her lips. "With this battle mask we anoint you as Queen of Strategy, Protector of Shade, Governor of the Guards and Overseer of Justice." She offered the battle mask, made from black leather and encrusted with sparkling crystals and sunstone. Crimson guided it to her face, and it immediately took to her skin like it was meant to be there. The mask pulsed, shooting magic vibrations through her head, sparking inside her skull and down her spine, fusing to her will. She lifted her chin and her mother smiled.

"Citizens of Shade, we present to you Queen Crimson, to whom you will vow love, respect and undying loyalty," Aunt Tilly boomed, sweeping the crowd her arms wide and wafting magic in gentle waves.

Everyone dropped to the floor on one knee, including all the Fortis and Crimson's own familiars. Her face burned hot, her heart raced and she couldn't believe that this was finally happening.

She was a Queen of Shade.

* * * *

Crimson had asked that only Jaggar accompany her to her home in the veil so she could retrieve the last of her can't-live-without things. She wanted him with her, not because she needed protection but because it was the only way, right now, for them to get some alone time.

And Crimson wanted to get Jaggar alone. She had things to say. They had things to do.

Important, long-overdue things.

Strangely, she felt nervous, jittery and couldn't stop blushing each time Jaggar's hands brushed against hers when she passed him the bags that needed to go back to the castle. She'd been weirdly hesitant to initiate anything with him. It was like she was a teenager all over again, unsure about Jaggar's feelings for her, even though she saw love and longing in his every glance her way.

"You made a comfortable home here," Jaggar said as he surveyed what was left of the cottage. Angelica's wild cats had destroyed the kitchen and sitting area, but the bedroom and back porch were still intact. Crimson might come back and fix it up at some point so she'd have a refuge if she needed it, but with all the work she had to do as queen, it might be hard to slip away.

"It was a small consolation to have found such a peaceful place." Crimson grabbed the last of the mementos she wanted to take to the castle, a vase that Talon had made for her out of mountain stone. "But it became our home while we were here."

"I'm sorry for that, Crimson." Jaggar's voice was garbled and edged with pain, like she'd brushed against a wound that still hadn't healed. "I shouldn't have lied to you. I should have come to tell you my plan."

"That's not what I meant." She turned to face him, guilt hammering her. "And it wasn't your fault."

She closed the distance between them, finally finding the courage to do what she'd wanted to do since he'd been freed from the binding spell. With her arms around his neck, she tugged him closer so she could kiss him.

He wrapped his hands around her waist and hoisted her higher, deepening their kiss until she couldn't think of any reason to delay their bonding.

"Jaggar," she moaned as she tore herself away, "we've lost so many moments already."

"We have much time to make up for, I agree." He brushed his thumb down the side of her face. "I've been wanting to…say some things."

"Me, too," she whispered, but instead of saying them she kissed him again, pressing into him so when he opened his mouth to hers, she entangled her tongue with his and savored the moment she'd been dreaming about since they'd been parted the year before. He devoured her just as fiercely as she did him, stroking him, exploring him, claiming him.

When he pulled away on a gasp of breath, she lunged forward, unwilling to give up the bombardment of sensation that she'd craved for so long.

"Crimson." His guttural voice turned her name into a command.

She pulled back enough to meet his eyes, shivers running along her skin.

"I will mark you before we go any farther," he said, as if expecting her to argue.

"What are you waiting for?" she teased.

A feral glint flashed in his eyes, and she knew his panther was rising to her challenge. He swept his hand along her throat to the back of her neck where her spine met her skull, a gesture of possession but one that Crimson had always craved from Jaggar. "I vow to you, Crimson, that I will forever be your partner, your lover, your mate and your friend."

The intensity of his stare made his words magical, and his power coursing along her spine jolted through every nerve ending, synapses firing, body heating, coming alive with Jaggar's power. It rolled over her, sinking in deep, routing along her skin, down her back and over her hips, infusing her with his essence.

She closed her eyes to relish the sensation.

"We belong to each other now," Jaggar's gravelly voice called to her.

She opened her eyes and nodded. "As it was meant to be."

He growled then kissed her again, fiercely, possessively, marking her with his lips.

He spun her to the bed, pushing her back so he could climb up on top, cradling her with his body, pressed against her with delicious weight that she wanted to sink into, become one with.

They shed their clothes slowly, revealing skin to kiss and lick and suck. Indulging in the time they'd stolen so they could be alone, knowing that after today, they'd forever be together with the rest of Crimson's harem.

And that was okay, something she was looking forward to, but right now, it was all about her and Jaggar.

She ran her hands down his torso, reminding her fingers of the ridges and dips, the cut of his muscles. He flexed his stomach as she teased her way to his pants then moaned when she slipped her fingers over his cock to encircle his shaft. He cupped one breast while he sucked greedily on the other, tweaking her nipples between finger and thumb and tongue and teeth. She arched into him as he moved down her body, forcing her to give up her prize and release his dick as he kissed and licked his way over her stomach, leaving a trail of fire that burned her to her core.

He shimmied the bottom half of her battle garb down her legs, stroking the insides of her thighs as he tugged her remaining clothing off then tossed it behind him.

He stared down at her, his eyes hungry, taking her in, making her quiver, desperate for more of his touch. She reached out, motioning him to come back, and when he didn't immediately comply, she ran her hands over her hips, up her waist, then played with her own tits, cupping, flicking, teasing, coaxing him to take over.

With a growl, he parted her legs, sliding his hands from her knees to her pussy. When she looked down at him, he was already between her legs, his lips curled in a wicked grin, his eyes hooded and sexy as hell. When he used his thumbs to open her lips, his hot breath tickled her wet pussy and she moaned, rolling her hips up, urging him to get closer, to touch her, to put her out of her agony.

"Jaggar," she whispered, urgency in her tone.

He chuckled softly, then dabbed her clit with his tongue, tentatively at first, gently, taking his time to lick her little nub, to torment her. She pinched her nipples, bringing pain to the surface, redirecting her focus so she didn't thrust her pussy into Jaggar's face and force him to get serious.

He was taking his time, enjoying himself and, she knew, reveling in her torment. He slipped his fingers along the edge of her pussy hole, touching so softly that she finally snapped, shooting her hand into his hair and gripping tightly.

"Jaggar!"

He laughed again, then thrust his fingers deep inside, rubbing along the wall of her pussy to find her G-spot while he finally got busy sucking on her clit, giving her the pressure she needed, the friction driving her wild.

Pleasure rippled through her, coiling in her belly, then radiating out to ping against every erogenous zone. He circled her clit with his tongue and stroked her G-spot, simultaneous sensations that made her buck into his mouth and against his hand. With her climax rising, she tugged on his hair, wanting him to finish the job with his cock nestled deep and her legs wrapped around his hips, their mouths pressed together.

Jaggar lifted his head, his eyes locking on hers, then continued to dab her clit, his sexy 'fuck me' eyes making her swoon for him, threatening to push her over the edge. How she had missed that look. Even if they'd never gone further than this in the past, she'd missed the breathtaking anticipation of seeing him so close to the edge of need and want and hunger for her.

The heat of his stare was enough to make her come.

Just when she thought it was better to give up, give in and let him bring her to orgasm, he pulled back, grinning madly, somehow knowing that she was a hairsbreadth away from climaxing.

He pulled his fingers out of her pussy then stuck them in his mouth, savoring the taste of her so much that he moaned, his eyes still zeroed in on hers.

He ran his hand along her waist, over her belly to her hips where he gripped her hard, then pulled her down and under him.

Jaggar cupped her face, looking at her like she was the most beautiful woman on the planet, then he kissed her softly, entangling his tongue with hers, the taste of her own juice an aphrodisiac all on its own. Her body revved, the nerve endings zinging, primed as he thrust into her for the first time, rolling his hips gently so she could savor each second of coming together. He pulled back, ending their kiss so he could hold her stare once again, his eyes flickering, telling her all the things she'd been craving hearing from him for the year of their separation. He was hers, heart and soul, and he would never leave her side again.

His markings flared along her spine, caging her ribs, soaking into her core and giving her the gift of completion, the satisfaction of getting what she'd always wanted. She wrapped her legs around his waist, coaxing him deeper as he kissed her jaw, her throat, his body melded so closely to hers that they moved fluidly, grinding each other toward the peak of their orgasm until fireworks exploded in a rush of bliss and love and bonding.

Epilogue

Crimson

Now that she was queen, Crimson had responsibilities that all seemed overdue. Selecting a team to help her with her investigation was a number one priority, then monitoring and mending any security breaches left over from Angelica's disruption and her troublesome cats' invasions was another. Posting around-the-clock guards at the statue containing her sisters and Angelica to make sure that the petrification process continued without a hitch was something she took personal satisfaction from.

And, along with those top priorities, she needed to visit Lucki one last time to thank her in person for her role in Crimson achieving her destiny.

"Oh gosh, you didn't have to come all this way for that!" Lucki sat across from Crimson at the large kitchen table in the cat house, where they'd sat the first time they'd met. She poured them both tea from a pot that Reuben had brought over, along with a tantalizing plate of treats.

"I did need to come, not only to give my thanks but to also give you this," Crimson said as she lifted the satchel she'd carried all the way from Shade. It'd been heavy, unwieldy and difficult to shift through the ether, but only because it contained something bursting with power. Even now, as Crimson *thunk*ed it onto the table, the contents shimmered the air around them.

Reuben had left to hang with the men in the back garden where Jaggar, Talon, Zephyr and Valor were already shooting the shit, as they liked to say, with the other shifters.

It made Crimson almost giddy to see their comradery. Just as it made her downright gleeful to be giving Lucki her overdue thanks, no matter how hard it had been to bring the gift here.

Lucki gasped as Crimson pulled the rainbow sparkling battle mask out of the bag.

"Is that...? Oh my gosh, Crimson, it's beautiful!"

And it was. Crimson had made sure to capture the very essence of Lucki—her generosity and bravery, her loyalty and compassion—in the mask. She'd hunted for the gems herself and, with the help of her mother and aunt, had woven the mask to fit Lucki perfectly.

"I thought you'd like to have your own," Crimson said as she held the mask up for Lucki's inspection. "Don't worry. I'm not going to ask you to pledge allegiance or anything."

Lucki laughed but still hesitated to take the mask.

"What's wrong? It's yours." Crimson frowned, suddenly concerned that she'd overstepped.

"I'm just not sure I deserve it. I'm not…" She waved her hand up and down. "You know, like you all…real witches of Shade and all that."

"You're an honorary witch of Shade and welcome to visit *or stay*, any time. I know you love Weeping Falls, but if you ever need a second home, please consider Shade that place. I hope we can be allies, and I promise that if you need our help, we'll be there for you, just as you were for us. You are a hero in Shade. I couldn't have achieved my goals to right the wrongs my sisters had done without you." Crimson leaned forward. "I hope, too, that we are friends, and as a friend, I'd like you to have this mask."

Lucki blushed, a smile tugging her lips. "When you put it that way…" She covered her face and sighed before running her fingers through her hair, then faced Crimson once again. "Of course we're allies and friends and honorary sister-witches!" She nearly leaped over the table to crush Crimson in a hug.

Crimson froze, unsure how to respond, not used to anyone hugging her other than her familiars. She'd never gotten affection from her sisters, and her mother, aunt and grandmother had always been more on the formal side of warmth.

"You've earned this mask." Crimson offered the mask again as they pulled apart. She cleared her throat, trying to dispel the awkwardness. "Try it on. I promise, you'll never want to let it go."

Lucki grinned then took the mask. "It's so heavy!"

"It's made from a special version of queen magic. My mother and aunt did most of the weaving." Crimson winked. "So obviously, it carries a lot of power. Once you put it on, it'll belong to you and meld into your signature, so it will respond to your commands, even, with time, your thoughts."

"That's the only thing I lack from my shifters... They've yet to become my mind readers. They can mind-talk to each other, much to my frustration, but I want them to know what I'm thinking so I don't have to explain things over and over again. Is that too much to ask?"

"Be careful what you wish for, Lucki." Crimson snorted. "I'm not sure we really want our shifters to know our minds all the time."

"Good point." Lucki laughed but she lifted the mask anyway and laid it over her face. "Oh, wow, this fits like it's a second skin."

Warmth spread through Crimson's chest, knowing how much work she'd put into making sure the mask would not only fit Lucki but suit her personality and magic signature perfectly. "I found you a special gem called 'rainbow core' and another one called 'cat's paw'. I thought they'd fit with your life the best."

Lucki ran her fingers over the top and sides of the mask. "It just stays on like this? No ties or anything?"

"When a mask is made for you, it stays with you."

"The Crystal of Shade wasn't mine to use," Lucki said with a nod, her green eyes peeking from the mask. "That's why it fell off so easily when I sent Angelica to Shade."

"Yes, exactly, and you have nothing to worry about with this mask. It's yours, and it won't fall off."

Lucki got up and moved to the front foyer. Crimson followed her there to find an ornate mirror, encased in filigree and dotted with non-magical crystals. She stood behind Lucki as she checked herself out, turning her head this way and that. "It's so beautiful." Lucki turned and hugged Crimson again, and this time, Crimson was prepared. She melted into it, wrapping herself up in Lucki's embrace, letting herself enjoy the closeness of another witch.

"So, how do I get it off now?" Lucki laughed when she pulled back. "I'm not stuck with it on forever, am I? I mean, it's gorgeous but..."

"No, you only have to command it off." Crimson smiled. "You can say 'release' or 'get off'...but usually I just tug on the sides, and it knows to let go."

Lucki did as Crimson said, and the mask slid from her face. "Totally cool."

"I can't tell you how grateful I am for your help."

Lucki entwined her fingers with Crimson's then squeezed her hand. "That's what friends do."

Crimson nodded, feeling her heart tug at the idea that yes, sisters were supposed to support one another, be friends to one another. Lucki had been a better pseudo-sister than Crimson's real sisters had ever been.

"I have to confess. I had another reason for coming." Crimson's sly tone had Lucki's eyebrows rising. "I need a bit of sisterly advice..."

"Oh?" Lucki leaned forward. "Do tell."

* * * *

Crimson had spent some time with her men, adding features to the ancient sacred chamber that she had always preferred for her spell casting. She'd worked tirelessly to not only find new, powerful gems, stones and crystals to add to the intricate inlay of swirling circles that she'd always loved in the chamber, but she'd also designed and had her shifters create an altar of sorts.

Now the polished stone table glistened in the beam of sun that cascaded from the opening in the roof of the chamber, its embedded crystals sparkling, beckoning Crimson to start her ritual.

She'd invited her shifters to the chamber at the specific time when the warm rays would shine just right, creating a glow in the room and heating it almost to sauna temperatures.

She wore nothing but her battle mask, so when Jaggar first stepped into the chamber, his eyes widened almost comically and his mouth dropped open. Jaggar being Jaggar, he recovered then quickly ushered the others inside before slamming the door shut.

"There are guards outside," he said, as if Crimson was showcasing her nakedness for all to see. "You should have warned us you'd be..." He waved his hand up and down.

"Obviously she has a privacy spell in play, brother," Talon said with a tap of his nose, like he could smell her signature. For the only shifter with no Fortis magic, he was the most skilled at detecting Crimson's powers, even if he didn't exactly know what she was using them for.

"A privacy spell... Yes, you're right, Talon, but also a 'look the other way' spell and a 'noise canceling' extra layer." She grinned as her men circled her, their gazes hot on her skin, fists clenching and unclenching like predators hunting prey. "I've been busy today."

"And what, exactly, do you have in mind for your next spell, Crimson?" Valor asked as he stalked her, his penetrating gaze trailing up and down her body, making goosebumps rise.

Her nipples were already hard as pebbles, but with her shifters staring so hungrily at her, she felt a tightening all over her body like her skin was taut, aching already.

"I thought we'd balance the scales today, boys." She stepped back, careful not to trip on the step that led to her new altar. "I thought I'd show you my appreciation for you all."

She crooked her fingers, beckoning Jaggar and Valor to her side.

"Set me on the altar." Her voice was husky and her body primed. Her pussy was already slick and pulsing, her body quivering, her belly coiled.

Jaggar and Valor lifted her under the arms with ease, lowering her gently to the warm stone surface like she was a delicate flower that needed careful handling.

"I wear each of your marks," she said as she nodded toward Talon and Zephyr, motioning for them to come closer as well. "But none of you bear mine."

She'd sought Lucki's council to find out how to make her harem whole, so that every one of her shifters were not only Fortis but imbued with her magic, just as Lucki's men carried hers.

Lucki had given her very simple instructions.

"Love them with your entire being then call the magic and charge it with your intention."

So that was what Crimson was going to do.

She lifted her arms, already channeling the magic from her battle mask, and felt her markings flare to life along her skin, searing her with her shifters' heat, knowing that as much as she loved them, they loved her more.

"Touch me," she commanded and pulled power from the gems and crystals and the sacred chamber itself. The ancient magic coursed into her, along her veins, through her hair, electrifying the tips of each nerve ending, and her men gave her what she asked for, their hands, lips, tongues. With the way her battle mask glowed, she couldn't see who was touching where at first and she reveled in the anonymity of that, feeling the indiscriminate lust and affection from her shifters.

Someone cupped her breasts while another teased her inner thigh. One kissed along her throat while someone else trailed a searing touch down her stomach.

She pooled the power that she'd called, and when it reached its peak, she pushed it out, gifting her men more power, more magic, more of her, so that they would all be connected, not just in tune with each other on a physical level but by their very essence.

"Talon, Valor, Jaggar and Zephyr, you are my heart, my life, my partners, and I cherish you," she said before enveloping them in her power surge, sparking streamers of magic through her skin to where their fingers, tongues, lips and hands connected to her, infusing them with ancient, powerful magic that would not only elevate but equalize them.

When her vision cleared and the glow subsided, she saw that Talon had become Fortis, doubled in size and bearing new markings that would give him magic just like the others. On each of her men were new magic markings, a kaleidoscope of color flaring across their hearts like claw marks, her own branding on their skin. When she flexed her magic muscles, each of those marks pulsed to life and all her men gasped, their chests surging forward as they puffed up, magically speaking.

"Crimson," Talon groaned, his fingers on his new markings, trailing them as he checked out his body.

"We train together, learn together and master this new magic together, as equals," she said.

Jaggar took her chin in hand and turned her face toward his. "You are amazing, and no one, ever, will be on equal footing to you."

Then he kissed her, his tongue probing, entangling with hers. He eased her back, his lips still on hers until she was stretched out on the altar like a sacrifice. Jaggar teased her nipples and caressed along her waist. She opened her eyes as she pulled away from Jaggar's possessive kiss, only to be taken by Valor next — his kiss leaving her breathless.

She felt her way up their bodies on either side of her, finding her prize when she gripped Jaggar's shaft in one hand and Valor's in the other.

When Valor groaned, she pulled her lips away and looked down her body to find Talon there between her thighs and Zephyr spreading her pussy lips wide for him.

Jaggar played with one tit, tweaking and pinching her nipple while Valor played with the other, his huge hands dwarfing her most sensitive parts. Talon stuck his face between her legs, his hot breath cascading over her wet pussy until she bucked up, encouraging him to go deeper.

He licked her from asshole to clit then slipped his fingers inside, rubbing along her wall until he found the sweet spot while Zephyr lowered his lips to her clit and sucked her in.

She moaned, then turned her head and guided Jaggar's dick into her mouth, taking him all the way back until his throbbing head nudged at the gate of her throat. She adjusted to his size, then opened her jaw wider and took him in all the way. She cupped Valor's balls gently while she sucked Jaggar's cock, pumping slowly as she slipped her mouth along his shaft, teasing his crown before letting him slip out. Then she turned toward Valor and took him down, using her saliva to lubricate her hand as she pumped Jaggar's cock at the same time.

Her body was on fire, every erogenous zone sparking, every sensation tightening the coil in her belly, ratcheting her orgasm tighter as it twisted and twirled. When Talon entered her with a quick thrust, her whole body rocked, sliding along the slick stone altar as he pumped her pussy, holding her hips so he could slam her harder, faster, making it difficult to continue sucking cock as she was.

But it didn't matter that she was failing at her job to give head and losing herself to the bombardment of delicious sensations, because the men rotated. Talon slipped out and Zephyr punched in, using his cock to drill her pussy relentlessly while the others offered their dicks to her mouth, helping her stay on task as she licked and sucked each of them in turn.

It was too much and not enough. She savored their tastes, salty spurts of pre-cum mingled with sweat. She reveled in the way they touched her, stroking her higher, until she knew she must be floating on euphoria.

When her climax reached its peak, she cried out, riding the waves as her men — in her, around her — spurted their loads. They filled her pussy, her mouth and coated her body until she was racked with spasms, her body convulsing as wave after wave of pleasure rolled over her, through her and she felt, for the first time, the simultaneous climax of her men, their pleasure connected through their new markings so that it all ricocheted in a never-ending loop of bliss.

And when they were finally spent, panting and slick with sweat and other things, they helped her up and collectively opened a portal to her private chamber where they started all over — touching, tasting, stroking and setting fire to one another again and again.

Later, after they were all spent and exhausted, heaving breaths that slowly turned to deep sighs of contentment and satisfaction, Crimson, cocooned in the embrace of her four shifters, knew that her heart finally was healed.

Want to see more from this author? Here's a taster for you to enjoy!

Wicked Distractions: Wicked Disclosure
Angela Addams

Excerpt

"Someone will see us," Trent breathed out the words, half a moan, as Sabine opened his pants.

"Yeah, maybe." She licked her lips, her hand on his cock making him jolt. "But no one will talk about it."

He opened his lips to mutter some other stupid shit then closed them again. Sabine licked him from balls to crown and he thought he was going to come from that alone. He tilted his head back, groaning when she sucked him, slowly gliding her lips over his shaft, swirling and flicking her tongue before easing his dick in. She pumped him, taking him past the gate of her throat, fucking him with her entire mouth. His brain misfired, thoughts fading to nothing but electric impulses of pleasure. She gently massaged his balls with her fingers, her moan vibrating along his cock. Everything coiled – his gut, his sac – ready to blow.

She slid his dick out of her mouth, slowly, pressing her tongue hard against his shaft, lingering to give him another couple of flicks just under the ridge of his crown. He sucked in a deep breath and looked down at her, her lips glistening and a wicked smile greeting him. His body uncoiled, pulling him back from the edge enough that he could think again. It would have been some embarrassing shit if he'd lost his load so quickly.

"I probably shouldn't be doing this. Conflict of interest," he said, then chastised himself. *Shut up, you stupid fucker. Shut up, shut up, shut up!* There was Sabine Cowan, CEO of an escort empire, heiress to a multi-corporation legacy and notoriously *hot* bad girl, on her knees with her lips…*oh fuck*…her lips wrapped around his… "*Fuck!*"

She popped her mouth off him again, the suction making him want to follow her, his dick bobbing, begging for more. "You're not working tonight," she said. She sat back on her heels and slid her hand up his chest, pushing him to sit down in his chair. "I wouldn't have invited you to my party if I thought you were on the clock."

"Why am I here, then?" His brain was exploding, lust driving his every thought. He watched her lips move, her tongue darting to lick the corner of her mouth.

"Well…"

She moved between his legs, pushing against his thighs, nipples popping like they'd explode out of her low-cut dress. He wished they would. He kept his hands gripped to the arms of his chair, not trusting himself to move and break the lusty spell she was weaving.

"You're here to see how I keep secrets, aren't you?"

"I'm here to get you to sign a confidentiality agreement." He nearly choked on those words. *Could that be any more of a buzz kill?* She'd refused to sign the agreement at their meeting earlier, scoffing at idle threats made on behalf of his boss.

She smiled, batting her lashes. "Well, I guess you're just going to have to convince me then, aren't you?" She took his balls into her palm, stroking one then the other. "You wanna fuck me, messenger boy?"

"Yeah," he croaked. *Screw the confidentiality agreement.*

She released him, pushing on his thighs to stand, her hand out to help him up. In a daze he took her offer, standing on wobbly legs, dick rock hard, leading the way.

"You might want to tuck that bad boy back in." Sabine chuckled. "We've gotta walk through a few crowds to get upstairs."

Confused, Trent glanced down, realizing in a daze what she was saying. He pushed his aching dick back into his pants and zipped up. He'd had blow jobs in his life. Many. But he'd never had one like that. It seemed as if Sabine had enjoyed it just as much as he had. Maybe he'd just gotten so used to his mundane sex life that he'd forgotten how good things could be. Either way, he wasn't going to put the brakes on this. He couldn't. This was a fantasy-in-the-making of epic proportions. And he believed Sabine when she said that discretion was a guarantee. Off the clock or not, he knew his boss would not be happy to hear that Trent had not only partied with the enemy but fucked her too.

And that potentially sobering thought — the risk of blowing everything he'd worked his ass off to achieve, a corner office as Morgan and Miller Limited's newest lead communications officer, a stellar and solid reputation for innovative promotional campaigns and the bank account to show for it—still wasn't enough to derail his lust.

The temptation was just too great.

Sabine had been a socialite first—a wealthy heiress who'd attracted the media spotlight for not only her stunning looks but also her outrageous behavior. Drugs, parties, sex tapes... She'd done it all. Done it and reveled in it. Her celebrity status alone made her a trophy bang, but add to that her smoking-hot body—voluptuous and plump in all the right places—combined with her I'm-gonna-fuck-your-brains-out aggression and Trent was a goner.

Sabine took him up the grand staircase, leading him, walking just a little ahead so he felt like her hand in his was more like a leash, guiding him in the right direction. Adam, her very watchful bodyguard, was standing a few steps up, flicking his gaze from Trent to Sabine, his frown firmly in place. Sabine paused long enough so she could lean in and say something quietly to the giant brute. Adam gave a tight nod, shifting to look straight ahead, like Trent didn't exist. With another sly smile over her shoulder at Trent, Sabine continued up. His dick was literally weeping for her.

There was another staircase leading to the next floor, probably where the master suite was, but Sabine didn't continue upward. Instead, she took him down the hall, wall sconces lighting their way. It was quieter up here, the sound of murmured voices from the many conversations muffled as they moved higher and deeper into the house.

The room she led him to was bigger than his hotel room, even bigger than his condo. But there was nothing suggesting a touch of Sabine, nothing made him think she'd invited him into her own bedroom, her sanctuary. He didn't know why that bothered him. Why it would matter that she wanted to fuck in a generic room?

"Is this a client room?" He pushed away the feeling of jealousy that had reared, surprised that it was there at all. While downstairs had been all about socializing and harmless flirting, upstairs was a different story. If there was any doubt in his mind that her legitimate escort business was a cover for more nefarious shit, the multi-room traffic of girls and older men they'd passed on the second floor had been enough to tell him otherwise.

Sabine smiled when she faced him, her hand on the door to close it. "This is a guest room."

She shut out the rest of the party then moved toward him to run her hands up his body and wrap her arms around his shoulders, pressing her lips to his. He melted into her kiss. Finally, he could taste her. Any other thoughts dissolved when she slipped her tongue into his mouth, exploring, entangling. He moved his hands to her hips, then over her ass, lifting her so she could wrap her legs around his waist. Her skirt hiked up under his hands and he brushed flesh. *She isn't wearing any panties.*

"You're bare," he said as he pulled away from her mouth.

She cocked her head in a coy gesture, one he didn't believe for a second. "Yeah, I was hoping you'd figure that out sooner and slip your fingers in for a bit."

"Downstairs?" He was taken aback then chuckled at his own shock. "Finger you in front of everyone?"

Sabine wiggled her way out of his grasp, kicked off her shoes then climbed onto the bed, facing him on her knees. "You'd be surprised how few people notice those kinds of things. And the ones who do either enjoy the view or look away."

Trent yanked off his jacket and shoes then crawled onto the bed, invading her space, making her move so that she was holding herself up, leaning back on her hands, her legs partially spread.

"Well, it would be a good show if they did watch." What he was really thinking was, *I sure as shit hope no one recognized me.* Instead of blurting out his panicked thoughts, he distracted himself with Sabine, letting his dick do the thinking from that point on. He ran his hand up her calf then down her thigh, slipping the skirt of her dress back to her waist.

She laughed, dropping her head back, and opened her legs wider. He ignored her offer, bypassing the view of her pussy, those plump lips bare of hair with the glint of a piercing on her hood, in favor of her luscious fat tits. Finding her peaked nipples hard, he lowered his mouth, sucking her through her dress before nipping her between his teeth, taking her by surprise so that she whipped her head back up to meet his gaze. Something sparkled there—intrigue, curiosity. She watched him move from one breast to the other, latching on to the top of her dress, yanking it down so that her tits spilled out.

She moaned when he nipped again at the lush bud that was hard, impossibly hard. He flicked his tongue against it, sucking while he fondled her other breast with his hand, cupping as much as he could, her ample flesh spilling out of his palm. He alternated between the two, flicking and teasing. He could play with her nipples forever, sucking them until they were hot and rosy red, throbbing against his tongue.

"Eat me, messenger boy." She rocked her hips, nudging against him, making his cock pulse.

He pulled away with a smile, feeling cunning, triumphant. Sabine Cowan was as good as begging him to lick her clit. He obviously had to oblige. He spread her legs wider, holding her knees as he lifted them, pushing back until they were nearly touching the bed. Her pussy was gloriously splayed, wet, glistening, the piercing a diamond stud, hot as hell. He licked his lips and she moaned, the sound enough to make his cock throb. He lay down between her legs, flicking at the piercing, rolling it around with his tongue before moving to her clit to give her a good suck. He licked his way down, probing her hole, lapping her juice. He glanced up and caught her watching him as she played with her tits, teasing herself, her eyes hooded.

He slid his fingers deep inside, stroking her G-spot, giving her the right kind of pressure, servicing her with his tongue and his lips, so that her orgasm would rise just as his had. And right when he got her writhing, groaning, her breathing hard, her eyes closed and back arched, he stopped.

It took her a few seconds to realize what he'd done. She cracked open her eyes, watching him, snaking her hand down to finish the job he'd started.

"Nah uh, sweetie." He gave a shake of his finger while he unbuttoned his pants with his other hand. "You're going to come around my cock."

Sabine froze in place and gave him a slow, knowing smile. She wiggled herself out of her dress, tossing it over his shoulder to land in a heap on the floor. He pulled his pants off, then his boxers and socks, followed by his shirt. After giving him another once-over, she crawled to the other side of the bed, swaying her ass in a tantalizing manner. She opened a drawer on the bedside table and pulled something out. Turning to face him, she tossed it against his chest.

Condoms. A row of them.

Trent smiled, his cock jolting, eager to be sheathed. She crawled to him, slipping her mouth over his dick at the same time that she ripped a condom from the row. When she sucked her way off, he mourned the loss but knew something much better was coming. She slipped the condom on him then spun around, wiggling her ass. He didn't need more of an invitation. With hands on her hips, he thrust into her, his balls smacking her skin. He moaned as her pussy gripped him.

She lowered herself so her face was against the mattress, his thrusts rocking her, her tits swaying. She slipped her hand down her front, likely to rub her clit. He couldn't actually see her fingers, but the thought of her touching herself had his orgasm rising fast. He reached one hand around to play with one of her breasts, cupping it then gliding his thumb down to flick her nipple. She cried out, her pussy spasming hard and fast, her moans bringing him to climax and cum spewing into the condom. It was a great release after months of nothing but his hand.

He pulled out of her, sitting back on his heels as he caught his breath — or tried to, anyway. She was on him in a flash, pulling the condom off, slipping her lips back on. Sabine soon had him hard and wanting her all over again. She slid another condom on then pushed him backward, nearly toppling him off the bed so she could straddle him. He knew he was in for the night of his life. With her eyes locked on his and his cock buried deep, she gave him a slow ride. All he could do was stare up at her and think that Sabine-fucking-Cowan was a goddess.

* * * *

He woke up with a sex hangover. His dick was sore, every muscle in his body felt strained—and he was smiling like a madman. *What an unbelievable night.* He shifted, rolling to the side, not really surprised to find himself alone. He pushed himself up on his elbows, noting that the bathroom door was open, the room itself dark. Sabine hadn't stuck around. That wasn't surprising, but, if he were honest, it was disappointing. He collapsed back onto the mattress with a sigh. It wasn't that he was complaining. He'd had an amazing night of hot sex, more times than he'd thought was possible. It had been wild, crazy, uninhibited, no-rules kind of sex in every possible position. Sabine's body and what she could do with it—he moaned at the thought—was like the best porno fantasy times a thousand. *No, times a million.* It was a story for the record books. His friends would likely do just about anything to hear about it. But no one was going to hear about it. That one was locked in the vault, meant for only his enjoyment.

He pulled himself out of bed, making a half-assed attempt to find his clothes, hoping that maybe Sabine was just downstairs getting coffee for them. His phone rang, a muffled sound from across the room. He narrowed his eyes at the pile of clothes, flung haphazardly on the floor. It took him a few seconds to find it, but by the time he did the call had gone to voicemail. There was a text from Roy, a link and nothing else. With a sinking feeling, Trent clicked it.

"Oh fuck," he breathed. The link opened to a popular tabloid where a grainy photo showed Sabine on her knees, looking up at Trent. *"Morgan and Miller Golden Boy Caught with His Pants Down."* There was a spread and a half dozen or more photos. Trent wanted to barf.

Another text came from Roy.

Not good.

Trent closed his eyes briefly, nausea sweeping through him. He typed a response.

I was promised discretion.

It sounded lame. He wanted to take it back the second he pressed Send.
No response.
Fuck. Trent typed.

I'll fix this.

Damage is done. Get your ass back here. I sure as shit hope you got the confidentiality agreement signed.

Trent cursed again. He dug into his pile of clothes, searching for the agreement. He found it crumpled up where he'd left it in the inside pocket of his jacket — unsigned, of course.
His phone dinged again. He looked down, expecting to see another text from Roy, but it was from Sabine.

Had to fly out this morning. Early. Didn't want to wake you.

A second text came.

Had a great time last night. XX See you around.

"Fuck!" Trent threw his phone against the wall, satisfied when it busted to pieces.

About the Author

Angela Addams is an author of many naughty things. She believes that the written word is an amazing tool for crafting the most erotic of scenarios and likes telling stories about normal people getting down and dirty and falling in love. Enthralled by the paranormal at an early age, Angela also spends a lot of her time thinking up new story ideas that involve supernatural creatures in everyday situations.

She is an avid tattoo collector, a total book hoarder, and loves anything covered in chocolate…except for bugs. She lives in Ontario, Canada in an old, creaky house, with her husband, children and four moody cats.

Angela loves to hear from readers. You can find her contact information, website details and author profile page at https://www.totallybound.com